"A delectable tale of murder and intrigue . . . This bake-shop mystery is a real page-turner, and we look forward to others in the series, just as tasty."

—*Portland Book Review*

"This delicious debut mixes a quaint bakeshop in Ore-gon, an eclectic community of artists, and a diabolical murder. Delicious pastries and food are a focus of this fast-paced mystery."

—*RT Book Reviews*

"With plenty of quirky characters, a twisty, turny plot, and recipes to make your stomach growl, *Meet Your Baker* is a great start to an intriguing new series, but what sets this book apart and above other cozy mystery series is the locale. Ashland comes alive under Alex-ander's skilled hand. The picturesque town is lovingly described in vivid terms, so that it becomes more like a character in the book than just a backdrop to the action."

—*Reader to Reader*

"This debut culinary mystery is a light soufflé of a book (with recipes) that makes a perfect mix for fans of Jenn McKinlay, Leslie Budewitz, or Jessica Beck."

—*Library Journal*

"Marvelous . . . All the elements I love in a cozy mystery are there—a warm and inviting atmosphere, friendly and likable main characters, and a nasty murder mys-

tery to solve . . . I highly recommend *Meet Your Baker* and look forward to reading the next book in this new series!"   —*Fresh Fiction*

"*Meet Your Baker* is the scrumptious debut novel by Ellie Alexander, which will delight fans of cozy mysteries with culinary delights."   —*Night Owl Reviews*

"Alexander weaves a tasty tale of deceit, family ties, delicious pastries, and murder against a backdrop of Shakespeare and Oregon aflame. *Meet Your Baker* starts off a promising new series."

—Edith Maxwell, author of *A Tine to Live, A Tine to Die*

A Battle of Life and Death

"Clever plots, likable characters, and good food . . . Still hungry? Not to worry, because desserts abound in . . . this delectable series."   —*Mystery Scene*

"A finely tuned mystery!"   —*Dru's Book Musings*

"A delightful cozy mystery that will keep you turning pages to see what Jules is going to get into next . . . Grab a few napkins, because you'll be drooling all over the pages as you read some of the delicious-sounding recipes these chefs are cooking up."   —*Fresh Fiction*

A Crime of
Passion Fruit

Ellie Alexander

St. Martin's Paperbacks

This is a work of fiction. All of the characters, organizations, and events portrayed in this novel are either products of the author's imagination or are used fictitiously.

A CRIME OF PASSION FRUIT

Copyright © 2017 by Kate Dyer-Seeley.
Excerpt from *Another One Bites the Crust* copyright © 2017 by Kate Dyer-Seeley.

For information address St. Martin's Press, 175 Fifth Avenue, New York, NY 10010.

ISBN: 978-1-250-08807-9

Our books may be purchased in bulk for promotional, educational, or business use. Please contact your local bookseller or the Macmillan Corporate and Premium Sales Department at 1-800-221-7945, ext. 5442, or by e-mail at MacmillanSpecialMarkets@macmillan.com.

Printed in the United States of America

St. Martin's Paperbacks edition / July 2017

St. Martin's Paperbacks are published by St. Martin's Press, 175 Fifth Avenue, New York, NY 10010.

10 9 8 7 6 5 4 3 2 1

Chapter One

They say that the heart is like the ocean; its rhythm shifting with the sand on the shore. My heart had found a steady rhythm in Ashland, Oregon, the quirky Shakespearean small town where I had grown up. It had been almost eight months since I had returned home to our family bakeshop Torte, and despite an occasional dull ache for the life that I had left behind, there was no debate in my mind that I had made the right choice. My heart belonged in Ashland.

During my years working as a pastry chef on a luxurious cruise ship, I had forgotten how much I loved Ashland's Elizabethan charm, its lush parks, the eclectic shops and restaurants, and most importantly its warm and welcoming community. Tucked into the southernmost corner of Oregon, Ashland, with its sunny, mild climate, abundant recreation opportunities, and fairy-talelike village, attracted tourists from all over the world.

This morning as I walked down the plaza past the bubbling Lithia fountains and a troupe of street performers who were dressed like modern-day gypsies, I couldn't help but chuckle. They waved and played me a spontaneous baking song on a harp and accordion. Only in Ashland, I thought as I took in the scent of the sulfur water in the basinlike fountain. The water was piped to the center of town from a rare, naturally occurring mineral spring. A stop at the fountain was a must for any tourist, not only because of the water's famed health benefits but also because it tasted like rotten eggs.

I crossed the street and passed Puck's Pub, an old-English-style pub with a massive wooden door and its oversized wrought-iron handles. Torte, our family bakeshop, was located on the far corner of the plaza. I walked along the tree-lined sidewalk. Magenta banners with gold lions flapped in the breeze. Antique lampposts, hanging baskets dripping with pink fuchsias, and collections of outdoor bistro tables filled the narrow passageway. Soon the plaza would be humming with tourists grabbing a bite to eat or window-shopping before the afternoon matinee at the Oregon Shakespeare Festival, but until the season officially launched, GONE FISHING signs had been posted in storefront windows and only a handful of locals lingered over leisurely lunches in the late-afternoon sun.

Torte's fire-engine-red awning sat like an anchor at the end of the sidewalk. My mom and dad had started the bakeshop when I was a young child, offering their delectable sweets, savory pastries, and artisanal coffee to townsfolk and tourists. Torte was more than a bakeshop—it was the heart of Ashland. That was thanks to Mom. When my dad died she took the helm and had been serving up home-style handcrafted food with a side of love ever since. She was part baker and part counselor. Her easygoing style and superb listening skills made strangers feel like family from the minute they stepped inside Torte's bright and cheery front door. Every touch and detail had been designed to make customers feel at home, from the chalkboard menu with a rotating Shakespearean quote and space for Torte's youngest patrons to display their art work to fresh cut flowers on each table, and its vibrant teal and red color palette.

Now it was my turn to continue her legacy. Not that she was going anywhere, but we were taking on a major renovation and I wanted to make sure that I was bearing the burden of our expansion plans.

Thanks to an art foundation's grant that my friend and artistic director of the Oregon Shakespeare Festival, Lance, had helped us secure, we were about to double Torte's square footage. It wasn't exactly something we had planned on. Mom and I had discussed Torte's future many times since I'd been home, but mostly in passing. We had both been content with the bakeshop's slow and steady growth and had saved up enough cash to upgrade our ovens. That project alone had us both reveling in how much more productive we could be, but when the opportunity arose to take over the property below us, neither of us could pass it up.

Real estate on Ashland's bustling plaza was always at a premium. If we didn't jump at the chance it could be years—or decades—before the opportunity might arise again. Mom had been managing the busy shop for ten years without me, and part of the appeal of returning home to Ashland was being able to take on more duties so that she didn't have to work so hard. She loved Torte, but I also knew that she was reaching a time in her life where she could travel and indulge in more leisurely activities. Without her gentle yet firm nudging I may never have followed my dream of going to culinary school, and I hoped one day she would do the same. She and the Professor, the town's lead detective and resident Shakespeare aficionado, were getting closer and it was her turn to set sail and explore. I just hoped that she would allow herself the same freedom she had allowed me.

Expanding into the basement space had already turned out to be a bigger undertaking than either of us had initially imagined. The property had been abandoned for years, and to make matters worse it had flooded numerous times, most recently after a monsoon hit downtown Ashland. Our first task was to pump the basement and have a new drainage system installed. No work on renovations or breaking through to Torte's upstairs could begin until we fixed the water issue. The problem was that our fellow shop owners were in the same boat. In a town the size of Ashland there weren't enough contractors to go around. We were in a holding pattern until the construction crew finished other repairs along the plaza.

As I reached Torte's front door I pushed my worries about our basement plans aside. I had other pressing things on my mind, like tonight's Sunday Supper. We had started offering Sunday Suppers at the bakeshop as a way to supplement our income during the off season and to showcase our cooking. Both Mom and I enjoyed cooking as much as baking, and Sunday Suppers allowed us to stretch our creativity. We served dinner family-style to encourage guests to mingle and help build an even stronger sense of community. Thus far the suppers had been a hit. Until now they'd all sold out, and we had a lengthy waiting list of guests who wanted to attend tonight. Yet another reason that expanding the bakeshop could be good for our bottom line. We simply didn't have enough space at the moment.

Although I had to admit that one of the reasons that demand for Sunday Suppers might be so high was thanks to my estranged husband, Carlos. He had been in town for a short stay and had entranced the town with his sultry Spanish accent and spicy tapas. His Latin-inspired feast had left the town hungry for more. With his succulent tapas still fresh in everyone's mind I had opted for a decidedly different cuisine for tonight's supper—Asian fusion.

"I'm back," I called, opening the door with my free

hand and tucking the box of vegetables I'd picked up from the market under my other arm.

"It's about time, boss." Andy, Torte's resident barista, winked from behind the coffee bar. He pushed up the sleeves on his Southern Oregon University football sweatshirt. "We've been dying without you." In addition to handcrafting creamy lattes, Andy was a student and football star.

"Right." I laughed, scanning the dining room where a couple was sharing a slice of Mom's chocolate caramel cake at a booth in front of the windows and a student with headphones was nursing a coffee as she studied. "It looks pretty packed in here."

"I'm serious. We can't get anything done around here without our fearless leader." He gave me a half salute and organized canisters of coffee beans.

I shook my head and passed by him. "Carry on. Just as you are." Torte's staff might be young but they were highly capable. Mom and I had often commented on how lucky we were to find such hardworking and talented help.

Walking around the coffee bar, I entered Torte's open kitchen where Mom, Sterling, our young sous chef in training, and Stephanie, another part-time college student, who had turned out to be an incredibly skilled baker, were working on the evening's dinner. Every time I entered the newly remodeled kitchen I had to smile. We had upgraded our old, clunky ovens with shiny modern beauties that not only sparkled but cranked out so much heat that we were still tinkering with finding the right settings. The team had painted the kitchen walls in an opaque teal about three shades lighter than the dining room. It gave the workspace a vivid feel and blended in with the cheery color scheme in the front.

"Juliet, did they have scallions?" Mom asked, whisking

a sauce on the stove. Her chestnut hair was tucked behind her ears, revealing a pair of coffee-cup earrings.

I placed the box of veggies on the island and held up a bunch of scallions.

"Excellent!" She dipped her pinkie into the sauce and gave it a taste. "I think that a nice bite of scallion will finish this off perfectly."

"You mean elevate," Sterling said from the opposite side of the island. His dark locks shaded one eye. He wore his apron around his waist with a dish towel tucked into it. It was a trick he had learned from Carlos. I could hear Carlos saying, "A chef must always have a towel, *sí*? You do not need to use these pot holders." He scoffed at the silicone oven mitts we used. "These take too much time. A towel it is easy and quick and you can use it for so many things." Sterling had taken Carlos's words to heart.

"Elevate?" Mom wrinkled her brow.

"That's what the professional chefs say." Sterling pushed up the sleeves of his black hoodie, revealing his tattooed forearms, and began kneading pork and spices in a large mixing bowl.

Mom grinned. "Well, I like the sound of that. I'm elevating my sauce. Very impressive."

"Since when do you pay attention to how professional chefs are talking?" I asked. "Elevate" wasn't a term I had ever heard Carlos use. He was more provincial in his approach to food.

Stephanie who as usual appeared uninterested in our kitchen banter busied herself assembling strawberry tarts on a tray and finishing each one with a sprig of fresh mint.

Sterling shrugged. "I've been watching a few cooking shows here and there. For *research*. You know."

He tried to sound casual but I knew exactly what he meant, and by the looks of Stephanie's cheeks, which matched the red strawberry tarts, I had a feeling I knew who he'd been watching cooking shows with. Stephanie was addicted to the Pastry Channel, especially the cooking competition shows, which had surprised all of us. Her somewhat sullen attitude and goth exterior didn't exactly match with cheesy culinary television. Which just proves that the kitchen is the great equalizer. People of all walks of life connect over food. It's one of the many, many reasons that I love being a chef.

The attraction between Sterling and Stephanie had been apparent to everyone in the bakeshop, but as of yet neither of them had been public about whether they were or weren't a couple, and I certainly wasn't going to ask.

Mom wiped her hands on her apron and joined me at the island. "That produce looks gorgeous." She ran her hand over a bunch of yellow peppers. I noticed that she wasn't wearing her wedding ring. Instead it hung from a simple gold chain around her neck. "Look at the color on these."

"I know." I nodded toward Sterling. "How is the pot sticker preparation coming along?"

"Good." Mom pointed to the pot she had left simmering on the stove. "The sauce is almost ready and as you can see Sterling is up to his elbows in the filling." To Sterling she added, "As soon as you're done incorporating the spices I'll show you how to fill them."

My mouth watered at the thought of homemade pot stickers. At least once a month when I was growing up my dad would make an Asian-inspired feast that always included hand-rolled pot stickers. The flavorful dumplings were always my favorite. We were using his recipe tonight. In addition to the pot stickers, we planned to serve an Asian noodle salad chock-full of cabbage, bean sprouts, julienned carrots, cilantro, and peppers tossed in a tangy peanut sauce. For dessert we would add a touch of whimsy to the table with coconut and chocolate deep-fried wontons.

"It's starting to smell amazing in here." I unpacked the rest of the vegetables and assembled piles of organic carrots and bunches of cilantro on bamboo cutting boards on the island.

Andy came into the back balancing a tray of coffees. As our resident coffee mixologist he was constantly experimenting with new drinks. No one ever complained about tasting one of Andy's creations. We usually fought for position to be the first in line for a taste. "Hey, so I thought it might be cool to do a drink pairing with your wontons," he said, passing us each a cup. "Give this a try and let me know what you think."

I cradled the warm mug in my hands and inhaled the scent of Andy's drink. The creamy tea smelled fruity and fresh. I took a sip and tasted a hint of pear mingled with just a touch of ginger. The balance of the spicy ginger and sweet pear was sinful.

"This is amazing," I said to Andy, taking another drink.

Sterling mumbled with his mouth full and gave Andy a thumbs-up.

"What's in it?" Mom asked. "Pear?"

A smile tugged at Andy's boyish cheeks. He wore a baseball hat backward, making him look even younger. "That's right, Mrs. C. Asian pear and a hint of fresh ginger. I used a custom blend of chai tea with coconut and almond milk. Do you like it?"

"I love it." Mom looked at me and widened her eyes. "He's done it again, hasn't he?"

"He has." I nodded enthusiastically.

Andy's shoulders swelled at the compliment. "I thought it might be unique."

"It's like we planned it," I said. "This will be great with

our dessert wontons. You should add it to the specials board."

"Awesome." The door jingled and Andy hurried to the front to help the customer.

I was about to get started on chopping purple and yellow cabbage when my cell phone buzzed in the back pocket of my jeans. Not many people call me. I am sadly way behind the digital trend after working on cruise ships for so many years, and practically everyone I knew in Ashland came to Torte at least once a day. Whenever my phone buzzed it always took me by surprise.

I rested the knife on the cutting board and pulled my phone from my pocket. My heart skipped a beat when Carlos's face flashed on the screen. Why was my husband—or should I say estranged husband—calling me?

Carlos and I had spent many blissful years at sea. If you had asked me on our wedding day whether I thought our love would last, I would have never guessed that we would end up oceans apart. But I never would have guessed that he would have hidden something so important from me either—the fact that he had a son. When I learned about Ramiro, I panicked and left the ship. At first I thought that Ashland would be a temporary stop until I recovered from the shock. I never anticipated leaving the life I had built with Carlos behind me for good. But then something unexpected happened as I settled into my familiar hometown. I fell in love again—with Ashland. Ever since, I had felt as if I were dancing between two worlds. I knew that soon I was going to have to decide once and for all where my heart was going to live, but I wasn't ready to face the fallout yet.

"Julieta, is that you?" Carlos's thick Spanish accent greeted me from somewhere halfway around the world. Carlos was the executive chef on the *Amour of the Seas*. It was fitting that the ship had been christened with a name like *Amour*. The kitchen staff used to tease me, saying that Carlos was the love chef. He'd earned his nickname by showering me with luscious food, Spanish wine, and quoting poetry in my ear when he would pass me in the ship's long hallways. Why was he calling me now? He rarely called, and certainly not in the middle of the day.

"What's going on, Carlos? Where are you?" I asked, clutching the island to steady myself. Hearing his voice threw me off balance. After a brief stay in Ashland last month, Carlos had returned to the ship. I hadn't expected him to follow me to Ashland and was glad for our time together. I think we both had had a chance to heal, but our future was shaky. As much as I loved him, and the chemistry between us was undeniable, we were worlds apart. Carlos was a vagabond at heart. He belonged to the sea. I belonged to Ashland.

"I am on the ship, *mi querida*." He paused for a moment. "I have a favor I must ask of you."

"Okay." I could hear the trepidation in my voice. Mom studied me. Her gingerbread eyes widened when I said Carlos's name. I held up my finger and waited for Carlos to continue.

"It is our pastry chef. He, how do you say it? He freaked out and quit."

"Why?" I glanced behind me. Sterling and Stephanie appeared to have everything in control, so I motioned to Mom and pointed to the window. She nodded while I hurried outside. Thankfully the sidewalk bistro table sat empty. I plopped down on an iron chair. "Why did he freak out?" I repeated.

"I do not know. Someone said he is angry because a customer complained that his flan it is no good." Carlos laughed. "I am with the customer. His flan it was terrible."

I laughed too. "There's nothing worse than a bad flan."

"*Sí, sí.* It is not a real loss. No one liked this chef, but this is our problem. We have a new pastry chef coming from a sister ship, but he can't arrive for over a week. He is already at sea."

"Uh-huh?" I stared at the tree above me. Its dainty green leaves quivered in the slight wind.

"Okay, so we want you to come."

"Me!" I shouted. Then I regained my composure as a couple strolled past with a bag of Torte pastries. "I can't come on the ship. I'm working—at Torte. You know that."

"*Sí,* I know, but it is only for a few days. We need someone good to come help until the new chef comes. The staff, they already know you. You know the ship. It will be easy for everyone and it makes the most sense."

"Carlos, I can't just leave Ashland and come back to the ship." A leaf floated down from the tree and landed on the table. I picked it up and ran my fingers along its spine.

"Only for five days. This is nothing. And they will pay you extra. Double pay."

"Double pay?" The cruise lines rarely offer bonuses or double pay.

"*Sí,* double. And I talked to the captain about your mom." Carlos sounded smug, like he knew he had won.

"My mom?" I glanced into the kitchen window where Mom stood next to Sterling at the stove. "What about Mom?"

"I thought it would be so nice if you bring her along. And the Professor too. They could have a vacation here on the ship while you are baking, no?"

"A vacation?"

"*Sí.* They can be my guests for free. No charge. They will each have a nice suite with a balcony and all expenses will be paid."

"Wow." I found myself at a momentary loss for words.

"It is a good cruise too. We will go to so many stunning locations, Julieta. You can show them the gorgeous white beaches, they can explore each port, and I will make you all such wonderful fresh food that you will never want to leave. What do you say?"

"I don't know what to say," I stuttered. "When? And how would it work with Mom?"

"I need you here in three days. You have your passport and you still have clearance, so it should be smooth and easy. The flights they can be arranged right away."

"Three days?" I ripped the leaf in half. That wasn't much time.

"Will you come?" I could hear the longing in his voice.

"I don't know." I hesitated and glanced inside again. "Let me think about it and I'll get back to you."

"Okay, but you must tell me soon. Otherwise we must find someone else."

"Why don't you promote one of the sous chefs?"

"No, the captain will not allow it. There is too much drama. One of the sous chefs left with the head pastry chef and the others they are not liking the vibe in the kitchen. It is a bad idea. You will be perfect because you will help things run smoothly until the new chef comes."

"I don't know." I wavered. Mom deserved a vacation, but there was so much to do at Torte.

"You think about it. Talk to Helen and then you let me know, okay?"

"Okay," I agreed and clicked off the phone. When I returned to the kitchen Mom pounced on me. "Was that Carlos?" she whispered. "Is everything okay?" I tugged her by the shoulder toward an empty booth in the dining room. I didn't want to have this conversation in front of our staff.

I explained everything and she nodded along with relative calm until I got to the part about Carlos's invitation to her and the Professor. Her eyes lit up. I could tell that she was excited about the idea.

"Would you have any interest in going?" I asked, carefully.

She tried to keep her face neutral but I could see the glimmer in her eyes when she said, "No, I mean that's a wonderful and generous offer from Carlos, but I wouldn't want to put you in the middle of something like that or make things awkward for you."

"I'm not worried about that. I'm worried about leaving Torte. We have so much going on right now, with the expansion."

Mom leaned her head from side to side and looked thoughtful for a moment. "True, but we're in a holding pattern for a while and it's only five days, right? I think the kids could handle things for a while, don't you?"

I nudged her in her petite waist. "You want to go, don't you?"

She shrugged and smiled wider. "I have to admit the thought of lounging by the pool with a good book and tropical drink is very appealing. It's been a stressful winter."

"Done. I'll call Carlos back right now."

"But, honey, wait. You don't need to do this for me."

"I'm not. You're right. A free trip for you, double pay for me, and there's nothing we can do here until they get the basement pumped out. Let's do it. Five days in paradise. What could possibly go wrong?"

Famous last words.

Chapter Two

For the remainder of the afternoon while we put the finishing touches on our Sunday Supper menu my mind whirled with thoughts of Carlos and returning to the ship. Mom's excitement was contagious. She raced to call the Professor and peppered me with a million questions as she diced scallions and danced around the kitchen.

"What should I pack? How formal is it? Do I need a cocktail dress? Should we go shopping? I don't own anything fancy." She pointed to her clogs. Mom's style was distinctly Ashland. She typically wore jeans or khakis and clogs to the bakeshop. She always looked put together and professional yet casual. Just like Torte.

"You'll be fine," I promised. "But we can go through your closet tonight."

Andy had closed up the front of the shop and was rinsing the last of the coffee mugs in the sink. "I've never seen you like this, Mrs. C. You're usually so calm."

She grinned. "I know. I feel like a kid. I can't remember the last time I went on a vacation like this." Her face turned serious for a moment. "Probably before your dad died," she said to me.

I saw her eyes mist briefly. She dabbed them with a tea towel hanging from her waist and clapped her hands together. "Now, what about the three of you? We might need to call in some reinforcements."

Sterling had finished assembling the pot stickers and was warming sesame oil in a wok. "We'll be fine. You both worry too much. OSF hasn't opened yet. We don't have any huge orders next week. We've got this."

While I appreciated his positive attitude and all of their willingness to help, I couldn't shake the nagging worry in my stomach. Sterling was right that if there was ever a time to be gone from Torte, this was it. Once the Oregon Shakespeare Festival kicked off its new season things would really start to heat up in the kitchen. Summer was by far our busiest time of the year, but the opening of the festival brought in double the tourists that we saw in the winter months. Before long Torte would be bustling, but for the next couple of weeks we would have a reprieve. I made a mental note of our current wholesale clients, any specialty cake orders on the horizon, and itemized our daily task list. Even with things being slower than normal, having both Mom and me gone would make a major impact on our daily operations.

I scooped coconut filling into four-inch-square sheets of wonton dough. "Can everyone gather around for a second?" I asked, motioning to the island.

Sterling removed the pan from the stove. Stephanie and Mom stood on the far side of the workspace, and Andy plopped into one of the high bar stools.

"Let's think this through," I said, dusting coconut from my hands and reaching for a notebook. "We can scale back our daily offerings for a few days. We go back to basics and don't take any specialty cake orders."

Mom nodded. "I agree. I'll call Chef Garrison at Ashland Springs. I'm sure he'll be glad to take referrals."

"Yes, and I'll talk to Bethany of the Unbeatable Brownie too," I said, making a note. Mom and I had met Bethany at the Chocolate Festival. She had recently launched a brownie delivery service and I knew that she'd been looking for commercial kitchen space. I had a feeling she might even be willing to do some of her baking at Torte in exchange for looking over our staff.

"That will give you a couple options to send our customers to, and we can offer them a ten percent discount on their next order," I said to the team. Then I frowned and looked at Mom. "What about our wholesale accounts? Do you think we should cancel those?"

"Hmm." Mom's forehead wrinkled. "It might not be a bad idea. That's putting a lot of responsibility on Stephanie."

"Maybe Bethany can help with the wholesale accounts too," I suggested.

Stephanie tucked her violet hair behind her ears. "It's no big deal. I can handle it."

"That's a lot of extra work." Mom hesitated. "Maybe I've gotten ahead of myself here. This might not be feasible."

"No way, Mrs. C." Andy jumped off the stool and walked over to the whiteboard. "You deserve a vacation and everyone in town knows that. We can handle it." He started to point at the wholesale schedule when a knock sounded on the front door.

I looked up to see Lance dressed in a three-piece silver suit, waving his fingers. Lance was the artistic director at the Oregon Shakespeare Festival and would easily win any award for best dressed in Ashland. He rarely ventured outside without a suit and tie, which he wore with an effortless confidence. Lance was about my height with a lean frame, dark hair, and catlike eyes. His expensive suit shimmered in the early evening light and the purple iridescent tie around his neck made him look even more regal than usual.

He rapped on the door again and gave me an exasperated look. I went to let him in while everyone continued to debate.

"It's about time, darling. Were you planning on leaving your dearest pal out in the cold?" He kissed each of my cheeks and swept into the room.

"What are you doing here?" I motioned to the sign on the door. "We're closed."

"Juliet, it's Sunday Supper. Is that any way to treat your most esteemed guest?"

I glanced at the clock. "You're early." Lance was never early for anything. He made a concerted effort to be fashionably late for everything.

"I know. I was hoping for a word." He gave me a devilish look. "You look divine as always, darling. Oh what I wouldn't give to set my hair stylist free on those ashen locks of yours. And that porcelain skin. It's straight from the pages of Shakespeare's works. You do your namesake proud, don't you?"

Lance was notorious for his effusive praise of my appearance. I knew that was mainly in jest. It was his little joke, but he was also relentless when it came to trying to convince me to take the stage. As a child I had acted in a few productions at OSF, and quickly came to realize that I much preferred the theater from the audience's view.

I ignored Lance's comment. "What do you need to talk about?"

For a brief moment his affect disappeared and his face looked severe, but then laughter erupted from the kitchen. He straightened his tie and breezed past me. "I see the entire team is here, and having a tête-à-tête, no less. Do tell, what is the scoop?" His demeanor shifted as he looped his arm through mine.

"Nothing. We're trying to figure out coverage. Mom and I are going to be gone next week. Well, I think we're going to be gone."

"Gone where?" Lance gasped.

"The ship. Carlos called and asked me to fill in for a few days, and to sweeten the deal they've offered to give Mom and the Professor a free cruise."

Lance threw one hand over his mouth. "How delightful." Then he wrapped his other arm through mine. "Say no more. I'm at your service. Come, come." He yanked me into the kitchen.

He immediately inserted himself into the conversation and took command. Clapping his hands together he said, "Not to fear, I'm here to help. These lovely ladies deserve a break and yours truly will take it upon himself to oversee things here at Torte while they are away."

Mom shot me a look. I shook my head. Lance tapped the countertop. "Now, what is our plan of attack?"

Sterling frowned. "We don't have one. We don't really attack when it comes to baking."

"Nonsense. Everyone attacks. That's the first rule of the stage. What's your motivation? Let's think Hamlet here." Lance loosened his tie as if limbering up to deliver a monologue. "His objective is to seek revenge for his father's death. What's Torte's objective?"

"Uh, to sell pastries?" Andy suggested with a snigger.

Lance waved him off. "No! You're not selling pastries. You're setting the stage. You're creating a vision—a delightful, a magnificent vision of sweets and comfort. Place yourself in your customers' shoes. Imagine them opening the front door." Lance proceeded to act out this process.

Stephanie rolled her eyes. Mom tried to reel Lance back in, but he had found a captive audience and wasn't about to let the moment pass him by. Within minutes we went from scaling back to Lance directing our young staff on the importance of artistry and production value in our pastry.

When he finally finished, Mom cleared her throat.

"Thank you so much for your generous offer. I never thought of our bakeshop like Hamlet, but now I will." Her eyes creased in a smile. "We couldn't ask you to take time away from the theater. I'm sure this must be an incredibly busy time of the year for you."

Lance waved her off. "It's nothing, dear Helen. It's the least I can do for an old friend."

Mom plastered on a fake smile. "Well, if you're sure?" She looked to me for support. I shrugged. There was no stopping Lance now.

He clapped his hands together. "Positive. Absolutely positive. Do not give another thought to Torte, my dear. Leave things in my capable hands and you won't even recognize the place by the time you're back."

"That's exactly what I'm worried about," I whispered to Mom under my breath.

Swatting me under the counter, Mom thanked Lance and hurried to open the doors for the other Sunday Supper guests who had begun to arrive.

"Wait, wait," Lance called after her. "Let me help greet the guests. Consider it my first act as Torte's director."

Once he was out of earshot Sterling, Stephanie, and Andy all complained in unison.

"Jules, you can't let him be in charge." Sterling stared with his steely blue eyes at the front where Lance re-arranged an orchid in one of the vases. "He'll drive us crazy."

"No way!" Andy agreed. "He cannot be in charge. He'll have us all quoting sonnets and make me figure out a way to sculpt Shakespeare's bust out of latte foam."

"Hey, that's not a bad idea," I joked.

Stephanie folded her arms across her chest and glowered.

"Don't worry. I'll take care of it," I promised. I knew that Lance meant well and I also agreed that he would drive my staff crazy. Lance's flair for the dramatic made him a master of the stage, but the kitchen was no place for drama. I could only imagine what he might do to the bakeshop—like painting it purple and black to give it extra flair.

"How?" Stephanie snarled, twisting a strand of hair around her finger. Lance would definitely approve of her alternative look.

"I'll give him a specific task. Maybe overseeing progress on the basement property. That should keep him out of your hair."

She didn't look convinced and I couldn't blame her. Lance and I had become friends since I'd been home but he was easier to handle in small doses. Mom was right. He had to be busy with the launch of the new season. Hopefully if we gave him something like keeping tabs on the basement renovation it would appease his need to be in the know and keep our staff intact.

I didn't have time to worry about it as our dinner guests trickled in. For Sunday Suppers we transformed the dining room, pushing the smaller four-person tables together to create one long shared table. Mom had covered the table with a white linen tablecloth and adorned it with votive candles and delicate bouquets of pink and yellow orchids. The space quickly hummed to life as I circled the room with bottles of sake and an Asian plum wine.

Sterling panfried the pot stickers, giving them a gorgeous golden-brown crispness, while still keeping the dumpling dough soft and slightly chewy on the inside. Mom served the first round of appetizers as Sterling and I plated my noodle salad.

"Give it a try," I said to Sterling as he scooped noodles from a stainless steel mixing bowl. One of the most important rules in the kitchen is to taste, taste, and then taste again. He twisted the thin noodles around his fork and took a bite. Nodding, he gave me a thumbs-up and took another bite. I followed suit, and was pleased with how the salad had turned out. The noodles were cooked al dente and tossed with a spicy vinegar-peanut sauce. The cabbage, bean sprouts, peanuts, and julienned carrots gave the noodles a nice crunch.

"This is great, Jules," Sterling said, returning to plating the noodles.

"Yeah, not bad," I said, sprinkling fresh cilantro and chopped peanuts on top of each plate and taking the first round out to the dining room. Lance sat at the head of the table. He held up his glass of sake in acknowledgment. "A toast to our chef," he said.

Everyone clinked their glasses, and I'm sure I blushed but I managed to quickly redirect Lance's attention by starting a conversation with him and Rosalind, the head of Ashland's downtown business association. Rosalind had been instrumental in helping us secure the grant funding and basement property. Once I delivered their plates, I mentioned to Rosalind that Lance would be keeping an eye on progress while Mom and I were gone. Lance beamed as I made sure to fluff his ego. "I feel very confident leaving things in Lance's hands," I said to Rosalind.

She wrapped her shawl around her bony shoulders. Despite being one of downtown's oldest members, Rosalind was a smart and savvy businesswoman who didn't let age hold her back. "Excellent, but I'm not sure you'll have much to do," she said to Lance. "After that last storm we are absolutely backlogged. I've called in help from Medford and even Grants Pass, but if memory serves I believe Torte is still maybe four or five spots down the list of businesses in line for pumping and new drainage systems."

I had already been told as much by our contractor, so it wasn't news to me. However, Lance launched into a new tirade. "What do you mean fourth or fifth in line? That's unacceptable. Torte is one of the plaza's premier businesses. They should be on the top of the list."

Rosalind sighed and rubbed her temples. "I know, dear, but there's nothing I can do about it. Everyone is in the same position."

"We'll see about that." Lance straightened his tie and shot me a knowing look.

I left to get another round of dinner plates, feeling slightly guilty for leaving Rosalind to deal with Lance. However, I felt validated that I was making the right decision in giving Lance some direction. Hopefully his attention would be directed at the poor construction workers and away from my staff. Or on second thought, maybe that was a bad idea.

Chapter Three

The next day flew by. There was so much to do before Mom and I left for the ship. Our first order of business was making sure the staff had a simple and clear day-to-day plan. Any special orders would be directed to Chef Garrison and Bethany at the Unbeatable Brownie. We touched base with our wholesale accounts, and scaled back the daily menu. On paper it seemed very doable, and I knew that Ashland would rally around Torte. We were only going to be gone for a few days, after all.

Bethany stopped by the bakeshop after the morning rush. She wasn't much older than Sterling, Andy, and Stephanie, but she had successfully launched a new startup, was almost done with culinary school, and had a commercial baker's license. "Great to see you, Jules," she said, offering me a basket of thick-sliced brownies. Bethany was active on social media and had attracted quite a following, especially students at Southern Oregon University who could place their order on Twitter or Instagram and Bethany would deliver it to their dorm room on her bike. She wore a pink and chocolate-brown T-shirt with the Unbeatable Brownie logo and hashtag #GetInMyBelly.

"These look delish," I said, breaking off a bite of a chocolate-mint brownie.

"I'm working on some new flavors. The Chocolate Festival was really inspiring, you know?"

Her brownie was equally soft and chewy. She had struck an excellent balance between the brownie being too cakey or too gooey. The white chocolate-mint drizzle gave it a crisp finish. "This is great," I said, taking another bite.

"Thanks, that means a lot coming from you." She blushed slightly. "So what can I do to help?"

"Make more of these," I joked.

"Consider it done." She tugged at her T-shirt.

"Actually, we were hoping you might be willing to do your baking here while Mom and I are gone. I heard that Carter took a job in Portland, and I know you've been wanting to test out industrial kitchens. This might be a good chance to get a feel for what it's like working in a bigger space. You can sell your brownies—the profit would go to you of course, and if you'd be willing to help Stephanie with some of the morning prep and wholesale accounts we would pay you."

"Yeah. I'm in!" Her long brown curls bobbed with enthusiasm. "That would be great. I've been feeling kind of lost now that Carter ditched me. I mean, don't get me wrong, it's great for him. I told him he had to go, but we were going to be a team. Now it's just me in my kitchen. Oh, and my cat." She grinned. Carter was a budding chocolatier who had planned to partner with Bethany before he landed an apprenticeship at one of Portland's premier chocolate purveyors.

Bethany continued. "You know, this is kind of like a real-world social media takeover. As long as it's cool with you I could document this on Instagram. I'll post pictures all week from Torte's kitchen. We can hashtag it #Torte-Takeover. I'll snap pics of everything—baking, your team, customers, whatever else you think would be good. It should be good PR for both of us."

"Sure, that sounds fun. I know the team will be into it. Stephanie has been trying to get us up to speed on social media for a while. She'll love this. Let me show you around." I motioned toward the back.

As predicted Stephanie cracked a smile when Bethany launched into her plan for a literal and virtual takeover. Knowing that Bethany would be another set of hands was a huge relief. It would also free up Sterling to oversee any movement in the basement. Once Bethany left to go start hashtag *#TorteTakeover*, Sterling and I did a walk-through (or more like slog-through) of the property.

"I don't think there's much you're going to have to do while we're gone," I said as we navigated the mossy steps leading to the basement. Torte sat on the corner of the plaza. Currently the only access to the basement property was around the back on a walking path known as the Calle Guanajuato. The brick path paralleled Lithia Creek and many of the shops and restaurants on the plaza had decks and patios off the walk that provided lovely views of the rushing creek.

The cement steps were slippery. I cautioned Sterling to use the handrail. He rolled his eyes, but did it anyway. Once we made it to the landing I noticed that the water had receded some. A week ago the landing had been flooded in inches of water. Today a small puddle was all that remained. I unlocked the door and pushed it open.

"Ugh!" Sterling threw his hand over his nose. "What is that smell?"

An overpowering stench of mildew assaulted us. Power had been cut off to the property for years, so it was hard to see but if the smell was any indication there was a ton of cleanup to be done. This wasn't news to me. I had already toured the basement many times, but the last deluge had made things soggier and smellier.

"Yeah, it's bad." I followed suit and covered my nose

and mouth with my sleeve. "That's why I don't think you're going to have to do anything. As soon as the excavation crew is done at Trickster we're next. The first thing they're going to do is gut all of this."

Sterling stayed in the doorway. "That's going to be a nasty job."

I stepped farther inside, noting that the water level was about two inches deep. The old carpet had been completely covered by water, and I guessed it was the main source of the smell. Had we made a mistake? It was impossible not to feel overwhelmed when taking in the state of ruin that greeted us. Rotting furniture, damp photos, and rusty cooking equipment littered the dark and dingy space. The only silver lining was that I knew that a brick oven was hidden behind the soggy Sheetrock on the far wall. I didn't venture farther in. I had seen enough for the moment.

"You okay?" Sterling asked as I locked the door and my eyes readjusted to the light outside.

"It's a mess, isn't it?"

The sun hit his face, making his eyes look like ice. "Yeah, it's bad, but if anyone can bring that place to life it's the Capshaw women."

"Thanks," I said, kicking moss from the bottom step.

"Hey, don't sweat it, Jules. Once they dig it out and dry it out it's going to feel—and smell—like new."

"I hope so." I continued up the steps, hoping that Mom and I hadn't gotten in over our heads.

We returned to Torte right as the lunch crowd began to pick up. I didn't have more time to dwell on the basement. Mom and I were leaving in less than forty-eight hours. I had lists to make, directions to leave for Sterling and Bethany, supplies to pick up. Then there was packing, making sure Mom had her passport, and figuring out our flights. Lance came by practically every hour to make sure we didn't need anything. Even Mom who was usually a model of patience snapped when he danced in with an armful of fabric swatches and his lead costume designer.

"I have a surprise, my darlings. What do you think about this?" He petted an eggplant silk swatch. "I was thinking I could freshen up the place a bit while you're away."

"No!" Mom shouted. She recovered quickly when Lance started and nearly dropped the load of fabric he was carrying. Mom scooted over to him and placed a gentle but firm arm on his shoulder. "That won't be necessary. We are so grateful for your help, but until we get the basement pumped out and functioning again we can't think about the design."

"Leave it to me, Helen. OSF's designers are the best in the world. We'll sketch out some ideas for you, won't we?" He turned and addressed the costume designer. "You know Tatiana, don't you?"

Tatiana gave Mom and me an apologetic smile by way of a greeting.

"I'm having her mock up a scale model of the future Torte for you. It's going to be brilliant. Breathtaking— absolutely breathtaking."

Mom tried to protest, but Lance waved her off. "You don't need to thank me, Helen. Consider it a gift from a friend. Ta-ta, darlings." He clapped twice and Tatiana followed after him.

"What are we going to do about him?" Mom said to me after he was out of earshot and we went over the reduced menu for the thousandth time. Typically Torte produces a variety of breakfast and lunch pastries along with specialty sandwiches, soups, and daily hot food items. In preparation for our trip I had stayed late last night and stockpiled containers of soup. Soup freezes well, so the team would simply need to remove containers of soup from the freezer and reheat them on the stove. We were ditching daily specials and hot breakfast items, and only offering a limited pastry menu—just the basic muffins, cookies, cupcakes, and layered bars. Andy could manage the coffee counter alone, Sterling would help Stephanie with prep and man the register, leaving Stephanie and Bethany in the kitchen. Knowing that Bethany would be around and was willing to step in relieved my stress. I cautioned Stephanie to keep that news on the down low as Lance would surely cause a commotion if he learned that he had competition.

"Hopefully he'll settle down," I said, highlighting the supply list. I wanted to make sure we were completely stocked so that no one had to worry about ordering extra butter or flour while we were away.

"Do you think that something's going on at the theater?" Mom asked.

"I don't know. Why?"

"It's not like him to be disconnected from OSF, especially right now. I think that there's more to the story. I tried to ask him but he changed the subject."

"What do you think is going on?" I thought back to the other day when Lance asked if we could talk alone.

"I don't know, but there's something going on. I'm sure of it."

Maybe that's why Lance had wanted to talk to me. I would have to find time to get a moment alone with him before we left. Add it to the growing list. Mom and I had meetings with our contractors, architect, city inspector, and an interior designer before our bright and early flight tomorrow. I wanted to make sure I had face-to-face time with each of our wholesale accounts, and had a ton of supplies to pick up. It was going to be a busy afternoon.

I untied my Torte apron and pulled on a thin cardigan sweater. "I'm off on errands," I said to Andy on my way out the door.

"Have fun, boss! The coffee will be hot when you get back."

Stepping onto the plaza always brought a smile to my face. Huge red and gold Shakespearean banners waved in the slight wind. They announced the new season of OSF. Every shop had gotten into the spirit with matching red and gold decorations, theater posters, and Elizabethan garb. I paused to admire our display. Stephanie and I had worked on it last week. We had swapped our chocolate display for red and gold ribbons with tiny gold clothespins that held pieces of chalkboard paper. Whenever a customer came in to order a pastry or coffee we asked them to be part of the display. There was a basket of chalk and a variety of sizes and shapes of chalkboard paper that Stephanie had cut out by hand. Customers wrote what they loved about Ashland and we clipped it to the ribbons. It was simple and sweet, just like our baking.

The window was starting to fill up with our customers' sentiments. What they had chosen to share was as varied as the town. One read "funky" while another listed friends' names and places around town like Lithia Park and Mount Ashland. There were Shakespearean quotes and a picture of a stick-figure family drawn by one of our youngest guests.

Pleased with the way the window was already filling in, I smiled and crossed the plaza toward the Lithia fountain.

"Juliet! Over here!" Richard Lord's voice boomed and shook me from my happy moment.

Richard Lord owned the rundown Merry Windsor Hotel across the plaza from Torte, and had taken an immediate dislike to me since the day I moved home. I let out a sigh and turned toward the hotel. Richard was dressed in a hideous golf outfit. I wondered if he was channeling Lance, with his purple and pink plaid shorts that were one size too tight and highlighted his rotund belly in all the wrong places.

"I want a word," he bellowed.

"What's going on, Richard?" I kept a safe buffer between us by standing on the sidewalk. He placed his hands on his hips and stared down at me from the faux front porch of the Merry Windsor. Like the other businesses on the plaza the Merry Windsor was designed in Elizabethan architectural style, but that was the only aesthetic that the hotel and Torte shared. Inside, the hotel had gaudy green carpet that didn't smell much better than the moldy basement property Mom and I had leased. Richard tried to mask the scent with fake apple air fresheners, but it didn't help. His food was equally uninspired.

"Rumor has it that you're leaving town." He chomped on the end of an unlit cigar.

"Mmm-hmm." I stuffed my hands into the pockets of my jeans.

"For how long?"

"Just a few days."

"How many?" His ruddy cheeks puffed with anger.

"Why does it matter?"

He glanced behind him. "I wouldn't want you to miss the big pretheater launch we have planned. I'm sure you've heard all about it."

"Actually I haven't."

"Ha! That's because your pal Lance is out of the loop on this one." Richard's cheeks reddened even more.

"What do you mean?"

"I went directly to the board and they unanimously voted to hold the official launch party here at the Merry Windsor."

"Great."

His smug grin widened. "Have you heard about our new menu? We'll be unveiling it at the launch."

"Nope." I could only imagine. The Merry Windsor was known for having some of the worst food in town. Richard preferred processed meats and prepackaged baked goods to anything fresh or organic.

"I hired a new chef who has completely transformed our dinner menu. Have you heard of the deconstructed movement? We'll be one of the only restaurants in town to offer diners a deconstructed menu. Too bad for Torte."

It took every ounce of control to stifle a laugh. Richard Lord offering a deconstructed menu was about as ironic as it could get. The deconstructed food craze had been wildly popular when I was in culinary school. Chefs would literally tear apart their creations. Instead of building an eight-layer torte they would smear frosting on the bottom of a plate and rip the cake into crumbles, sprinkle edible flowers on the top, and call it art. Food critics raved about the movement, but most pastry chefs stuck with tradition. I hoped that Mom and I would be home in time to witness Richard Lord unveil his deconstructed menu. I would pay a hefty price to watch him or his new chef try to describe how they've torn apart one of his greasy cheeseburgers or stale shepherd's pies.

"Deconstructed. Interesting," I said to him.

"So you have heard of it."

Richard was one of my least favorite people in town, but I didn't have the heart to tell him that he was late for the trend.

"Yep." I nodded.

"Don't get any ideas." He pointed the cigar at me.

"Not to worry. I promise you I won't."

"So should I reserve a seat for you and your mom?" Richard asked, his voice thick with gloating.

"Please. That would be great." I started on. "I have to get going. Good luck with the new menu." I walked away before Richard could say more. Never would I have imagined that the Merry Windsor of all places would launch a deconstructed menu. Classic. However, now I wanted to talk to Lance more than ever. Why would the board have gone against his wishes? I knew that the Merry Windsor was the last restaurant in town that Lance would have picked for the launch event. Mom was right, something must be wrong.

Chapter Four

Unfortunately I never had a chance to talk to Lance before our flight. I spent the day running around, picking up supplies, packing, and triple-checking that Sterling, Stephanie, and Andy were confident and ready to manage Torte in our absence. When my alarm buzzed at five the next morning, I woke up feeling mostly excited but also slightly nervous, hoping that there wasn't anything I'd forgotten.

"It's too late to worry now, honey," Mom assured me as we drove to the airport. "The kids are amazing. Torte is in good hands, and between Bethany, Chef Garrison, and Lance they'll take care of anything that might come up."

I wished I had her confidence. I couldn't shake the feeling that I'd forgotten something, but she was right, there wasn't much I could do about it once we were on the other side of the country. Mom and I picked up the Professor, who emerged from his town house wearing a Hawaiian shirt, khaki shorts, and sandals. I'd never seen him without his tweed jacket. He looked like a different person, as did Mom, who wore a floral sundress and strappy sandals. Their energy was contagious. I allowed my worries about the bakeshop to fade away as we drove to Medford and they peppered me with questions about what to expect on the cruise.

We chatted about our itinerary and the Professor reached for Mom's hand and said, "You brought your dancing shoes, didn't you, Helen?" The Professor and Mom had been dating for over a year and had been friends for much, much longer. Last winter he had hinted that he was interested in taking their relationship to the next level. I had been waiting for him to propose, but so far nothing had developed. I hated keeping a secret from Mom, but I didn't want to ruin any romantic surprise the Professor might have planned. Although at this point I had begun to wonder if maybe I had misinterpreted his words.

Mom caught my eye in the rearview mirror. "I did, but it's been years since I danced. I hope I remember how."

"Your feet never forget," the Professor replied with a smile.

Our first flight took us from Medford to Portland, followed by a cross-country flight to Miami, where we would board the ship. To my surprise when we landed in Florida, Carlos was waiting for us at baggage claim. He held a bouquet of roses and looked more gorgeous than ever. His dark skin was beautifully bronzed and his relaxed white linen shirt and pants only highlighted his tanned skin. He scooped me into a long hug and kissed my forehead. "Julieta, you look so wonderful."

My heart and stomach flopped at the sight of him and the touch of his lips on my cheek made the room spin. "You didn't have to come to the airport," I said, secretly glad that I had opted to wear my A-line black travel dress instead of my standard attire of jeans and a T-shirt. I knew that the black contrasted with my pale blond hair and accentuated my narrow waist. I'd also left my hair long. Carlos loved it when I wore it down.

"I wanted to see you, *mi querida*." He greeted Mom with a friendly hug and kiss on her cheeks, and shook the Professor's hand and kissed him too. Carlos was effusive when it came to physical contact. When Carlos had been in Ashland he had helped the Professor with a case and the two of them had become friends. "Welcome to Miami, my friends. We will get your bags and then I will show you around town, *sí*?"

Mom grinned and looked at the Professor. "It's been a long day," the Professor answered for all of us. "Maybe just a quick bite?"

"Of course, of course. You want to rest. I understand. I will take you to my favorite tapas bar, and then we will get you to the hotel for rest, *sí*?" He winked at me. Carlos knew that I had a weakness for tapas.

"That sounds perfect," Mom said, squeezing his hand. "What time do we board the ship?"

"This is up to you to decide. Julieta and I will need to board early. You have special permission from the captain to come on with us if you would like a tour, or if you want to spend the day seeing the Miami sights that is fine too."

Mom glanced at the Professor. "What do you think, Doug?"

"Ah, Helen, your wish is my command." He gave her a half bow.

Pointing at her suitcase, Mom moved closer to the carousel. "Let's decide tomorrow, as long as that's okay?" She looked to Carlos for confirmation.

"*Sí, sí.* It is no problem." Carlos reached for her bag. He zoomed us through Miami's sweltering streets in a candy-apple-red sports car that he'd borrowed from a friend. He zipped around alleyways and floored the gas pedal as we sped around corners. Mom and I clutched each other's hands in the backseat. My hair flew in my eyes, but I had them shut so tight it didn't matter.

"This is fun!" Mom shouted over the wind.

"Yeah." I shielded my face as we slammed to a stop, Carlos narrowly avoiding plowing down a group of teenagers who were eating dripping ice-cream cones and paying no attention to the road. He cranked the wheel and paralleled into a space that looked like it would barely fit a bicycle. "Aha, here we are." He opened the door, brought his seat forward to let Mom and me out. Then he pointed to the neon above the restaurant. "This is the best place in Miami. You will love it. Come, come."

The restaurant's interior reminded me of a Latin dance club. Ten-foot palm trees were backlit with soft pink light. Plastic flamingos peered out from each palm. Wait staff appeared with pitchers of sangria before we had barely taken a seat.

"This is wonderful, no?" Carlos unbuttoned the top button of his linen shirt. "You must tell me, how is Torte?"

Mom sipped a glass of bloodred sangria and filled him in on Torte's expansion plans. A wistful look passed across his face as she explained how we had applied for and been awarded a grant from the city. He caught my eye and managed a partial smile. I could tell this wasn't news he was hoping to hear. "Ah, this is a big project for you and for Ashland, no?" he asked Mom when she finished.

I wasn't sure if she had caught the look that passed between us, but she kept her tone upbeat and proceeded to tell him about our renovation plans.

More sangria arrived at the table along with bowls of spinach and white bean soup. Carlos encouraged us to eat. "This is a simple Spanish stew with salt cod. You will love it." He turned to the Professor who inhaled the steam. "How are your cases?"

The Professor looked thoughtful as he blew on his spoon. "Static. Which is good. I must say that since we boarded the plane detective work has become a distant memory."

Dinner was a production. In true Carlos form, he knew

the head chef, who brought platter after platter of tapas and wine to our table. After hours and hours of gorging on paella, succulent shrimp skewers, and spicy Spanish sausages, we threw our hands up in protest.

"I can't eat another bite," Mom said, rubbing her belly.

"Nor can, I." The Professor folded his napkin over his plate in a show of solidarity.

"But you must stay for dessert," the chef protested. He waved over a waiter who carried a tray filled with flan, custards, fruit tarts, and a tres leches cake.

Carlos reached for a slice of the cake and handed it to me. "This is your favorite, *sí*?"

I couldn't resist the milky cake. Carlos had introduced me to the popular Latin American dessert years ago, and I made my own version of the creamy milk-soaked sponge cake on the ship. The light cake was always a hit among the guests—especially after a heavy meal. Tonight the restaurant had soaked vanilla sponge in a combination of milk, heavy cream, and evaporated milk. Then the cake was refrigerated and served cold with whipped cream and a dusting of cinnamon and nutmeg.

"Espresso?" the waiter asked.

I started to decline, but Carlos ordered a round of decaf espressos for the table and shared plates of flan and fruit tarts with Mom and the Professor. My stomach groaned at the thought of putting anything else in it, but the tres leches cake was so delicate and moist that I couldn't stop eating.

"It is good, *sí*?" Carlos asked.

"Yeah, but at this rate they're going to have to roll me onto the ship tomorrow," I replied.

"Me too." Mom laughed. "You don't eat like this every night?"

Carlos nodded. "*Sí, sí*. Of course, but in Spain we have

our meal in the middle of the day. It is better this way. You take a siesta and come back for more." To prove his point he stabbed a slice of chocolate cake and took a bite.

The Professor nibbled on his tart. "As the Bard says, 'Strive mightily, but eat and drink as friends.'" He held up his espresso in a toast. "Many thanks, Carlos, for such an enjoyable and ambrosial feast."

Carlos clinked his ceramic cup to the Professor's. "*Sí, sí,* my friend. It is wonderful to share this meal with all of you. And then tomorrow we sail the seven seas and it will be my great pleasure to cook for you."

I knew that Carlos meant what he said. Food was a language of love for him. He believed that we infuse our feelings into the food we prepare. He used to tell novice chefs never to cook mad. "It is no good for the food. You must use your hands in a loving way when you roll out the empanadas or stir a soup. We must always cook from here." He pointed to his heart. "Never from here." He finished, pointing to his head.

It was one of the things that had made me fall hard for him, and also a lesson that had stuck with me. Mom might not have had Carlos's romantic tendencies when it came to baking, but she'd been infusing her baked goods with love for decades at Torte. I knew that it was one of the many reasons our customers returned again and again for warm scones and velvety lattes. Carlos was onto something—food and love went hand in hand. I just hoped that I could keep my own heart in check and not get swept up into his sultry cooking. I was here to do a job, and then I intended to return where I belonged—Ashland.

Chapter Five

I'd forgotten the level of excitement and frenzy involved in setting sail. I woke early the next morning with a sense of eager anticipation and a slight headache from too much sangria. After downing two cups of terrible hotel coffee, I showered and repacked my bag. Carlos knocked on my door as I was running a light gloss over my lips and dusting my cheeks with blush. I've never been much for makeup. Foundation and eye shadow aren't usually a match with a humid and hot kitchen, but I wanted to look professional on my first day back on the ship. Then I tied my hair into a ponytail and opted for a pair of khaki slacks and a plain black T-shirt. Once on board I would be issued a chef's coat along with the crew uniform.

"Good morning, Julieta," Carlos said, greeting me with a kiss and a latte.

"I could kiss you again," I said, grabbing the latte and taking a long sip. The coffee was perfectly balanced—rich and creamy with notes of chocolate and nuts.

"You did not like the hotel's coffee, no?" He held out a paper bag. "I also bring you breakfast."

"You are a lifesaver." I peeked into the bag and spotted a flaky butter croissant. "And a dream."

He took my bag and I followed him to the elevator. "What did your mom and the Professor decide?"

"I think they're sleeping in." I noted the DO NOT DISTURB sign hanging from both of their doors. "It's still early on the West Coast. None of us have adjusted to the time change yet."

Carlos glanced at the watch on his wrist. "But of course. It is very early back home, *sí*?"

"*Sí*." I didn't want to think about the fact that five A.M. in Miami was two in the morning back in Ashland. I'd always found it easiest to immediately put myself on the same schedule as whatever time zone I was in. I might pay for it later, but for the moment with a strong coffee in hand, I was ready to start the day and familiarize myself with the ship.

"Are you nervous?" Carlos asked.

My hands trembled slightly as I clutched the coffee cup tighter. "Maybe a little. It's been a while. I hope I remember everything."

"You will be fine, *mi querida*. Do not worry." He brushed my cheek with the palm of his hand. His familiar touch was comforting and made my heart pound even harder.

I tried to follow his advice as we embarked on the *Amour of the Seas*. The boutique ship catered to foodies and passengers seeking a more luxurious and intimate cruising experience. The smaller size allowed guests to mingle and build camaraderie. It attracted clients interested in the finest cuisine and amenities like butler service for each cabin. The other benefit of sailing on a smaller ship was that the *Amour of the Seas* could reach secluded harbors and dock at undiscovered spots. Recently the *Amour* had pioneered the concept of overnight ports— allowing passengers to experience local nightlife and stroll along starry beaches until the wee hours of the morning.

As I walked up the gangplank I ran my hand along the oiled wooden railings and took in the ship's impressive refined design. No detail had been spared in its yachtlike style from its expansive balconies with teak Adirondack chairs and wispy yellow and navy flags to Edison bulb lights strung from each deck.

It took a while to sign my temporary contract and make sure all of my paperwork and documents were up to date. By the time I finished and had been assigned a temporary cabin and issued a chef's coat, the sun had risen. The smell of industrial cleaner and long narrow hallways below the main decks was instantly familiar. As were some of the faces of the crew. It took me almost a half hour to get to the kitchen because I stopped to greet old friends and catch up briefly. Once I had stowed my bags in my cabin and changed into my uniform I took a long breath and made my way to the kitchen.

The purser was waiting for me. He introduced me to the staff—many of whom I already knew—and explained that I would be in charge of pastry service until the replacement *pâtissier* arrived next week. Fortunately I had spent almost three years on the ship, which was a rarity in the world of cruising. Most assignments lasted for four to nine months, but thanks to Carlos's status as executive chef and his sought-after cuisine we had been lucky enough to stay on the same ship for a long stretch. I knew every passageway on the ship and most of the crew. Hopefully that would help ease my adjustment back into the fourteen- or fifteen-hour workdays that lay ahead.

Even the captain made a brief appearance and greeted me with a handshake and salute. "Nice to have you back on board, chef." He stood at attention. His graying hair gave away his age, but otherwise he was trim, with the muscle mass of someone half his age. His pristine white uniform fit him perfectly. The navy shoulder board on his starched uniform had three gold ribbons and two gold stars. Matching gold wings were pinned on his left chest.

"Thanks, Captain." I squared my shoulders in response to his posture.

"At ease, chef. We're happy to have you in the kitchen." He leaned closer and lowered his voice. "Any chance you'll be making your jelly roll this trip?"

"Count on it." I nodded.

"Not sure if you heard but we're tracking a mass of cold air from the north converging with the warmer air here that could throw a wrench in our plans. I'll keep you and the crew updated, but there's an outside chance we could lose a day depending on how far the system extends. We should be able to skirt it, but I want the crew informed in case."

"Got it." It wasn't uncommon for cruise ships to navigate around bad weather. By losing a day the captain meant that we might not make our first port of call. Ports had extremely tight docking schedules, and if we missed ours, even by a few hours, we would have to continue on. Depending on how far off course the captain had to take us, passengers might be stuck on board for an extra day. A weather system like this probably wouldn't be more than a blip on the radar for the mega cruise ships that housed thousands of passengers and boasted onboard putting greens, movie theaters, spas, shopping promenades, and more restaurants than Ashland, but for a ship our size even a minor storm could make things a bit rocky. If we encountered wind or rain it shouldn't really impact my team, but it could mean logging more hours baking. Typically the majority of passengers booked excursions at each port of call. We planned accordingly, scaling back our pastry production on those days.

The captain cleared his throat and called my staff to attention. "Folks, it's looking like we're going to have to go out and around some weather. We're working on navigating a new course on the bridge, but there's heavy commercial traffic in some of the channels so we'll keep you posted as we go. Stay alert. We'll be pulling out soon." He gave everyone a salute and then marched away.

"Do you need anything else?" the purser asked me. "Appetizer service is due on the pool deck by three o'clock sharp."

"Understood." I glanced around the kitchen where my team stood like culinary soldiers, with rolling pins as weapons and crisp navy and white uniforms. "I think we've got it from here. I'll let you know if something changes."

He seemed impressed, but gave me a firm look and repeated, "Appetizers plated and ready to serve by three o'clock."

I nodded and waited until he was out of earshot before I told my team that they could stand down. They all looked relieved and gave me a warm welcome. "We're so glad it's you," one young chef said. She reminded me a bit of Stephanie, only without the purple hair. "It's been a nightmare around here."

I gave them a few minutes to vent. I've found that when there's drama in the kitchen it's best to hash it out and move on, instead of trying to bottle it up. That would be a recipe for disaster. The last thing I wanted was for one of my sous chefs to explode in the middle of service.

"Okay," I said, reviewing the plan for the day. "Our first task is the send-off party and as I'm sure you just heard we need to deliver by three. Where do we stand with prep?"

While the staff explained what remained to be done I made sure that I was familiar and happy with the appetizer menu. Whenever a ship sets sail the guests are treated to a send-off party. This afternoon's party would take place on the pool deck. The appetizers were the star of the show

and the first taste of the food to come for the next few days.
I wanted everything to be perfect.

A steel-drum band would play as passengers waved to
people on the shore and noshed on sweets and tropical
drinks. The send-off parties were always a festive atmosphere and called for whimsical pastries. We would be
making mini kiwi tarts, chocolate and marshmallow fruit
skewers, baked brie and sundried tomatoes in puff pastry,
and grilled pineapple shortbread.

We had plenty of time but we'd also be baking on a
much bigger scale than I was used to at Torte. The ship was
nearly full, which meant that over six hundred guests
would be boarding in the next few hours. My kitchen staff
would work a minimum of eighty-hour weeks with very
limited time off for even the most basic things like lunch
breaks. We would be baking tarts and puff pastries by the
thousands. I had to quickly shift gears and focus on large-
scale baking. At Torte a busy day might mean selling out
of a hundred pastries. That wouldn't even scratch the
surface on the ship.

I organized the staff into three groups. The first would
focus on the sweet pastries for the send-off party, the second would work on savory pastries, and the third would
begin dinner prep with me. In addition to the party fare,
we were responsible for the dessert bar after dinner, as well
as sweets for the late-night snack buffet, and delivering
baked goods to the espresso bar and café on the second
deck. I'd forgotten how much strategy was involved when
it came to baking in mass quantity. Much of my role as
head pastry chef was to keep everyone on task and out of
each other's way.

Soon the kitchen was a blur of activity. My staff was
rolling out four-foot sheets of pastry dough and hand-
pressing hundreds of pie crusts. I weaved my way be-

tween the teams, checking on progress and giving minor suggestions on technique. Running a kitchen this size was more about control and structure and less about baking. No wonder I had fallen in love with Torte. In Ashland there wasn't a day that went by where my hands weren't coated in flour or my arms sore from kneading dough. That wasn't the case on the ship. The staff would do the vast majority of the prep and baking, leaving me to oversee them and the menu.

For the dessert buffet we would showcase sugar art and a variety of design techniques. Not only did the ship's guests expect our pastries to taste delicious but they wanted to be dazzled by tiered cakes and stunning displays of fruit sculptures. Lance would love this, I thought. I'd have to send him a picture later.

While my staff tempered chocolate and whipped mounds of fresh cream, I reacquainted myself with the kitchen. The galley was located two decks below the dining room. The pastry kitchen was next to the main kitchen where Carlos orchestrated a staff the size of the entire company at OSF. Every so often I could hear his Spanish accent over the sound of whirling mixers and sautéing pans. There were two other kitchens onboard. The members of the onboard culinary staff included butchers, sushi cooks, pantry cooks, pastry cooks, buffet cooks, and dozens of line cooks and sous chefs. Feeding six hundred passengers as well as the crew three meals a day, plus a never-ending rotation of snacks and treats, was no small feat.

Before I finished taking stock of the equipment and reviewing the inventory in the ship's massive pantries, it was time to start assembling the sweet trays for the send-off party.

"Where do you want these?" a young chef asked, holding

up an industrial stainless steel tray with sliced pineapple that had been sprinkled with cinnamon and a touch of sugar.

"Take those to the pool deck. We'll grill them fresh," I instructed. Time to start the show. Part of baking on a cruise ship was about performance. I reached for a clean chef's jacket and headed for the pool. I took the crew corridor (also known as the artery) to the crew stairwell and upstairs. The crew had its own elevators, stairways, mess hall, bars, and game rooms. There was an entire world below deck that passengers never saw.

I was a few feet away from the crew stairwell when I spotted a woman wearing ripped jeans and an oversized sweatshirt ducking out of one of the supply closets.

"Excuse me," I called, assuming she was a passenger who had gotten turned around since she wasn't in uniform. "Are you lost?"

The woman whirled in my direction, causing her long blond ponytail to swing. She slammed the closet door behind her. Her eyes reminded me of a deer caught in headlights. They were wide and filled with fear.

"Sorry," I said, approaching her. "I didn't mean to startle you. I just wondered if you need help getting to the passenger decks. It's easy to get lost around here."

She backed up. "Oh no. I'm good. Sorry." Without another word she sprinted down the corridor.

I felt bad for scaring her. It wasn't as if a passenger would get in trouble for being on the crew levels. Her reaction was strange, but then again some guests developed a mystique about the crew. They had a tendency to want to get a glimpse of what went on behind the scenes, especially cruise fanatics. There were entire Web sites and tours dedicated to giving outsiders a peek into life below deck. I blew off the young woman's response to that. Part of me wanted to follow her and explain that working on a cruise ship was far from glamorous, but work beckoned so I continued on.

Polished teak floors and the scent of salty air and grilled meat greeted me as I stepped onto the pool deck. A wave-less blue-tiled pool sat in the center of the deck surrounded by creamy yellow and navy lounge chairs. Two hot tubs enclosed in glass flanked each side of the pool. To the aft (or front of the ship) a bar, named Top Shelf, was designed with the same teak wood and yellow and navy awnings.

Every passenger was greeted with a tropical drink. A steel-drum band pounded out rhythmic beats on the star-board side. The atmosphere was alive and festive. I couldn't help but smile as I took it all in. It was impossible not to get swept up into the excitement as guests waved happy good-byes to everyone waiting on the shore. I was about to set sail again and I was actually looking forward to a few relaxing days at sea. But I didn't realize how wrong I would be.

Chapter Six

Guests devoured our pastries. I had to send runners back to the kitchen for extra platters and keep an eye on the young chef grilling the pineapple. His interpretation of lightly charred was much darker than mine. I wanted each slice of pineapple to be grilled with beautiful char marks and warmed, but not blackened. The smoky char mingled with the sweet and juicy fruit and a hint of spicy cinnamon was always a crowd favorite.

One woman wearing a two-piece shell bikini came back three times. "These are so good," she commented with a mouthful of pineapple. "I've never had it grilled before."

"That's why we're here," I said with a smile, handing her another hot slice. "Our goal is to introduce you to new flavors native to the regions we'll be visiting." The food philosophy of the *Amour of the Sea* was to infuse the cruise with flavor. It was one of the reasons that Carlos had been drawn to work on this ship. Food was a centerpiece of every voyage.

"I just want to eat this for the next four days."

"I'm sure we can arrange that." I grinned.

Mom and the Professor weaved through the crowd. They were both glowing and wearing matching pink and white orchid leis. "Hey, you two, can I offer you some grilled pineapple?"

The Professor took a slice and offered one to Mom. "This is quite a production." He pointed toward the band who were draped with colorful beads and pounding the drums with gusto. On deck six above us passengers waved from the crow's nest where more blue and yellow flags flew in the breeze.

"This is nothing. Have you toured the other decks yet?" I asked. They both shook their heads. "You have to do that next. There's an art gallery, the ballroom, a library, and an outdoor espresso bar on deck four. And if you need help don't forget to summon your butler. They will assist with all of your needs from unpacking your bags to delivering hors d'oeuvres to your room."

"Is every cruise like this?" Mom asked. She held a strawberry daiquiri with a paper umbrella in one hand. Her halter dress matched the yellow lounge chairs and brought out the natural honey highlights in her hair. "I knew they were elegant, but I didn't expect this."

"This isn't even the most opulent ship on the sea right now."

"Wow, I had no idea." She sipped her drink and surveyed the hopping deck. The ship's horn sounded three times, signaling that we were about to embark.

"Ladies." The Professor raised his drink in a toast. "To our maiden voyage, Helen." His voice was husky as he clinked his glass to Mom's and gave her a peck on the cheek.

The band paused momentarily as a short, bald, and very tan man took the stage. He wore an aqua-blue T-shirt that read: LET YOUR DREAMS SET SAIL. "Welcome, welcome!" His booming voice echoed in the mic. "I'm your cruise director, Rocky, and I'm here to pamper your every need for the next four days."

Everyone cheered. Rocky reached for a drink and turned around to point at the back of his shirt. The slogan on the opposite side read: SHIP FACED. "Now, I want you all to enjoy yourselves. This is a place to let loose. We have an incredible lineup of entertainment planned for you. I don't want any of you hiding out in your cabin. You're here to live it up and party! We have the absolute best food in the entire fleet on this ship. Not to mention incredible cocktails, the finest wines from around the world, and an assortment of imported microbrews that rivals a German beer hall."

This encouraged another round of whoops and cheers from the crowd.

"You are going to be treated to a sensory buffet and my specialty is to get you ship faced!" He finished his drink in one gulp and slapped one of the drummers on the back. "Hit it, boys."

The steel drums pulsed as the ship slowly lurched forward. Even Mom and the Professor ran to the side to wave good-bye. We were off. There was no turning back now. I watched as Rocky mingled with the guests, making sure that everyone had a full drink and a heaping plate of party food. He caught my eye and motioned for me to wait for him. I had worked with Rocky a few times. He was what the staff referred to as a "lifer," having worked in the industry for nearly three decades. Rocky's personality was a match for his job. The cruise director's responsibility was to keep everyone happy and entertained. He did that well, but was a bit too enthusiastic for my taste, and would be a much better match for one of the massive ships. Carlos wasn't a fan. He had asked the captain on more than one occasion to let Rocky go in favor of hiring a more refined cruise director—preferably someone with food knowledge. "He knows nothing of serving from the heart," Carlos would complain to the captain. "My food it is meant to be savored and eaten slow. Not for Rocky's crazy show."

"Jules." Rocky slapped me on the back so hard that I wondered if it would leave a mark. "I heard that you had returned. Welcome, welcome!"

"Thanks, Rocky. It's just a few days until the new pastry chef arrives."

"Sure, that's what they all say. You know that the water is in your blood. Once a cruiser, always a cruiser."

"Well." I hesitated. I had to look down to meet his eyes. He only came to my shoulder. I knew I was on the tall side, but Rocky was short.

"You can't fool me. I see it in those baby blues. You're home again. I know someone who is pretty happy about that. Where is your hunky husband? He's supposed to be up here to greet my guests." Rocky looked around for Carlos.

Mom and the Professor danced back over with the Professor twirling Mom through the crowd of happy passengers. His reddish beard glowed with the sun, as did Mom's skin.

"Rocky, let me introduce you." I offered introductions, feeling relieved that I didn't have to explain my temporary gig in more detail.

"I see the resemblance." Rocky fawned over Mom. "A beautiful mother and daughter. Welcome, welcome to my ship. You two are going to have the time of your lives." He stopped and stared at the Professor's empty glass. "What's this? An empty cocktail glass. Unacceptable. You need a refresher, my friend." Rocky glanced around for wait staff who were circulating with drinks but no one was in sight. "Hold on, I'll be right back."

The Professor tried to stop him. "Don't bother," I said. "He's on a mission now. You're both going to have an entire tray of drinks. You heard him, his goal is to get everyone ship faced."

Mom's eyes widened. "Oh no, I'm barely sipping this and am starting to feel a bit rocky myself."

"That's the movement from the ship," I assured her.

She chuckled. "Oh right. I guess I'm not used to moving at all. We're pretty landlocked in Ashland, aren't we?"

The Professor looped his arm through hers. "That's the way we like it."

"I suppose I'll get used to this?" Mom asked me.

"You will. Give it a little time. Soon you won't even notice it." I actually hoped that would stay true. The captain had warned us that a few other ships our size had experienced high seas in the Atlantic. I wasn't worried. The weather in the Caribbean in March is usually about as perfect as it gets. We should be sailing on smooth seas and steer clear of the storm. Of course, one thing that I had learned from working on a ship for over a decade was that weather at sea can change in an instant. I would have to cross my fingers and toes that we didn't hit any rough patches. I wanted Mom to relax and enjoy herself for the next few days, not have to worry about being seasick.

As expected Rocky returned with a tray of drinks and handed one to each of us, ignoring everyone's protest. "Hold up your glasses," he commanded. "A toast to Jules and her mom. I'm going to see to it that you have the cruise of your life."

Mom gave me a pained smile and sipped her new drink. Rocky got pulled away by another group of guests. After he was out of earshot, Mom whispered, "He's enthusiastic."

"Don't worry about Rocky," I said. "His job is to be enthused. He has an entire crew of regulars that he has to please, so I'm sure he'll lose interest when he realizes you aren't going to rebook."

"Rebook?" The Professor raised one brow.

"That's the goal. Rocky's job—in addition to making sure everyone is happy and entertained—is to get guests to book another cruise."

"But we've barely left port." The Professor stood on his toes to see over the crowd. Miami's waterfront was vanishing behind us.

"Exactly."

"I had no idea." The Professor sounded incredulous.

"That's the world of cruising. You know, there's quite a contingent of people around your age who book back-to-back cruises. They basically live from ship to ship."

"You mean they've given up their personal residences?" the Professor asked.

"Exactly. If you love cruising, which most of our guests do, it makes sense. It's not really much more expensive than paying rent or a mortgage, especially when you factor in meals and entertainment."

The Professor turned to Mom. "What do you say, Helen, should we retire and sail around the world?"

Mom frowned. "I don't know. I think I like land better." She clutched his arm tighter as the ship picked up speed. "Not that I'm not thrilled to be here, Jules."

"You don't have to worry about me. I'm not going to try to get you to book another cruise, but watch out for Rocky." I winked, which ended up contorting half my face.

Mom laughed. The Professor gave me a half bow. "On that note, what do you say we take a spin around the dance floor?"

"I'm already spinning," Mom said, handing me her full drink. "Might as well spin some more."

"Have fun! I'll see you both at dinner," I called as the Professor whisked her away. Good. I hoped that she could enjoy herself, and I was pretty confident that the Professor had the same goal in mind. Turning my attention back to the task at hand, I checked on the cook overseeing the grill and made sure the trays and platters were stocked. Everything seemed to be going off without a hitch, so I decided it was safe to return to the kitchen.

I weaved through the crowd, allowing my feet to move to the beat of the drums. I had to credit Rocky, he definitely knew how to throw a party. There wasn't a sad face in the crowd. Everyone was in the spirit and the energy was contagious. Once I had made it to the far side of the deck I took in one last glance at Mom and the Professor who were right in the mix. I let out a small sigh of relief and headed for the back stairs.

To my surprise I spotted the young woman whom I'd bumped into downstairs stuffing pastries and appetizers into the front pocket of her sweatshirt. What was she doing? Didn't she know that food, drinks, and gratuity were all included in the price of her ticket? If she wanted a late-night snack or had a craving for chocolate cookies she simply needed to dial zero and a butler would appear with her request within minutes.

I watched as she wrapped a caramel nut bar in a napkin and crammed it in her pocket. Then she glanced around the pool deck and hurried over to the crew stairwell. What was she up to? I pushed past a couple wearing matching navy boat hats and spinning on the dance floor and followed after her.

As I opened the heavy metal door, I almost ran into Rocky. He had his back to me and was yelling at the woman. When he spotted me, the woman ran down the stairs, her long blond hair bouncing with each step.

"Hey, what's going on with her?" I asked, pointing below.

"Huh? It's nothing. Just a drunk passenger," Rocky replied, keeping his gaze on the woman fleeing down the steps. He sounded casual but his face had lost any trace of humor. A door slammed on the deck below and the woman disappeared.

"Already?" I asked. "That has to be a record."

A fake smile returned to Rocky's leathered face. "No. Not even. Once I had to have medical escort a woman off board who was plastered before we even left shore."

"Yikes. I don't envy you."

"It comes with the territory. Every cruise has to have at least one drunk or disorderly passenger. I told her to go sleep it off. She'll be fine by morning."

"Right. But I think I just saw her hoarding food. She was stuffing her pockets with appetizers. Isn't that weird?"

"Hardly. Don't even get me started on some of the weird things I've seen over the years. You never know with the drunks." Rocky held his ground in the middle of the staircase. I almost had the sense that he was trying to block me.

"Yeah," I agreed, but something about the woman was bugging me. She didn't look like she was drunk, and why had she been down below earlier and using the crew stairwell? I pushed past him. "Good luck with the rest of the party. Everyone seems to be having a great time."

He gave me a salute, took the stairs two at a time and opened the door on the deck below for me. I couldn't shake the feeling that whatever I had just witnessed with the blond woman was more than a case of her having too much to drink, but pastry was calling me and I didn't give it another thought.

Chapter Seven

I couldn't believe how easily I fell into my old routine. Once I returned to the galley I was calling out commands and tasting soufflés and custards as if I had never left. The *Amour of the Sea*'s pastry kitchen was different from Torte in size, scope, and design. Unlike Torte's homey vibe and royal color scheme, the ship's sterile and spotless kitchen was constructed entirely out of stainless steel from the ceiling to the countertops. The floors were cement, which made them easy to hose down after each shift. Every square inch of the kitchen would be scrubbed and polished between lunch and dinner service.

Maintaining strict cleaning and safety standards was critical. With so many bodies working in close quarters and so many hands touching food, a bug could spread like butter on hot bread and sicken the crew and passengers. I intended to ensure that didn't happen on my watch.

Next door I could hear Carlos blaring Latin dance music and teasing his staff. He had a reputation for being the biggest prankster on the ship. According to one of the cake designers, his latest antic involved playing Russian roulette with cartons of boiled and raw eggs. Before we set sail he lined up his staff in two teams and made them toss eggs back and forth. No one knew which eggs had been hard-boiled and which were raw. Whenever someone broke a raw egg they were out and assigned cleanup duty. However, Carlos rewarded the losers as well as the winners with cheesy omelets and champagne. His whimsical nature endeared him to his staff. He also made a concerted effort to dine in the mess hall whenever possible.

On many cruise ships the crew dines based on their rank. There are separate mess halls for officers versus the crew. But the *Amour of the Seas* took a unique approach to building comradery by offering one communal mess hall where everyone from the captain to the dishwasher and cleaning crew dined together. Carlos believed that the only way to really know a person was to break bread with them. He took this philosophy to heart and lingered over late-night dinners in the mess hall, listening as line cooks and deckhands shared their life stories. The food for the crew was as diverse as the many nationalities represented on board. From vegetarian and vegan options like Ethiopian lentil and sweet potato stew to Filipino lumpia with chicken and shrimp, the crew menu offered tastes from around the globe as well as American standbys like grilled hamburgers and French fries.

Before I knew it, dinner service was plated and ready to deliver to the dining salon. I took the opportunity to return to my room and change. My cabin was located one deck below the galley, and thanks to my temporary role as head pastry chef it sported a small porthole. I made my way along the artery's polished laminate floors past framed plans of each deck on the ship that were mounted to the walls. In the event of an emergency each member of the crew was responsible for a specific area. The color-coded plans directed crew members where to go and indicated different evacuation routes.

I took a few minutes to unpack my bags and brush my hair. Formal attire was recommended in the dining salon, so I opted for a knee-length black flared skirt and white silk tank top. I tied my hair back with a thin black scarf and finished my outfit with strappy black sandals and a matching black onyx necklace and earrings. Not bad, Jules, I said to myself in the mirror. Then I took the stairs to the dining room. The crew elevators tend to be busy no matter whether it's day or night, but I knew that during the peak of dinner service they would be in constant use.

The upper decks were nothing short of opulent, with marble staircases, crystal chandeliers, and art work that could rival that on display in the best galleries in the world. As head pastry chef I had access to each deck and had been invited to dine with Mom and the Professor. I spotted them right away when I stepped into the glowing dining room. Their table was on portside with floor-to-ceiling glass windows providing a stunning view of the sea. I weaved through tables draped in pristine white cloths and set with gold-decorated china and crystal stemware. Wait staff in black tuxedos circled the room with bottles of sparkling wine. Grecian columns divided the room into four sections and a three-tiered chandelier the size of a small yacht hung in the center of the room. It dripped silver light in every direction, making silverware shimmer and casting flecks like starlight off the walls.

Mom waved when she caught my eye. She and the Professor were already seated and taking in the view of the fading purple sky outside. "Honey, you look gorgeous," Mom said, squeezing my hand as I took the seat across from her.

"You do too." I returned the compliment. She looked incredible in a soft chiffon sundress with spaghetti straps that revealed her well-toned arms. She always claimed that years of kneading bread dough and rolling out pie crusts was the only workout she needed. "See, you didn't need to worry about what to pack," I teased.

She twisted her wedding ring that hung around her neck. "I'm out of practice when it comes to formal wear."

The Professor cleared his throat. "Ladies, I must say that you are the two most beautiful women in the room regardless of what you're wearing."

"Oh, Doug." Mom hit his arm playfully. "You would say that if I was wearing a flour sack."

He pretended to be injured and looked to me for support. "Juliet, a little assistance, please."

"I'm not getting in the middle of this one." I picked up my water glass and took a sip. "But I will say that I think we all are making Ashland proud, even you, Professor."

Grinning, he raised his wineglass in thanks. It was true. No one at Torte would recognize us. Maybe most of all the Professor in his navy suit with nautical tie. "I like that you've gone with a cruising theme," I commented.

He held out the tie. "Why, thank you. I had quite forgotten that I even owned it until I unearthed it from my closet. It's quite fitting, don't you think?"

"Quite," Mom bantered.

At that moment I felt a hand on the back of my neck and turned to see Carlos standing behind me. My breath caught at the sight of him in his tailored black suit. He had slicked his hair down and tucked a single red rose into his lapel. "Julieta, you are a vision," he said, kissing the top of my head.

"I didn't know you were joining us." I squeezed my fingers together under the table to maintain my composure.

"But of course. The Professor invited me to dine with you. How could I say no?" He nodded to the Professor, then removed the rose from his lapel and handed it to me.

"Helen, how beautiful you look too," Carlos said to Mom with his dazzling smile.

My heart thumped in my chest. Why did he have to have such a visceral effect on me? He scooted his chair close to mine so that our knees touched. I felt a spark of electricity shoot up my spine.

The conversation turned to food as the waiter brought our first course—sea scallops sautéed in butter and fresh herbs. While we sipped prosecco and ate the succulent scallops Rocky appeared on the small stage at the far end of the dining room. "Hey, hey, foodies. How is everyone doing tonight?" His bald head glistened under the chandelier.

Carlos muttered under his breath. "Idiot. He knows nothing of food."

Rocky continued in his over-the-top tone. "It's customary to give you a taste of our entertainment lineup while you get the first taste of the award-winning cuisine you'll be eating for the next few days." He paused and placed his hand over his forehead like a visor. "I thought I saw our executive chef out there." He scanned the crowd, finally landing on our table. "There he is! Chef Carlos, can you stand up and give a wave?"

Carlos scoffed, but plastered on a charming smile, and followed Rocky's request. I noticed a group of older women at a table nearby nudge each other when he smiled at them. He was used to this kind of attention. As executive chef it was his duty to mingle with the passengers and talk up his food.

Rocky clicked his fingers in Carlos's direction. "Ladies and gentlemen, as I'm sure your taste buds are already telling you, you are in the hands of a master. Loosen those belts and get ready because you are about to eat some of the finest cuisine you'll find anywhere in the world. Isn't that right, chef?"

Carlos gave a half laugh and sat down. I could sense the tension in his body as Rocky proceeded to rave about the food and went on to introduce the ship's wine steward. I held my breath, hoping that he hadn't noticed me. Unlike

Carlos, I didn't enjoy being the center of attention. Fortunately Rocky motioned to the other side of the room and a young guy with a guitar slung around his shoulder joined him on stage.

"Now folks, as you know, in addition to the best cuisine we have a top-notch entertainment lineup for you. Some of the huge ships like to talk about how their shows are Vegas style. Not here on the *Amour*. Our mission is love. Love of food, romantic music, salsa dancers to get you in the mood. Be sure to check with your butler for your personalized daily activity schedule. From literary discussions in the library to wine tasting, I've got your every need covered while you're on board with us. And tonight I have someone special to introduce—Grayson Allen." He clapped his arm around Grayson's waist. Grayson towered over Rocky. "Grayson is a singer-songwriter who will make you swoon and make you drink lots more wine. If you were at the send-off party this afternoon, you know that it's my mission to keep you happy and ship faced and I can't think of anyone better to get you in the mood for a little romance than Grayson."

Grayson and I had worked together on my last cruise before I walked out on Carlos. I remembered the first time I heard his poetic lyrics and tender voice. Carlos and I had slipped away to take in the late show. We sipped champagne with our arms around each other and swayed to Grayson's romantic melodies. He dedicated the show to us. I wasn't sure if it was because he could sense our connection or if Carlos had slipped him a twenty before the show.

Rocky moved off the stage while encouraging everyone to clap. A round of applause broke out in the dining room as Grayson sat on a bar stool and tuned his guitar. The two men were polar opposites. Rocky looked like a typical cruiser with his bulky body and slick attitude whereas Grayson reminded me of a trust-fund hippie in his intentionally ripped jeans and Chuck Taylors. His long curly hair fell from his knit beanie.

"Excuse me," a woman's voice sounded behind me. "I think this is my table assignment." She motioned to the empty chair next to me.

"Sure, have a seat." I scooted even closer to Carlos to make room for her to squeeze in. Carlos instinctively wrapped his arm around my shoulder and left it there. I thought about moving away but his arm felt good.

"I'm Babs," the woman said to the table. I guessed her to be about Mom's and the Professor's age. She wore her dark hair in a severe, spiky short cut and was dressed from head to toe in black leather. Thick silver hoop earrings the size of tea saucers hung from her earlobes and a collection of heavy chains weighted down her neck.

After a round of introductions we learned that Babs was a music producer from Miami. "What sort of music do you produce?" Mom asked, but Babs shushed her and pointed to the stage where Grayson was beginning his first set.

Grayson's lyrics were about heartache and longing. I felt acutely aware of Carlos's arm around my shoulder and his breath on my neck as Grayson strummed on his guitar and sang love song after love song, and course after course arrived at our table. Familiar feelings flooded my body. I had a hard time concentrating on Grayson's performance with Carlos so close. At one point, Grayson moved from the stage and weaved through the tables. I was impressed that he could play and move so seamlessly. He looped through the back and then found his way to our table.

I watched Babs study him, and wondered if that was part of the gig. As a pastry chef I find it impossible not to analyze taste and flavor when I'm eating someone else's pastry. I figured the same must be true for Babs because she scrutinized his performance, watching intently as Grayson's fingers flexed and bent his guitar strings.

He must have noticed her attention as well because he locked eyes with her and sang directly to her. Instead of being pleased by this Babs glared and turned to stare out the window. Grayson shrugged, dropped to one knee, and serenaded Mom.

Carlos squeezed my shoulder as a steady blush crept up Mom's chin. The Professor leaned back in his chair and watched Grayson croon his love song from bended knee. When the song was over Grayson reached for Mom's hand and planted a kiss on it. Her cheeks turned a shade darker, but she smiled and clapped along with the rest of us.

Grayson returned to the stage and finished his set. When he was done Mom waved her hands in front of her face. "Whew, I've never had that happen before."

The Professor ran his fingers over his ginger and gray beard. "I believe our young singer has most excellent taste, don't you agree?" he asked Carlos with a twinkle in his eyes.

Carlos removed his arm from my shoulder and sat forward in his chair. "*Sí, sí*, Helen. He knows beauty when he sees it."

"In the business we call that pandering," Babs scoffed. I thought back to the first time I'd heard him play and wondered if she was right.

"I'm sure he gets extra tips that way." Mom chuckled, trying to cut the tension.

Babs rolled her eyes and drummed her fingers on the table. "That's about all he's going to get. The kid has no talent, and honestly, how many times can you hear the lyric 'lost in love' without wanting to throw up?"

Carlos caught my eye and made a face. I wasn't sure what Babs's issue with Grayson was. He sounded like he had talent to me, and the rest of the dining room appeared to agree. Before we had a chance to dive deeper into her music background, Rocky hopped onto the stage again. "How awesome was that, cruisers? Let's give it up for Grayson Allen." He led everyone in another round of applause. "Now that we've got the romantic vibe rolling, we're going to kick it up a notch and heat things up in here.

"How many of you like to dance?"

A number of passengers shouted and hands shot in the air.

"All right, then put your hands together for the hottest dancers around. We're going to crank up the tunes and get your booties shaking with Maria and her Salsa Sisters!" He leaped off the stage in synch with rhumba music that played overhead.

I tensed up as a leggy dancer with cascading locks of jet-black hair and a skimpy sequined skirt and bra shook her way onto the stage. I knew Maria. She and her Salsa Sisters had been one of the most popular entertainment acts on the *Amour of the Seas* for years. She had also had a thing for Carlos and hadn't made any attempts to disguise her interest in my husband. Carlos snapped his fingers and swayed to the beat as Maria and the Salsa Sisters strutted between the tables in a flurry of sequins. Carlos didn't appear fazed by the fact that I had stiffened, but Mom caught my eye across the table and frowned.

There was no denying that Maria was gorgeous. She had curves in all the right places and could contort her body in ways I never thought possible. But seeing her ignite the room made jealousy bubble inside me. I didn't like the feeling, and I really didn't like the idea of someone else capturing Carlos's attention.

I tried to plaster on a smile and pretend that I was enjoying the dance. Maria made a point of shimmying up to every man in the dining room, including Carlos, and shaking her assets.

"Now that's an act I can get behind," Babs said, leaning over to me while Maria spun in a circle around our table. "That is real talent."

"Right," I said, reaching for my wineglass and taking a huge sip.

The Salsa Sisters promenaded out of the room. Maria on the other hand stopped at one of the tables at the far side of the dining room. At first I thought she was posing for a picture with a fan, but then I realized she was talking to the mysterious woman I had bumped into in the crew corridor earlier and spotted swiping food at the send-off party. The woman had ditched her jeans and sweatshirt and wore a skimpy silver dress and matching stilettos. Her bottle-blond hair had been tied in the same ponytail and she had the same frightened look in her eyes. Maria grabbed her by the wrist and dragged her out of the dining room. Who was this woman? I had to fight back the urge to race after them.

Rocky jumped back onto the stage and reviewed the evening's lineup and where each act could be found on the ship. "Before you go," he said as wait staff cleared our dinner plates. "I have a quick message from the captain. He's getting a brief update about a little weather system out there. He wanted me to officially welcome you aboard. Usually he does that himself at our first dinner, but he'll be with us tomorrow night and have a noon update for you tomorrow. Not to worry, I personally assure you that we will have smooth sailing for the next few days. That's it for my announcements and the sampling of our awesome entertainment. Now let's have some fun and get ship faced tonight!"

Babs downed the last of her wine, excused herself from

the table, and marched to the stage in her ankle-high black leather boots. I wondered if she was going to ask Rocky about Maria and the Salsa Sisters.

"A weather system," Mom said. "Should we be worried?"

"No, no, this is nothing, Helen. Do not worry. The captain will keep us far, far from it." Carlos pointed to the black sky out the window. "See? The water it is perfectly calm."

Mom didn't look convinced, but smiled and nodded.

I glanced at my watch. It was nearing ten, and I had a huge day tomorrow. "I should go," I said. Carlos pushed back his chair when I stood.

"*Sí*, I will walk you to your cabin."

I almost told him no, but after seeing Maria again something unfamiliar and unwelcome had come over me. I took his hand and let him lead me away. This wasn't good. I couldn't hold on to Carlos just because someone else might take him, but at the same time I didn't want to let him go.

Chapter Eight

I slept like a baby, probably thanks to the gentle rocking of the ship and the fact that I had been on my feet and moving since before dawn. When I woke the next morning I felt refreshed and ready to tackle the day, which was good considering that I had multiple meals to oversee.

After a quick shower, I tugged on a pair of capris, a V-neck white T-shirt, and my tennis shoes. I wanted to get a morning walk in before the rush of pastry production kicked into high gear. One of my favorite memories of my time on the ship was my early morning walks on the pool deck. This morning was no exception. The sea was as smooth as rolled pie crust. Stars faded into the dawning sky. I breathed in the salty air and let the mist hit my face. This is just how I remember it, I thought to myself as I started my first lap around the running track that circled the pool deck.

Unlike yesterday's send-off party the deck was deserted. Most of the lounge chairs had been washed and stacked. Soon deckhands and cleaning staff would restock blue and white striped beach towels and position sun umbrellas strategically around the pool, but for now the space was mine.

The teak floors and hand railings smelled of wood

polish. A flock of seagulls squawked above me, signaling the slow rise of the sun. Water stretched in every direction. The enormity of the ocean brought me a strange comfort. There was something about endless sea that always made me feel like I was part of something bigger.

I breathed in the cool early morning air and rounded the front of the ship. I paused and took a minute to drink in the mellow waves and fading stars on the horizon. For hundreds of years sailors had cut through these same waters, seeking adventure, foreign lands, and fortunes. What was I seeking? Or maybe the better question to ask myself was, had I already found what I was seeking? I was pretty sure that I already knew the answer, but I wasn't ready to face it at this hour of the morning.

Continuing on I passed by the Top Shelf bar on the far end of the deck. Its yellow and navy awning had been closed for the night, but I thought I saw something move behind the stacks of bar stools lined up next to the bar.

I blinked twice. There was nothing there. The bar had been locked up tight. You're seeing things, Jules, I told myself as I kept walking.

Then I heard something that sounded like a motor running. I glanced around me and spotted the source of the sound. Grayson, the guitar-playing lounge singer, was passed out on one of the deck chairs. Someone must have had a late night. He snored so loudly that I couldn't believe he hadn't woken himself up. His guitar was tucked under his arm like a security blanket. With each heavy inhale the guitar rose and fell on his chest. How had he slept like that? It looked very uncomfortable. He must have really imbibed last night.

I continued on my lap ignoring Grayson's snores. As I rounded the hull, I saw another flash of movement. Someone else was up here. I called hello, wondering who else had my idea of walking before the sun came up. Then I realized it was the crew. Three deckhands were at work polishing the wood and mopping the floors. Like so many other members of the staff aboard the *Amour* they were probably an hour or two into their workday while the guests were cocooned into their cozy beds.

One of the deckhands dropped his mop as I approached and raced to the edge of the ship. Then he proceeded to get sick. Oh no.

"Are you okay?" I asked, hurrying over to see if I could help.

His navy uniform blended into the milky sky. A gray plastic cart packed with cleaning supplies, mops, and brooms was shoved up against the railing. He looked up at me, held out his index finger, and then threw up over the handrail again. Poor guy.

"Can I get you anything?" I asked.

He shook his head and clutched the railing. His face was as green as a kiwi and his eyes were having trouble focusing. "I think I'm good," he mumbled.

"You don't look so good."

"I can't keep anything down. It feels like I'm on a roller coaster."

I glanced out to the calm, still seas. "This is as smooth as it gets."

He frowned and made a moaning sound. I thought he might get sick again, but he gulped and looked at me with wide eyes. "Really?"

"Really." I nodded with an apologetic smile. I'd seen this before. There are some people who just don't take to the sea. Personally I love the gentle rocking and motion of cutting through miles and miles of open ocean, but there were plenty of crew members who couldn't handle advancing through the sea. No amount of medicine or time acclimating to slicing through waves helped. There were some people who weren't cut out for cruising. I suspected that was the case for the deckhand. If he was struggling now when the water was like glass, he would be in bad, bad shape if we hit even a minor patch of bigger waves.

"My bunkmate told me that fresh air might help."

"Is it?"

He ran his hand through his wavy brown hair, which looked like it hadn't been washed in days. "Not really." He was young—probably in his early twenties, like the team at Torte. His face was pocked with acne and there were a few spots with crusty scabs that looked as if they'd been scratched too hard.

"I'm Jules," I said, not offering him my hand. He was clutching the railing so hard that his hand had lost all color. I had a feeling if he let go he might pass out. "I'm the pastry chef. You should come down to the bakery and I'll get you a cup of peppermint tea. It might help some."

"Thanks." He swallowed hard. "I'm Jeff. The new deckhand. Although I guess you probably already figured that out."

"Is this your first cruise?"

"Yeah and probably my last."

"Give it some time," I suggested. "It might get better."

"You think?"

I shrugged. "To be honest, I've seen it go both ways. Sometimes people adjust, and sometimes they decide that life on solid ground is better."

"My bunkmate said I'm lucky. They assigned me to the pool deck, so at least I get fresh air while I'm working."

He was right. Most deckhands and crew for that matter spent the vast majority of their days below deck. There was strict hierarchy in terms of who could go where. Many crew members weren't allowed on the upper decks and rarely saw the light of day unless they were on break. Status mattered when it came to interacting with guests and mingling at parties. As head chef Carlos had access to all floors of the ship, but he was only one of a handful of crew members who were allowed to mix with the passengers.

When Carlos and I lived together on the ship, our joint cabin had a small window and built-in bathroom, which was considered luxurious. Most of the crew slept in bunk-style rooms below without any windows. Many people found it claustrophobic and couldn't handle feeling trapped under the water line. I understood the feeling. When I took my first job as a sous chef on another ship, I spent my first two years at sea living in a tiny cabin with three other crew members. The lifestyle isn't for everyone, but the perks are pretty spectacular, like seeing nearly every port of call and building friendships with people from all over the world.

"Fresh air should help," I said to Jeff. "Do you think you can make it down to the kitchen?"

He nodded. "Give me a few minutes."

"Sure. I'm going to finish my lap, but if you need me just holler."

"Thanks." He gulped again and looked like he was about to vomit.

I continued on toward the pool, greeting the two other deckhands, neither of whom looked green. Poor Jeff, what a crummy way to start a job. I didn't want to give him false hope, but fingers crossed, maybe with some air and hot peppermint tea he could get his stomach to settle and get back to work. The sun was starting to break through the dark sky. In the next few hours passengers would begin to trickle from their cabins to the breakfast buffet. I told Mom and the Professor that the best way to experience breakfast aboard the ship was to grab a coffee and a plate of sweet rolls and bring it up to the pool deck. Most guests didn't start filling in the upper decks until later in the morning. Enjoying a relaxing morning coffee with a warm breeze and briny air was nothing short of divine.

Thinking of coffee made my stomach rumble. As soon

as I finished my lap and checked in with Jeff I was heading straight for the espresso machine in the kitchen. The thought of a dark nutty Americano made me pick up my pace. I turned and followed the pathway along the railing around toward the pool and stopped dead in my tracks.

The dwindling moonlight reflected in the pool's surface, giving it an otherworldly glow. The smell of chlorine and salt assaulted my nostrils as I stepped closer to its tiled edge. I tried to make sense of what I was seeing. Were my eyes playing tricks on me or was that a body floating facedown in the water?

Chapter Nine

I gasped. There was no mistaking what I had seen. A woman with flowing blond hair was floating facedown in the saltwater pool. Without thinking I dove in headfirst and swam with all my might to reach the woman. Part of me knew that she was already dead, but I couldn't stop myself from trying to revive her. My lungs burned as I kicked toward her body. I swam underneath her and rolled her over. It was the mysterious woman whom I'd seen yesterday. Her face was devoid of color and a terrible shade of ashen white. She wasn't breathing.

"Help!" I screamed as loud as I could as I treaded water and held on to her back. I couldn't start rescue breathing in the water, and although I was pretty sure it was a lost cause, I had to try. I looped my arm under her neck and starting dragging her toward the shallow end.

"Help! Jeff, Grayson! Anyone! Help!" I shouted again. My voice sounded like it was coming from somewhere else. I screamed even louder and tasted salt on my tongue.

No one was coming, so I kicked as hard as I could and dragged the woman's lifeless body with me. The water was frigid. The pool wasn't heated. It didn't need to be. By the time passengers made their way to the sundeck the tropical afternoon heat would naturally warm the pool and guests would welcome a refreshingly cool dip in its salty waters.

By the time I got her to shallow water both Jeff and Grayson along with the two other deckhands were waiting for me. Grayson looked like he'd been run over by a train but he jumped into the shallow end of the pool and sprinted toward me. Jeff stood at the edge of the pool looking even greener than before. Oh no, the last thing I needed was to have him hit the deck too.

"Go get help," I ordered him. Hopefully having a task to focus on would help him forget his motion sickness.

"What happened?" Grayson called, reaching me and positioning himself on the other side of the woman's body.

"I don't know. I just saw her floating in the pool and dove in."

"Let's lift her out, on the count of three, okay?" Grayson moved closer to the edge. He counted down and we both heaved the woman's body onto the deck.

In one easy, fluid motion Grayson pulled himself out of the pool and checked for a pulse. "She's not breathing."

I waded to the stairs. My capris and T-shirt clung to my skin and my tennis shoes squirted out water with each step. "I know."

Grayson started rescue breathing. Every member of the crew from the captain to the line cooks was trained in first aid and CPR. I watched feeling helpless and starting to shiver. The adrenaline of diving into the icy water had started to wear off and my body quaked in response. She was dead. Grayson's attempts at pounding on her chest and breathing into her mouth were futile. I didn't blame him for continuing, but it was hard to watch him pour everything he had into trying to revive her lifeless body.

Voices and footsteps sounded behind us. Jeff had returned with the captain, head of security, and doctor.

They pushed us out of the way and the doctor took over. He placed a hand on Grayson's shoulder and checked the woman's vitals. A minute later he looked up at the captain and shook his head.

My breath caught in my throat. She was dead.

The captain removed his hat and held it against his chest. He said a few words as we stood in stunned silence for a moment. Who was the woman? Her hair was platinum blond and hung to the middle of her back. She looked young this close up, barely twenty maybe. I'd seen her in the closet on the crew corridor, arguing with Rocky after stuffing her pockets with food, and then being dragged away by Maria last night. What was her story? Could Rocky have been right about her being drunk? Maybe she'd ignored his advice to sleep it off in her cabin and returned to the pool deck for more imbibing? Could she have been drunk and stumbled into the pool? Questions spun in my mind as I tried to push the sight of her bloated face from my memory.

Clearing his throat, the captain returned his hat to his head and shifted his demeanor. "Does anyone know who this woman is?" he asked, as if reading my mind.

Everyone shook their heads.

"Is she a member of the crew?" He directed the question at Grayson.

"I don't recognize her, sir, but she could be." Grayson stood and nearly lost his balance.

The captain frowned and stared at me. "Chef, do you know her?" His stark white uniform was almost blinding in contrast to the shadowy sky.

"I saw her yesterday. She was near the pastry kitchen. Then I saw her again at the send-off party and at dinner. I don't know who she is though. Or if she's a passenger or crew. I've been gone for a while and there's been some turnover, you know."

Grayson scowled. "Oh, Jules, that's right, I heard you were back. I didn't recognize you soaking wet."

The captain nodded and went around to each member of the crew. Everyone denied knowing the young woman. "I'll pull the passenger manifest. Before we do anything we need to determine who she is."

Jeff appeared to my left wheeling his cleaning cart and holding a stack of blue and white striped beach towels. "I thought you might be cold." His hands quivered and sweat poured from his brow.

I took two towels and wrapped one around my shoulders and the other over my head. "Thanks," I whispered.

"Is she dead?" He stared at his feet.

"Yeah, I'm afraid so."

He dropped the towels and raced to the side of the ship to get sick again. If he couldn't get his stomach settled the purser would probably cut him loose at the first port. The captain motioned for me to come over to him. I rubbed my arms to keep from shaking and moved in his direction.

"Chef, I'm told that one of your guests on board is in law enforcement, is that right?" His posture was erect and commanding.

I tried to match his stance and force my feet to steady themselves. How did the captain know about the Professor? My mind felt like it was churning through a vat of butter. Had I introduced them?

Then I realized he must have heard about the Professor from Carlos. As executive chef Carlos often dined at the captain's table with VIP guests. Some of my favorite memories of our time on the ship were lively dinners at the captain's table. Carlos loved taking the captain's special passengers on a tasting tour of his cuisine. He would liberally refill wineglasses while explaining his braising technique or how he had discovered a rare jaboticaba fruit while on a rain-forest tour in South America. The captain enjoyed Carlos's food adventures as much as the guests did. As the commander of the ship he was responsible for his crew and made an effort to learn as much as he could about each of his staff members. I was sure that Carlos must have convinced him to allow me to invite Mom and the Professor along.

"Yes, my mom's . . ." I paused, wondering how I should refer to the Professor. "Uh, friend is a detective."

"Can you go find him?"

"Of course." I started to leave, but he stopped me.

"How are you holding up?" he asked, appraising me with his sharp eyes.

"I'm okay. It's a shock, but I'm fine." My hands betrayed me by shaking.

"As soon as you find the detective be sure to go change out of those wet clothes." He said this like an order.

"Will do." I almost offered him a salute in return.

"And, chef, any chance your lemon jelly roll will make an appearance soon?" A smile cracked on his serious face. I knew he was trying to lighten the mood.

I grinned and wrapped the towel tighter. "Consider it on the menu." The captain had a not-so-secret addiction to my lemon-curd jelly roll. When I worked on the ship I would often make a jelly roll just for him and have one of my staff members deliver it to the bridge.

He gave me a salute and I went to find the Professor. I didn't want to ruin their vacation, but I knew that the captain would only ask if he needed assistance and I also knew that the Professor would gladly offer his services.

Their cabins were three floors below. My shoes squished and I had to hold tight to the railing to keep from slipping on the metal steps. When I arrived at Mom's cabin I paused for a moment. It was early. I hated having to wake them, especially on their first official day of vacation, but this was an emergency after all. I decided to try her door first and knocked softly. To my surprise Mom swung the door open right away. "Good morning, Juliet." She was fully dressed and holding a steaming mug of coffee.

"Mom, what are you doing up so early?"

"Is it early?" She wrinkled her nose. "This is late for me."

I hadn't thought about that. Mom had been working baker's hours for three decades. Rising before the sun was in her blood. "How did you sleep?"

"Like a baby. I had the best night's sleep that I've had in years." She looked like it. Her walnut eyes were bright and her skin glowed with a hint of a tan.

"Do you want a coffee?" she asked, motioning for me to come in.

I peered over her shoulder at the door that joined her cabin with the Professor's. "Do you know if the Professor is awake?"

She glanced behind her. "I'm not sure. I thought I heard movement next door. He may be getting dressed. Speaking of, what happened to you?" Her face shifted to a look of concern. "And how about that coffee?"

"A coffee would be great." I scrunched my hair with the towel as she made me an individual cup of dark espresso. Each cabin on the ship came equipped with in-room coffee makers. They used to be time-consuming for the cleaning staff, but thanks to advancements in coffee technology the ship had upgraded to Keurig machines for quick-and-easy cleanup and storage.

Mom hit the start button on the coffee machine and pointed to the single chair in front of the desk. "Sit down and spill, young lady."

There was no arguing with her mom tone. I followed her directions and took a seat. Before I could explain why my clothes were soaked and I was wrapped in a towel, a knock sounded from the adjoining room.

Mom went to open it and the Professor emerged, wearing shorts and yet another Hawaiian-style shirt. This one was black with a cream and yellow papaya print.

"I thought I heard voices. Good morning, Juliet." He gave me a small bow and kissed the top of Mom's head. Watching the two of them share tender moments like a simple kiss made my heart swell. I was thrilled to finally see Mom happy and in love.

Mom squeezed his hand and retrieved my coffee. "Cream?"

"Sure, just a splash."

The Professor frowned. "You look as if you've had a splash."

I couldn't muster the energy to laugh. Instead I rubbed my temples and launched into an explanation of what happened. "There's been an accident."

"Accident?" Mom froze with a container of vanilla cream in her hand. "What kind of accident?"

"A woman was found dead in the pool this morning."

"What woman? And by who?" Mom's mouth hung open. I thought she might spill the cream for a minute. "Oh no, Juliet, you didn't."

"I did." I nodded.

"That's why you're wet?"

"Yeah. I jumped in thinking that I could save her, but it was too late." My voice sounded funny as I trailed off.

Mom stirred my coffee, handed it to me, and sighed. "Oh, honey. I'm so sorry. Are you okay?"

The mug instantly warmed my hands and the scent of the earthy brew calmed my nerves. "I'm fine. A bit shaken and cold, but okay."

The Professor's entire demeanor shifted. "The captain asked for my assistance."

I sipped the coffee, which wasn't the best I had ever tasted, but in the moment it was as close to perfection as I could imagine. "He did."

"Does he suspect foul play?"

"He didn't say."

"Mmm-hmm." The Professor ran his fingers through his sandy beard. "Hold that thought for one moment, please." He returned to his cabin briefly.

"You don't know who the woman was?" Mom asked.

"No. I mean not exactly." I explained my strange run-ins with the mysterious woman. "In fact no one at the scene knows who she is."

"What does that mean?"

"Probably that she's a passenger. If she was on staff I'm sure at least one person would have recognized her."

"Has anyone been reported missing?"

The Professor returned to the room with a Moleskin notebook and four-inch pencil in his hand. "Exactly what I intended to ask, Helen."

Mom blushed slightly then moved to sit on the edge of the bed.

"If you don't mind, Juliet, can you please walk me through everything that happened while it's still fresh."

I agreed and explained what I had witnessed in as much detail as possible. I included seeing Rocky and the blond woman fighting in the stairwell yesterday. I also told him about seeing Grayson passed out on deck and how Jeff the deckhand had a terrible case of motion sickness, and how Maria had pulled the woman out of the dining room last night.

The Professor jotted down notes as I spoke, and stopped me once or twice for clarification. When I finished he closed the notebook. "Shall we go meet with the captain?" he asked.

I finished my coffee and thanked Mom again.

"There's no need to thank me or to apologize, Juliet. I'm fine. You two go take care of whatever needs to be done. I'll meet you for breakfast later, Doug," she said to the Professor.

"Don't wait." He looked at me. "We might be a while."

"I have a book," she replied with a soft smile. "Go do what you need to do. I'll be here."

The Professor held the door open for me. Once we were outside in the hallway he glanced back. "Your mother is one remarkable woman."

"I know," I said, leading him to the employee stairwell. I just hoped that the Professor wouldn't get wrapped up in the investigation. He and Mom both deserved a vacation.

Chapter Ten

Even more crew members had gathered around the pool. A few deckhands in matching navy uniforms stood at each corner blocking anyone from viewing the body. It wasn't necessary. None of the passengers were up and moving yet, but I appreciated that the captain was conscientious about protecting the woman's privacy.

"We're here to see the captain," I said to one of the deckhands who was taking his guarding duties seriously.

"Name?" he asked.

"Jules. I'm the pastry chef."

"This area is secured. We don't need any food."

"I know." I pointed to my wet clothes. "I found the body. I'm here with a detective."

The deckhand scowled and moved out of our way.

"I could use someone like him on my team," the Professor joked.

Fortunately someone had covered the woman's face and body with a beach towel. Even so I kept my gaze focused on the horizon as we stepped past her. "Captain, this is Doug Curtis, Ashland, Oregon's lead detective." It felt weird to use the Professor's real name. Everyone in Ashland had called him the Professor for as long as I could remember.

"Thanks for coming." The captain shook the Professor's hand. "I could use a set of fresh eyes on the scene."

"At your service." The Professor returned his handshake and followed it with a bow. "How can I be of assistance?" I was struck by the similarities between the two men. They were about the same age, and while the Professor's beachcomber shirt didn't exactly match the captain's crisp whites, they both conveyed an air of authority balanced with a genuine caring. I knew the dead woman was in considerate and capable hands.

"First I'd like you to take a look at the body. Something about it doesn't look right, but I can't put my finger on what it is. My staff physician has taken photos and assessed the body."

They spoke like I wasn't there. I wanted to go take a shower and get out of these uncomfortable clothes, but I was also intrigued by the captain's response. He hadn't said anything about the body earlier. Had he wanted the Professor's help because he was concerned that the woman had been killed?

A shudder ran down my spine as I watched the Professor kneel next to the woman and remove the towel. The ship's doctor scrolled through photos he had taken on his phone and pointed out an area of bruising on the woman's neck and wrists. The Professor made more notes and walked around the body three times.

"She was found where exactly?" he asked the doctor.

The doctor pointed to the deep end of the pool. "Right there. Facedown. By my estimate she'd been dead at least thirty minutes before she was discovered. Maybe longer. This isn't my area of expertise though. Time of death is usually a window."

"I understand." The Professor removed a pair of reading glasses from the front pocket of his Hawaiian shirt and placed them on the tip of his nose. "And in addition to Juliet, who was on the scene when the body was found?"

The captain proceeded to call Jeff and Grayson over. He noticed me for the first time. "Chef, I didn't realize you were still here. You can go. You must be miserable."

"Sir, I didn't want to leave without permission." That was true, but a shower would be nice. My toes were numb and my fingers felt like Popsicles.

"Go—go! That's an order. We'll take care of everything from here." He dismissed me with a curt nod.

I wanted to go, but I had to know if they had learned more. "Any luck figuring out who the passenger is?" I asked, wrapping the damp towel tighter around my shoulders. "I saw the woman with Rocky and Maria yesterday. You might start with them."

He scanned the deck and then returned his focus to me. "Thanks for the tip. We haven't had any luck with identifying her yet. I'm calling her Jane Doe for the moment. As soon as we finish here and remove the body, I'm going to make an announcement over the loudspeaker, and then we'll have the crew start going door to door and knocking on each cabin. I'm hoping that we'll discover her identity in the next hour, maybe even sooner."

"How terrible for her family. Can you imagine hearing that news?"

The captain frowned. "I can't imagine how I'm going to break the news."

"Oh right." What a horrible job, I thought to myself, noting the silver and gold medals pinned to the captain's chest. He had obviously received numerous awards and accolades during his career, but I wondered if he had ever had to do something as awful as this.

He patted my shoulder. "Thank you for your help and for getting the detective. Go change. I'll see you at breakfast, chef."

"As long as you're sure." I hesitated.

"That's an order. Shower! Now." He winked and waved me off.

I trudged back to the stairwell and started down to my cabin. When I made it to the landing of the first flight of stairs I heard a woman's voice speaking in hushed tones.

"Darling, there's no need to worry. No one saw us. It's done. Go get some beauty sleep and I'll see you later." She sounded like she was trying to pacify whoever she was talking to.

A door slammed and I heard high heels clicking on the stairs. I leaned over the railing and saw Babs, the Miami music executive, stroll away. She was wearing the same skintight black leather jacket and leather boots she'd had on last night. Who was she talking to, and what did she mean by "no one saw us"? Could she have something to do with the mysterious woman's death?

I had to resist the urge to follow after her. I was already late for breakfast prep and in desperate need of a shower. I would, however, make sure to mention it to the Professor and see if I could find out anything more about Babs.

Peeling my wet clothes from my damp and clammy skin was a bit of a challenge. My shoes were a lost cause. I would have to send them to the laundry to dry out. Fortunately I had packed a pair of comfortable closed-toe flats. They would have to do. Open-toe shoes or flip-flops are a terrible idea in a commercial kitchen. With so many feet flying around the tight and busy workspace it would be too easy for someone to step on a toe or have a cast-iron skillet land on an ankle.

The hot shower revived my senses and icy skin. I stayed in longer than I meant to, but the scalding water felt like the jolt that my body needed to make it through the rest of the morning. That and coffee. If my kitchen staff didn't have strong coffee brewed and waiting for me, I might go on a rampage and fire them all. Not really, but I could use a cup or two of joe right about now.

After my skin had turned a bright shade of pink and color returned to my face I dried off and pulled on a new pair of capris and a dry T-shirt. It felt like déjà vu as I walked down to the kitchen where the staff was already plating platters of coconut and pineapple muffins and filling huge carafes of coffee. "Morning," I greeted everyone. "If I could I would give you all raises on the spot because that coffee smells so good."

Someone handed me a cup before I finished my praise and pulled on my chef coat.

"We heard what happened," one of the sous chefs, kneading bread dough, said.

"I heard you found the body," a dishwasher added.

"It's true." I figured it would be better to get everything out in the open and on the table so to speak. I had learned that full disclosure is the best policy. Otherwise rumors start and can quickly spin out of control, especially on a ship where everyone lives and works together. "The captain is going to make an announcement soon. You should be prepared to answer any questions that he or the detective in charge have for you."

"Detective? Since when do we have a detective on the ship?" someone asked.

"Just a lucky turn of fate," I replied, and then proceeded to explain the Professor's background.

"Is this an investigation?" The dishwasher loaded heavy trays into the industrial washing machines.

"It is, but it's nothing that anyone should worry about. The biggest issue right now is identifying the woman. If any of you know who she was you should let the captain know immediately." My voice sounded reassuring and confident. Even if I was still feeling shaky I wanted my staff to focus on baking.

"Like a murder?" a cake decorator asked. Her hand worked in rapid, effortless motion as she piped pale purple buttercream on rows and rows of cupcakes.

"They don't know, but right now we need to worry about breakfast service and let the captain handle it."

Everyone agreed and returned to their workstations. There was a palpable tension in the air as flats of strawberries and melons were sliced for fruit salad and the crepe station. Like Carlos, I didn't want my staff's concern over Jane Doe's death to impact the summer spread I had planned for breakfast.

"How about some tunes?" I asked, walking over to the built-in stereo. "Anyone have a preference?" The gleaming stainless steel galley suddenly felt stark. I felt a wave of homesickness come over me. What I wouldn't give for Torte's cheery interior, one of Andy's Americanos, or some friendly banter with my small staff right now. I even missed Lance's dry humor and ability to make me laugh in the worst circumstances. Hopefully some music would help liven up the cool space.

No one offered a musical preference, so I opted for a Calypso band. The upbeat pulse of the drums quickly changed the tone in the kitchen. People looked lighter and moved with less tension between chopping and plating stations. For breakfast I was making my signature crepe cake. The technique involves layering thin vanilla crepes with mascarpone and whipped cream and topped with fresh strawberries. It isn't difficult, but it does require patience. Each individual crepe was browned to perfection and slathered with the rich cream mixture. Then the process was repeated until the crepes were stacked in a tight layer. Finally we would slice the finished stack like a cake and top each piece with strawberries and a dusting of powdered sugar.

I organized an assembly line of crepe makers, fillers,

and a plating team. Crepes are like a painter's blank canvas. They are so delicate and light that they can be paired with almost anything from lemon curd and raspberries to Nutella and bananas. The cakes we were making this morning consisted of twenty paper-thin layers of crepes, which meant that the team cooking the crepes had to be at the top of their game.

"You only need three tablespoons of batter," I said, swirling an already buttered saucepan with the batter to cover it. Then I waited until the edges of the crepe started to brown and carefully flipped it with my fingers. "Just give it five or ten seconds on the other side. It doesn't need much. Only a second or two to give it a nice crisp."

My team watched as I cooked a few more crepes to show them the proper technique. While I waited for my examples to cool, I folded whipped cream into the mascarpone base and used an offset spatula to spread a thin layer of the mixture on the crepes. I continued the process until I had a completed example. "Anyone want to give it a taste?" I asked, placing luscious sliced strawberries on the top.

Everyone's hands shot in the air. I chuckled and cut tasting slices for my staff. The cake was decadent without being overly sweet or too rich. "What do you think, a perfect breakfast cake?"

I received a round of applause and thumbs-up. "Great. Let's get to work. We'll want to chill each cake for an hour before we serve them."

As I was about to start on my next project, the sound of Carlos's voice interrupted me. "Julieta, can we talk?"

Carlos was rarely up and moving at such an early hour. He leaned against the door frame wearing a pair of well-cut shorts and a classic white polo. I gave him a quizzical look and wiped my hands on a dish towel. "Keep working on those. I'll be right back," I told my staff.

"What are you doing up this early?" I asked.

He pulled me away from the kitchen. "I was woken by the crew. Have you not heard the news?"

"Oh right."

"You have heard, then?" His dark eyes pierced through me. Regardless of where things stood between us there was no debating my attraction to him. I felt my body pull toward him, as if he were a magnet.

"Yeah." I nodded, not meeting his eyes.

"What is it, *mi querida*?"

"I found her," I mumbled.

"What?" Carlos clutched my shoulder. "You found the woman? How is this possible?"

I shrugged. "It wasn't as if I intended to find her. I went for a walk on the sundeck this morning and found her in the pool." My jaw tightened as I spoke. I tried to blink away the image of her bloated face.

Carlos must have noticed because he pulled me into his arms and wrapped me in a hug. The smell of his earthy aftershave and the feel of his muscular body made my knees go weak. I allowed myself to melt into him. "It is okay, *mi querida*," he whispered, kissing the top of my head and running his fingers along the back of my neck.

"She was so young." I fought back tears.

"I know. It is terrible."

He held me tighter. Neither of us wanted to let go, and I might have stayed there in the safety of his embrace indefinitely, but the sound of someone coming toward us forced us apart. Carlos's presence had a calming effect on me. The second he released me I could feel anxiety begin to build again.

"Sorry." Grayson the lounge singer walked past us with his guitar looped over his shoulder. "You haven't seen the captain by chance, have you?"

"No." I shook my head. "The last time I saw him he was on the pool deck."

Grayson bit his bottom lip. "He's not there now."

I wanted to ask him about Babs, the music executive, but I didn't think that was such a good idea in front of Carlos.

Grayson continued past us. "If you see the captain, will you tell him I'll be in the lounge?"

"Sure," I replied.

Carlos returned his attention to me and frowned. "What is it, Julieta?"

"What's what?" I pretended not to understand what he was inferring.

"What is going on? Why is he asking you to tell the captain? Is it something with the woman?"

"No. I have no idea why Grayson wants to talk to the captain."

Carlos's full lips turned down. "I do not want you to be involved in this. It is not good. This is work for the captain."

"I know. I'm not. In fact, the Professor's in charge at the moment."

This news brought relief to Carlos's golden skin. "Ah. *Sí.* This is good. The Professor, he will know what to do." He reached for my hand. "You must promise you will bake and stay in the kitchen, *sí*?"

"*Sí.*" I squeezed his hand. "I should get back in there."

Carlos looked like he wanted to say more, but he let me go and I was acutely aware of the fact that his gaze was burning into me as I walked into the kitchen.

Chapter Eleven

The crepe-cake production was in full swing. My staff had already assembled eight cakes. They looked incredible with tight layers of brilliant white cream and juicy slices of bright red strawberries piled on the top. I knew they were going to be a hit with the passengers. "These look great," I said, instinctively reaching for a Torte apron and then realizing I was already wearing my chef whites. Every member of the pastry crew wore ship-issued white uniforms. The first chef I worked for on the cruise line, before I climbed my way up the ranks, took the kitchen uniforms to heart and treated the staff like we were his personal military—barking out orders and rapping the stainless steel countertops with a rolling pin whenever someone made a mistake. I preferred Carlos's approach of bringing fun into an otherwise shipshape environment.

I grabbed my clipboard and reviewed what needed to be done next. Staff worked around the clock on the cruise ship. The night crew had already baked enough bread for French toast, regular toast, and the lunch hour sandwich platters. We needed to bake sweet breads, rolls, and savory potato and egg dishes. In addition to the spread that my staff would prepare, there would be a crew of chefs on-site at the breakfast buffet to whip up omelets and waffles, and carve an assortment of breakfast meats. Every meal was a production on the ship, much like the staged productions back home at OSF; guests weren't just fed, they were entertained by dazzling food displays and the sheer enormity of choices. Fortunately as head pastry chef I wasn't responsible for any live baking or cooking. That fell under Carlos's reign.

I jumped into the mix, grabbing an armload of butter and dumping it in one of the industrial mixers. The staff had given all of the mixers names. Mine was called Big Bertha. There was also Honking Huge Hugh and Monster Matt. Bertha could whip twenty pounds of butter in less than a minute. If I was going to get my mind off Jane Doe, the best way was to immerse myself in baking. I decided to make a peach coffee cake. Like its cousin the blueberry buckle, the peach coffee cake didn't require any time to rise and would bake in thirty minutes. To give it a tropical twist I would top it with a spiced mango crumble.

As the butter churned into a light daffodil color I added eggs, sugar, vanilla, and buttermilk. Then I sifted in flour and baking soda. Once the batter had thickened I turned the mixer onto low and incorporated healthy chunks of peeled peaches. I didn't want to risk juicing them, so gave the mixer a quick spin and then began spreading the batter into greased glass pans. For the crumble I forked together room-temperature butter, brown sugar, oats, nutmeg, ginger, and chopped dried mangoes. My mind wandered to thoughts of home. I hoped that things were going well at Torte without Mom and me. As soon as I had time to take a break, I would head down to the employee lounge and send Lance an e-mail. The peach coffee cake and act of actually baking something made me even more nostalgic for Torte.

Sprinkling the crumble over the peach batter, I took a taste. The peach flavor definitely came through and should mingle well with the spicy topping. I slid the peach cakes into the oven and checked on the status of each station. Everything was running smoothly. We looked to be in great shape to deliver breakfast to hungry guests as soon as the buffet opened.

I decided to e-mail Lance now. My coffee cake was baking and my staff was on task. I left my sous chef in charge and headed to the employee lounge, which was located one deck below. The lounge housed a variety of TVs, gaming stations, computers, tables, and a snack bar. During breaks employees could hang out and watch a movie or e-mail friends and family. Waving to a couple of housekeeping staff battling on the Xbox, I booted up one of the free computers and entered my employee log-in code.

The only issue was whether or not I should tell Lance about finding Jane Doe. Back in Ashland, Lance had been notorious for inserting himself into investigations. I knew that he would be hurt if he didn't hear the news from me, and despite his tendency toward the dramatic he had been a good sounding board and support for me in the past. Since the Professor was involved I figured there was a high likelihood that he would be in communication with Thomas. If Lance learned from Thomas that I had discovered a body he would never forgive me.

Considering my words carefully I constructed a non-inflammatory e-mail about the trip so far, asking how everything was going at Torte, following up with why OSF was hosting the season launch party at Richard Lord's Merry Windsor, and letting him know about Jane Doe. My finger hovered on the send key. Should I tell him? Or was that going to make things worse? I scowled at the e-mail and reread it twice. Just send it, Jules, I told myself, and forced my finger down on the key.

There's no turning back now, Jules, I thought as I

scooted my chair away from the desk and stretched. The housekeeping staff called me over to watch their battle. Video games are not my skill set, but I enjoyed watching their bodies lurch with each move on the controller and hearing their friendly trash talk. After a few minutes I grabbed a cup of coffee from the snack bar and returned to the computer to e-mail Sterling. I knew that he would give me the real scoop on whether Lance was helping or hindering them.

I was halfway through drafting my e-mail to Sterling when the computer beeped, signaling that I had received an e-mail. Lance had already written me back. What time was it in Ashland? Early. Too early for Lance, that was certain. I wondered what he was doing up and checking mail at this hour. When I opened his mail he answered the question for me.

> *Greetings from our humble hamlet, darling,*
>
> *Your message was quite timely. I've been suffering from the worst case of insomnia thanks to that maddening new young lead I hired. He thinks that he's a modern-day Romeo. It's vexing me to no end. I thought the ladies would swoon over his devilish looks and tight abs, but it turns out he's just a devil. His ego is so inflated I'm surprised the costume department has been able to find a hat to fit his head.*

I had to pause and laugh on reading that line. Talk about the pot calling the kettle black. Lance's ego wasn't exactly miniature. His voice came through perfectly as I read on.

> *Do not even get me started on that buffoon Richard Lord. For reasons unknown to yours truly he has managed to convince the board that the Merry Windsor's new deconstructed menu will dazzle the company's biggest benefactors. Between Richard and my pompous young lead I'm being driven to*

drink. Quite literally, in fact. I'm sitting in my living room backlit by candles with a martini in hand. Wish you were here, darling.

Now on to the deliciousness. Poor Jane Doe! Gasp.

Or really, darling, to lighten your mood you should have a little fun with it and call her Jane Dough. Dough, ha! Sometimes I'm astonished by my brilliance. Such a mystery. Who is this Jane Dough and what nefarious acts could have landed her facedown in the pool? Oh how I wish I was there. We would be on the case. You must fill me in. I want to know everything that you learn about Jane Dough. And I want daily—hourly—updates.

Everything is fine at Torte. Don't wrinkle your porcelain skin. I have it all under control. That cheeky brownie girl that you have helping is an absolute delight. Although for some odd reason she seems to be under the impression that she is in charge. Not to worry, I've set her straight.

Sorry to hear that you have a murder on your hands, but I have to warn you that you might have another by the time you get home. I'm about to play nurse to my young Romeo and send him a special elixir.

Ta-ta!
Lance

Had I mentioned murder? I read back through my e-mail, and confirmed that I hadn't. Leave it up to Lance to decide that Jane Doe (or Dough) had been killed. I sent him a quick reply telling him not to jump to conclusions, that she had probably had one too many mai tais. Although even as I typed I wasn't sure that I believed my own assertions. Something about her death was strange, and I had a feeling that the Professor suspected there was more to the woman's death than imbibing too much. Lance's flippant tone was typical, but I couldn't shake the feeling that something was amiss with him. Why would the board ignore Lance's input on the opening party? Lance always threw elaborate bashes for the company throughout the season. And I suspected that his young lead was really getting under his skin. I would have to follow up again.

Next I sent Sterling an e-mail to see what his take was on how things were going at Torte and make sure Lance wasn't meddling too much. Once I'd finished my message to Sterling I shut down the computer. My coffee cake should be ready and I wanted to make sure that we delivered our portion of breakfast early. "See you later," I said to my gaming friends and headed for the galley. On my way down the hall I spotted Grayson coming out of a supply room—the same closet where I'd first seen Jane Doe yesterday.

"Jules, hey. Good to see you again." He flinched when he caught my eye and looked to his left and right. "What are you doing here?" He yanked the supply room door shut and blocked it with his body.

"Nothing. What about you?" I'm sure my curiosity must have showed on my face.

"I was looking for towels. Had a spill in the lounge and I couldn't find any towels. Wouldn't want to damage my guitar, you know? My strings are my life."

"Right. I'm guessing you didn't find any?"

Grayson's hands were empty. His guitar was nowhere in sight either. This was the first time I'd seen him without his guitar slung over his shoulder.

"Huh?"

"Towels. There weren't any in the storage room?"

He cracked his knuckles. "No, no, I couldn't find them. I was going to go check with housekeeping."

I didn't have to be a detective to deduce that he was lying. His body betrayed him. He shifted his feet from side to side and kept cracking his knuckles. "Did you know Jane Doe? I saw her down here yesterday."

"Here?" Grayson rapped on the closet door. "You mean in the closet?"

"Yeah. Isn't that weird?"

He shrugged and ran one hand through his mangled curls. "Probably just came down to sleep one off. I've done that once or twice myself."

His words echoed Rocky's statement yesterday, but I didn't buy it. Who would "sleep one off" in a supply closet?

"Did you ever find the captain?" I changed the subject and decided I might as well push him if he was already nervous.

"Huh?" He glanced behind him at the supply closet door and straightened his spine. "No, I haven't had a chance to go find him. I've been working out a few new songs for tonight before all the guests are up in our business, you know?"

I nodded. "Was there something specific you wanted to see the captain about?"

"Nope, nothing. Just needed to talk about the performance tonight," he said loudly.

"Does the captain usually give you input about your performance?" I'd never heard of captains getting involved at that level with the crew.

"Sure, sure. He loves my stuff. He's always asking to hear new stuff." His voice was noticeably higher.

I could have sworn that I heard a bang coming from the storage closet. Grayson started and then intentionally slammed his elbow against the door. "Ouch, sorry. Did the ship move or was that me? I lost my balance."

"I didn't feel anything."

"Weird." He cracked his knuckles again, but didn't move from his position in front of the door.

"I guess I should get back to the kitchen."

"Yeah, yeah. Good talk. Good talk. You have to come

see my show tonight. I'll reserve a seat in the front row for you."

"Thanks. Actually can you reserve three seats?"

Grayson kept one hand on the door handle. "Three seats. You got it." He made a clicking motion with his free hand. "Consider it done."

"Great." I continued on toward the kitchen. When I glanced back at Grayson he was still standing guard in front of the closet and gave me a wide smile and nod. What was he doing in the storage closet? Was he looking for something? It was obvious that he didn't want me to see whatever he'd been doing. That made me more resolved to go take a peek at the closet as soon as he left his post. He'd been actively looking for the captain earlier, but when I asked him just now he blew me off and made it sound like it was no big deal. He was definitely up to something.

I felt like Lance as I entered the kitchen. I hated to admit it but I was already wrapped up in the mystery of Jane Doe and Grayson had been acting suspiciously earlier. Could his behavior be connected to the morning's events? What had he been up to in the storage closet?

Focus, Jules. I forced myself to concentrate on breakfast service. Orchestrating multiple staff members and delivery carts of pastries, fruit platters, and my crepe cakes was going to take all of my attention. Fortunately the staff were well trained and everyone knew where they were supposed to be. We created an assembly line of plating, with staff whose sole role was to adorn trays with a dusting of powdered sugar or a strawberry cut like a rose.

I was impressed with our work when I saw the final display in the dining room. Of course the first guests would graze through the buffet and dismantle our designs, but my staff would be at the ready with fresh trays and platters to constantly restock the breakfast spread. Breakfast service would last for three hours, so we had our work cut out for us. When the doors to the dining room were opened guests swarmed in and loaded their plates with slices of crepe cake and my peach coffee cake. There were tropical fruit parfaits, melon slices with yogurt dip, doughnuts, pastries, and breads with honey butter and lemon cream cheese.

Suddenly I found myself hungry. Assured that my staff had everything under control I returned to the kitchen to make sure that we were churning out second and third rounds of baked goods and to grab a bite to eat. On my way through the artery I noticed flyers for an all-crew party and notices asking crew members to swap shifts. Suddenly I found myself at the supply closet where I had seen Grayson earlier. I scanned the well-lit corridor and without thinking opened the door and slipped inside.

The storage closet was nondistinct, with shelves, mops, brooms and dustpans. There were rows of cleaning supplies, toilet paper, and toiletries on one side. The other rack was stocked with towels—beach towels, bathroom towels, and rags. Grayson had definitely lied to me.

I moved stacks of towels and containers of cleaning supplies around in search of . . . something. To be honest I had no idea what I was even looking for. My heart pounded in my chest. What was I doing?

This was ridiculous. I didn't have a clue what I was looking for and odds were good that a member of the cleaning crew would find me snooping. I was about to give up my search when something shiny caught my eye from beneath a yellow industrial bucket. I bent down to see what it was, and discovered a silver earring on the floor.

Suddenly I had an idea why Grayson had been barricading the storage room. Could it be that he didn't want me to see him with the earring? What if the earring belonged to Jane Doe? I picked it up and held it to the light. The sterling silver earring was about an inch long with a contemporary design. Single silver stems were linked to globes of polished silver that reminded me of balls of yarn. I'd never seen anything like it.

Had Jane Doe been wearing earrings? I tried to picture finding her body. The memory of rolling her over made my stomach turn. The image of her flowing luminous hair on the surface of the turquoise pool came to mind, but I didn't remember her wearing earrings.

Maybe Grayson took it earlier. Or maybe you're leaping to conclusions, Jules, I told myself. The earring could belong to one of the cleaning crew or another passenger.

I tucked it into my chef's coat pocket and would give it to the Professor as soon as I found him. It might be nothing or it might be a major clue in Jane Doe's death.

Chapter Twelve

The earring felt heavy in my coat pocket as I made my way to the galley. I wasn't sure if it was connected to Jane Doe's murder, but it was definitely suspicious. What other reason could Grayson have possibly had for lurking in the supply closet?

The sound of a guitar strumming made me pause as I passed the staff lounge. Speak of the devil. Grayson was sitting on one of the couches playing his guitar.

"Hey, again. Long time no see," I said. It was curious that Grayson had picked the staff lounge to practice. What happened to his spill? He almost looked as if he was intentionally trying to appear relaxed and casual. The guys who had been gaming earlier were gone and there was no sign of any other crew members. On the ship staff typically work ten-hour days with thirty-minute lunch and dinner breaks scheduled strategically so that no department is ever understaffed. Staff work around the clock. If a guest calls the kitchen at two o'clock in the morning for a cheeseburger or a bottle of wine, their request will be delivered to their room within twenty minutes. Customer service isn't a priority on a ship—it's *the* priority. I wasn't surprised that the lounge was empty. All hands were on deck for breakfast service.

Grayson stopped strumming his guitar and looked up at me. "Oh, it's you." He sounded disappointed. Then he scrunched his already messy shaggy hair.

"Is that the new song you're working on?" I pointed to a yellow legal pad on the coffee table in front of him. It had scribbles, musical notes and bars.

He rested the guitar on a pillow. Then he picked up a pencil and scratched out one of the bars on the legal pad. "No. I'm stuck. I can't figure out the chord sequence. It's making me crazy."

"When I get stuck on a recipe I try to take a break. Usually I'll head outside for a walk to clear my head and suddenly the exact ingredient I need to complete my dish will pop into my mind," I offered.

"I've tried that. Trust me, I've tried everything." He looked behind me where two members of the wait staff wheeled a cart of pastries down the corridor. Then he moved the guitar between his knees and patted to the empty seat next to him. "Can I talk to you for a minute?"

"Sure." I sat on the couch. The earring felt like it was burning a hole in my pocket, but there was no way I was going to mention it to Grayson. He had had quite a shift in attitude since I had seen him a few minutes ago in the hallway. Although by the looks of his disheveled curls, rumpled hemp T-shirt, and bloodshot eyes I got the impression that he hadn't changed—or slept much—since last night. He reminded me of the indie singer-songwriters who graced the green stage in Ashland. OSF hosted free afternoon Green Shows outdoors on the plaza during the summer months. The shows were beloved by locals and theatergoers for their wide variety of offerings. Everything from juggling to modern dance and African conga had been performed on the green stage, but singer-songwriters like Grayson were particularly popular in Ashland. He would blend in with the town's low-key artsy scene.

He flicked the strings on his guitar. "I know you must think I'm crazy or something."

"Why do you say that?" I figured the best way to get him to open up was to stay neutral and listen.

"The supply closet. I'm sure you realized that I wasn't looking for towels."

"Well, you did seem a bit jumpy," I confessed as I restacked a collection of well-read magazines on the coffee table. The staff lounge smelled like Top Ramen—the lingering scent of a crew member's snack. Unlike on the passenger decks the décor was far from plush. The neutral laminate cabinets and flooring felt more like a school cafeteria than a luxury liner.

He plucked one of the guitar strings so hard I thought it might snap. "Yeah."

I thought he would continue, but he stared at his guitar and sighed.

"Is everything okay?" I asked.

Grayson sighed again and knocked on the guitar. "No."

"Look, I'm not sure what's going on. I think I might have an idea, and if you want to talk about it I'm here to listen."

He looked at me with a sense of recognition. "Right. You've been through this before, haven't you?"

"Been through what?" I could hear the confusion in my voice.

He leaned closer and whispered, "A work romance."

"You mean me and Carlos?" This wasn't the response I had expected. I hadn't known Grayson well when I had worked on the ship. He had been hired right before I left, so I was slightly taken aback that he brought up Carlos. Then again gossip spread like wildfire on the ship—as it did in Ashland.

"Yeah. Why didn't I think of that before? You're the perfect person to talk to about this, and I have to get it off my chest. The stress is stifling my creativity."

"Are you dating a coworker?" I thumbed through an old copy of *Cruising Today*.

He shook his head. "No. A guest."

"Oh." Did he mean Jane Doe? Is that why he'd been in the supply closet? I took a minute to compose my thoughts before I responded, pretending to study an ad for a Christmas cruise through the Baltic Sea. Staff were allowed to date with one stipulation—supervisors had to be informed, but dating guests was strictly prohibited and cause for immediate termination. There was no gray area when it came to staff and guests getting romantically involved. Even senior staff members who were allowed to mingle with guests during dinner or chat at the bar, were banned from dating passengers.

"Right?" He sighed again and plucked a guitar string. "I'm going to get fired if anyone finds out."

"Does anyone know?"

"I don't think so. You do now." He clutched his guitar to his chest.

"I won't say anything, but I would advise you to tap the brakes. You're stepping into risky territory. If word gets out that you're romantically linked to a passenger the captain will have no option other than firing you."

"That's what it says in our employee manual, but do you really think he's that by-the-book? He's a good guy. I've been on this ship for two years now and haven't had any issues with him. I'm sure you've heard horror stories about other captains but ours is a good guy."

Placing the magazine back on the stack, I gave him my best serious face. "It's not about being a good guy. That's a direct order from corporate. It isn't his call."

"The thing is I can't cut it off, not yet."

"Why?" A voice in the back of my head wondered if he couldn't cut it off because the woman was dead. Was he talking about Jane Doe?

"This passenger is my ticket out of here." Our conversation was getting weirder by the minute.

"I don't understand."

He leaned closer and whispered. "It's Babs. She's really into my music and said she can get me a recording contract. If I break it off with her that will go away."

Grayson didn't sound like he was upset about ending things with Babs because he was lovesick. He sounded like he was motivated by greed, which was probably one of the reasons the company had originally instituted the "no-dating-guests" policy.

"You're in rough waters," I said. "I think you would be wise to let things lie and see what happens when we get back to shore."

"Is that what you did with Carlos?"

"That's different. He and I were both members of the crew." I felt slightly uncomfortable talking about my personal life with Grayson. Despite the fact that Carlos and I had been public with our relationship on the ship, I tried to maintain as much privacy as I could and rarely shared details of our love life with my fellow crew members.

"But you were in love." Grayson caressed his guitar. I got the impression he was more in love with his instrument than anything or anyone else.

"Yeah and we got married." I reached into the pocket with the earring to make sure it was still there. Could it belong to Babs? Maybe that's why he had been trying to hide it. But why wouldn't he have just given it back to her?

Grayson picked up the guitar and threw the strap around his shoulder. "Right."

I needed to get back to the kitchen, so I stood and assured him, "I'm sure you'll figure it out, and I promise your secret is safe with me."

"Thanks." He returned to his guitar.

As I walked to the kitchen I wondered if I could keep

my promise. In terms of Grayson dating Babs, I would definitely keep that to myself, but if there was a chance that their romance had anything to do with Jane Doe's death I would have to tell the Professor. Babs had said that Grayson had no talent. Could they really be having a secret fling? My conversation with Grayson left me more confused. Is that why he had been hiding in the supply closet and acting so weird? And why had he been on the pool deck before dawn? Had he really just been sleeping off one too many late-night cocktails or could Jane Doe have stumbled upon him and Babs in a passionate embrace or lovers' quarrel? What if she had been at the wrong place at the wrong time? Or seen something that Grayson decided she needed to be silenced for? I shuddered and smoothed my chef's coat before returning my attention to pastry.

Chapter Thirteen

My staff was hand-twisting cinnamon dough and pressing buttery pie crust into tart tins by the thousands when I stepped into the galley. "One hour left," I announced. "Let's keep up the great effort. The word from the dining room is that they can't keep the trays stocked. The guests are devouring your creations."

Someone shouted, "Is that good news or bad news? Means more work, right?"

"Right." I chuckled. Then I loaded my arms with two giant platters of hot croissants and balanced them up the stairs to the dining room. I could have taken the service elevator but the stairs were so much quicker and I wanted the exercise. After I delivered the platters to the buffet line, I spotted Mom sitting alone at a table drinking a mimosa. "You look content," I noted, taking the empty seat across from her.

She ripped off a piece of flaky croissant. "This is going to sound terrible, but even with everything that happened this morning and Doug being called to help, I feel so relaxed. Maybe it's the water?"

"Maybe you really needed a break."

"It could be that too." She winked. "These are pretty good. Not as good as our croissants at Torte, but good."

"I don't think we can compare. We're making close to a thousand croissants this morning."

"Wow." Mom's eyes widened. "How long do you think it would take us to make that many back home?"

"Weeks?"

She laughed. Her cheeks held a hint of pink from the sun and she smelled like coconut lotion. Breakfast and lunch on the ship were much more casual than dinner service. Mom looked right in place with the rest of the passengers in her periwinkle swimsuit wrap and sandals. "Did you hear the news?"

"Is there more news?" A waiter came by with a carafe of coffee and both Mom and I turned over the ceramic mugs on our table for him to fill. "Do I want to know?"

"The captain made an announcement that the ship is making a mandatory change of course to meet up with the Coast Guard."

"He did?" I hadn't heard an announcement.

She nodded. "He didn't say anything about the young woman's death, but he did ask passengers for any information they might have on a missing person aboard and explained that his staff would be coming door to door over the next few hours."

How had I missed the announcement? Maybe when I'd been baking earlier. The kitchen can be quite noisy, especially when all of the mixers were in use. A shudder ran up my spine as a new thought invaded my mind. If Jane Doe's death wasn't an accident, if she had been killed, that meant one of us had done it. We were in the middle of the ocean and there was no way off the ship. There could be a killer on board.

"He didn't say anything about having a dead body on board?"

Mom pursed her lips. "No, but look around. You can tell that rumors are starting to spin out of control."

She was right. The dining room had a much tenser vibe than at dinner last night. Guests chatted in hushed tones and eyes followed staff members like hawks. Obviously the captain's announcement had unsettled the happy vacationers. I wondered why he hadn't informed the passengers of Jane Doe's death, but as the highest-ranking member of the crew it was his call.

"I'm sorry that I had to involve the Professor in this," I said, taking a long drink of the coffee. It had a smoky, almost peppery roast.

"Don't give it a thought." Mom reached under the table and grabbed a turquoise and green striped beach bag. She removed a book, floppy straw hat, and pair of sunglasses. "I'm fine. I'm going to plop myself into one of the deck chairs with my hat, my book, and a cold drink."

"The Professor is lucky to have you." I squeezed her hand.

"I'm lucky to have him." She put her things back in the colorful bag. "I'm serious, Juliet, I feel guilty about how relaxed I am. I haven't worried about Torte once. And between the gentle motion of the ship and the warm air, I feel ten years younger. I have a new appreciation for how hard it must have been for you to leave."

"It was, but I was ready for a change."

She gave me a knowing look. "Change isn't always easy."

A simple look from her could bring me to the verge of tears. I understood her meaning. Leaving the ship hadn't just been about changing where I lived. It had changed me completely on every level. Being back felt familiar and fun, but in my heart I knew I didn't miss this nomadic life. I had made the right decision and as much as it hurt to know that staying in Ashland would likely mean losing Carlos, I belonged on land.

"No." I shook my head and blinked away a tear. "It's not."

A faraway look crossed her face. "I wish I could tell you that it gets easier as you get older, but I'm not sure that it does. I suppose the only thing we can do is embrace the not-knowing and dive in."

"Are you worried about change?" I asked. Her words had meaning behind them that made me wonder if she wasn't as sure as I thought she was about her relationship with the Professor.

"No," she answered with a smile. "I'm not worried, but I know that change is brewing in my life." She held up her coffee cup and smiled at her unintentional pun. "And I know that means things are going to change at Torte."

"How did we get into such a serious conversation?"

"I don't know. I need to get back to my relaxed attitude and beach read. I worry about you, honey, that's all."

"I worry about you too, Mom."

She finished her coffee. "There's no reason for that. I'm doing great. My joints are loving this weather and I'm going to go soak up a little sun." Packing up her things, she stopped and kissed the top of my head. "Meet you later for lunch?"

"For sure."

As I watched her walk away I couldn't help but feel like she was holding something back. What change was she really worried about?

Chapter Fourteen

Carlos was leaning on the door frame when I returned to the kitchen. My heart lurched at the sight of him, but I could tell from the way he had his arms folded across his muscular chest and his lips turned down that he was unhappy.

"Where have you been?" he asked, staring behind me.

"In the dining room. Why?"

He tugged me closer to him. "Julieta, I have spoken to the captain and the news it is not good. He has confirmed that the young woman has been murdered. It was not an accident. And, Julieta, she looks like you. I do not like this. There is a madman on board."

"Looks like me? What does that have to do with anything?"

"*Sí*, you must be very careful. They think the killer might have been following her on board. This madman—how do you say? A serial killer on the loose. And he could be hunting women who look like you."

Maybe it was a strategy to downplay my stress, but when Carlos said the words "serial killer" all I could think about was Lance's e-mail. Lance would call a crazed madman something punny like a "cereal" killer for sure. I had to stifle a laugh before I said, "Carlos, this isn't like you."

Carlos was passionate about food, but he was usually levelheaded when it came to situations like this. He put a finger to his lips as a crew of housekeepers walked past us with buckets of cleaning supplies. He greeted them in fluent Spanish and promised there would be tapas at the crew mess hall later. Once they were out of earshot he whispered, "This is very bad. The captain is changing our course to the nearest port. The ship must now sail through choppy waters. I don't like the idea of being stuck on board with a killer. It is dangerous."

He was right. There was something unnerving about the thought of a killer roaming the ship.

"I have an idea who it might be," he said, leaning so close that I could smell his minty breath.

"Who?" I tried to keep my voice level.

Carlos's dark eyes darted toward the ceiling. "Rocky."

"Rocky? What?"

"*Sí, sí.*" He looked behind us and then raised one eyebrow. "Do not say his name so loudly. He is the one who suggested you return to the ship. What if this was his plan? What if he is stalking beautiful blond women?"

"Carlos, you can't be serious?"

He firmed his lips. "Julieta, I am serious. You must be careful. I have never liked the man. Never. He belongs on a circus ship, not the *Amour*. We must wine and dine our passengers, not encourage them to get ship faced."

The smell of sautéing onions and garlic wafted from the kitchen. My stomach grumbled. I understood that Carlos didn't like Rocky's style, but worrying about him being a serial killer was a stretch. "I agree, but I don't think Rocky's stalking me."

Carlos pursed his lips tighter. "We will see. I want you to stay far from him."

"Okay." I took in the succulent scent of charred peppers.

"Have you not noticed what's happening?" He continued in the same hushed tone.

"Noticed what?"

Planting his feet firmly on the floor he held both of his arms out to his sides to form a T. He stood like a statue, easily maintaining his rigid posture. Then he lifted one leg and balanced like a crane.

"How?" All of a sudden I realized what he was doing. "Oh my gosh, that's crazy. How are you doing that?" I asked. Even on calm seas it would be difficult to hold a position like that on a moving ship.

He placed his foot back on the ground. "Did you not feel the thickness in the air outside?"

I hadn't, but I also hadn't been outside in hours.

His pupils dilated as he spoke. "The waters are like glass. It is bad. It is a bad omen."

"Carlos, this isn't like you. You're not superstitious."

His face clouded. *"Sí,"* he said softly. "But we have never had a murder on the ship."

I couldn't argue with that.

"You remember how I sailed through the typhoon in the South Pacific?" He paused as more crew members passed by us.

I nodded. Carlos told the story of his harrowing experience on a commercial fishing boat every time we hit a bad patch of weather. He would assure me that any motion or slight clamoring of dishes was nothing compared with surviving a massive squall in the Tasman Sea. Every time he relived the experience his face tensed as if his muscles remembered the fear.

"Sí, it is like this. That is the only time I have ever felt such stillness in the middle of the ocean. This is not good."

I hoped that Carlos was wrong but his eyes held a mix of intensity and vulnerability. "How do you know that Jane

Doe was killed?" I asked, changing the subject. If this was the calm before the storm there wasn't much we could do about it.

"Jane Doe?" When Carlos scrunched his brow it made his chiseled face look softer.

"The woman in the pool."

"I spoke with the captain and your Professor. They both agree that it was murder."

"You're sure?"

Carlos nodded and pointed toward the kitchen. "They do not want to inform the staff. They do not want word to get out to the passengers yet."

"Okay."

He kissed me on each cheek. His touch sent a wave of shivers through my body. "You must be careful, *sí*?"

"I promise."

"I will come and check on you later, but you must promise not to get in the middle of this investigation. I do not like this, Julieta. I have a bad feeling about all of it. Being stuck on a calm sea it is not so bad, but if we get a weather system, I do not like that. And then this mysterious woman is dead and no one knows her. It is all connected, I think."

"You think that her murder has something to do with the storm?"

Carlos frowned. "No, no, but I do not like any of it."

We parted ways and I tried not to let my face reflect any worry as I put on a clean chef's coat and greeted my staff. "Well done on breakfast, who's ready for lunch?"

A chorus of groans sounded in the kitchen.

"I know, I know, but lunch is much easier than breakfast." I picked up the clipboard and began assigning tasks. The pastry kitchen was responsible for bread and rolls that would be served for sandwiches and to accompany soups and salads. We would also produce a variety of lunchtime desserts. The lunch-hour dessert buffet wouldn't be as elaborate as our after-dinner desserts, but still required time and effort.

Today's pastries would include tropical cookies, brownies, and bars. I planned to serve cheesecake and flans with the evening meal so for lunch we would offer minitarts, cream puffs, and slices of Bundt cake. Everything would have a tropical flair and a touch of the exotic.

Once I had my staff on task, I started on a new recipe that I had mapped out back in Ashland. I creamed butter and sugar together, slowly incorporated eggs, and poured in a splash of pineapple juice. Next I sifted in flour, baking soda, and salt. Then I added oats, coconut, white chocolate chips, dried papaya, golden raisins, and macadamia nuts. The batter was thick and chunky. As I scooped two-inch round balls onto parchment-lined baking sheets, I thought about Carlos's warning. He couldn't really think that there was a killer loose on the ship, could he? And why were the captain and Professor convinced that it was murder?

I slid trays of my cookies into a hot oven and checked on the status at the other stations. A cake designer piped gorgeous pasty cream into golden rows of cream puffs. Another dusted the top of dark cherry tarts with crystallized sugar. The kitchen smelled like a combination of baking bread and a sandy beach.

"Juliet," a voice interrupted my thoughts.

The Professor walked into the kitchen. I went to meet him. "How's it going?"

He gave me a pained smile. "Might I beg a cup of your divine coffee from you?"

"Of course. Have you had a chance to eat? I can make you a plate."

"That would be most appreciated." His kind eyes wandered around the room. "This is quite the production. I had no idea."

"It's a little bigger than Torte," I joked. Pointing to the

office in the far corner of the galley, I said, "Go have a seat. I'll be back with breakfast and a hot cup of coffee in just a minute."

He smiled his thanks.

I piled a plate with croissants, butter, orange marmalade, and fresh fruit. Then I poured the Professor a mug of coffee and added a splash of cream. "Breakfast is served," I said, opening the office door and handing him the plate.

"You are too kind." His voice sounded heavy, and I noticed that he had removed his reading glasses and placed them on the desk.

"Have you learned anything about the woman?"

He rubbed his temples and dipped a croissant into the marmalade. The subtle lines around his eyes appeared more creased than usual. "We have determined that her death wasn't accidental."

I didn't tell him that Carlos had already mentioned that. "How do you know?"

"Bruising patterns. She has contusions on the back of her neck. The doctor and I agree that she was likely pushed into the pillar next to the pool and then landed in the water."

"Is that what killed her?"

"Most likely. We won't know until the medical examiner is able to perform an autopsy." He paused and savored his coffee.

"And have you figured out who she is?"

He sighed. "Alas, we haven't. At this point we are proceeding under the assumption that the woman is a stowaway."

"A stowaway, really?" That made sense. I thought about her spooked reaction when I spotted her fleeing the supply closet and stuffing food in her pockets. "What about Maria or Rocky? Have they said anything?"

Brushing flaky pieces of croissant from his arm, he

shook his head. "No. No one has come forward with any information. Indeed. It's most unusual, according to your captain."

In all my years of working on the cruise line I'd never heard of a passenger stowing away. Ships were locked down these days. Boarding without a passport and documentation would be nearly impossible. Embarking took hours and required more scrutiny than even airport security. How had Jane Doe gotten on board?

As if reading my mind, the Professor continued. "The captain has shifted his focus to interviewing the crew. He believes that the most likely scenario is that someone on staff was involved with helping Jane Doe board the ship."

"Yeah, that makes sense, but why?"

"My thoughts exactly." He tapped his scruffy chin with his long fingers. "Have you heard this passage by the Bard? 'There is a tide in the affairs of men, which, taken at the flood, leads on to fortune. Omitted, all the voyage of their life is bound in shallows and in miseries. On such a full sea are we now afloat, and we must take the current when it serves, or lose our ventures.'"

I shook my head. "No, what does it mean?"

"It means that once all is revealed I think the motive for this killing will be quite clear, but for the moment as I'm sure you know we are simply afloat."

"Literally and figuratively," I agreed.

"Ah." He gave me a slight nod. "Yes, you've noticed."

Then I remembered the earring in my pocket. I pulled it out and handed it to him. "I found this in a storage closet near the kitchen." The Professor examined the earring as I explained seeing Grayson in the closet earlier and told him that Grayson had confessed to having a fling with Babs.

He looked thoughtful. "It is almost too convenient, isn't it? At least for the moment. Time shall tell." Dabbing his cheek with his napkin, he paused and savored his coffee.

"Did the captain say anything about changing course?" I held out my arms and showed him how stable we were. "Carlos thinks this is the calm before the storm."

"I'm afraid that's out of my domain." He polished off his croissant and folded his napkin over his plate. "Speaking of domains, we are planted firmly in the middle of yours, and aside from craving one of your most exquisite pastries, I must confess that my motives aren't entirely tied to my sweet tooth. I came to ask a favor."

"Sure, anything."

He hesitated. "Unlike in our township, I know no one on board, which may give me a distinct advantage in some ways, but in others I fear it might hinder my investigation. I'm hoping that you might consider assisting me."

The Professor had asked me to keep my eyes and ears open when a murder had occurred at Torte right after I moved home, so I wasn't entirely surprised by his request. However, since then Mom and Carlos had not appreciated me getting entwined in the Professor's cases so I was taken slightly off guard that he was asking for my help again.

"Sure—in what way?"

He looked toward the busy kitchen. "Listen, pay attention, as you normally do. If you hear any gossip or chatter about our Jane Doe, let me know. Oh, I rhymed there. That was unintentional, I assure you."

"Is there anything specific you want me to ask about?"

"No, not at all. You are in an excellent position to overhear the crew. They know and trust you and will be much more at ease around you than, say, an authority figure such as the captain or even me. I have the sense that our killer is scared, and fear usually makes us stumble. I'll be at the ready when that happens, but first we must learn as much as we can about our mysterious stowaway."

"What about the Coast Guard?"

"The problem is we are out in the middle of the Atlantic for the moment. As you know, we are sailing in international waters so maritime laws are in play. As soon as we reach whatever port we're being rerouted to, the Coast Guard and FBI will take over the investigation. But I'm afraid it's up to you and me at the moment. As the saying goes, we are dead in the water until we reach the nearest port."

I swallowed. "Right."

"No need to worry, Juliet. I trust your instincts implicitly. Your lineage is like royalty on that account. I've sent fingerprints to Thomas and we've sent photos to the medical examiner. Technology for its many faults certainly has some pluses in this instance. I was able to take photos of the fingerprints and e-mail them to Thomas. Quite amazing, isn't it?"

"Yep. I always feel like I'm behind in the digital world after spending so many years here." I picked up his plate. "When will Thomas be able to get back to you?"

"I wouldn't suspect that it will take him too long." His eyes focused on the small clock on the desk. "Although I doubt he's even awake yet."

"Right."

He stood and bowed. "My deepest thanks."

"Not a problem. I'll let you know if I hear anything."

"Until later then," he said with a nod and strolled away.

I had a new sense of direction. Not only did I have a double batch of chocolate to start melting, but I had a double mystery to solve: who was Jane Doe, and why had she been murdered?

Chapter Fifteen

I could smell my tropical cookies before the oven timer dinged. One tip that I always gave to new bakers was to use their sense of smell. Baked goods will tell you when they're done. When the scent of a cake starts to fill the kitchen it's usually the first sign that it's done even if there is still time left on the timer. Sliding a silicone oven mitt over my arm, I pulled the trays of cookies from the hot oven. They were definitely done, golden brown and slightly crispy. The chunks of papaya, coconut, and macadamia nut gave the cookies a hearty texture. They reminded me of the "everything but the kitchen sink" cookies that we serve at Torte. With creamy melted white chocolate chips and oats serving as the plaster to hold the cookie together, I had a feeling that these were going to go fast. I let one cool for a moment and then broke off a bite to taste. The flavors mingled perfectly and the nuts and crisp oats gave the cookie just the right amount of crunch.

In addition to providing bread and sweet offerings for the main dining room the pastry kitchen was also responsible for stocking the bakery and espresso bar on the second deck. Passengers who didn't want a sit-down breakfast, or who preferred to grab a latte and scone and sit under a sunny umbrella, could feed their sweet needs at the espresso bar. The bar was staffed by trained baristas who would handcraft a dark chocolate iced mocha or a strong cold brew coffee that guests could sip as they strolled around the soaking pool or rested on a lounge chair. We tried to keep our pastries varied at each restaurant on the ship. For the espresso bar we tended to feature items that were easy to grab and go, like slices of lemon-glazed pound cake and ham-and-Gruyere croissants.

With lunch prep moving along as planned I went to check in with the espresso bar manager. On my way up to deck two I ran into Maria. She was even taller than me and had legs that seemed to stretch to the sky. Despite the fact that it wasn't even noon she wore a skintight sequined top that left nothing to the imagination, a tiny sparkly skirt that barely covered her backside, and platform heels that made her look twice her size. Her shiny black hair fell in loose waves and her skin looked airbrushed.

"Hi, Maria," I said with a touch of jealousy. When Carlos and I first met, Maria had been less than subtle in her attempts to win him over. She used to hang around the main kitchen before her show wearing even less than what she had on today and speak to him in their native tongue. It wasn't unusual to hear a variety of languages spoken among the crew. In fact, most of the crew were international, the vast majority originating from the Philippines. However, I got the sense that Maria intentionally spoke in Spanish so that she could keep her conversations with Carlos private, especially from me.

She appraised me with her long fake lashes. I suddenly felt self-conscious about my baker's attire and that I'd done nothing more than pull my hair back in a ponytail after my early morning swim.

"Good morning," she said too sweetly. "I did hear that you had made a return, but it is temporary, right?"

Part of me wanted to lie just to spite her, but instead I nodded. "Yep, I'm filling in for a few days."

"Yes, Carlos told me." Her face was passive but her tone challenging.

"You look like you're ready for a show." I ignored her attempt to get under my skin.

"Rocky has asked me to do a special lunchtime performance since we are not going to reach port as planned."

"You don't usually perform midday shows, do you?"

She tossed her curls to one side. "It is a favor for Rocky. He begged me to dance for the guests. How could I say no?"

"I'm sure you couldn't."

"No, I could not." She stuck out her chest and flipped her hair again. "The guests must be entertained, no?"

"For sure. Hey, are you missing an earring?"

She flipped her hair back to reveal her ears. "No. Nothing must get in the way when I dance. It is me, the music, and the energy of the room." She pulsed as she replied.

I had to resist the urge to say something I might regret, so I changed the subject and followed the Professor's request. "I saw you at dinner last night."

Maria tossed her hair over her shoulder and wrapped it around her index finger. "Yes, I dance every night on the ship."

"No, not that. I saw you after the performance—talking to Jane. You yanked her out of the dining room."

"Jane? You mean Annie." Maria realized what she had said and threw a manicured hand over her mouth.

"Annie? Is that the stowaway's name? Annie?"

A brilliant blush spread up Maria's tanned cheeks. She waved me away with both her hands. "No, no. I don't know. I heard someone say that her name was Annie, that was all."

"Who?" I couldn't contain my excitement. This was an important clue. Knowing who Jane Doe was would be critical to figuring out why someone wanted her dead.

Maria brushed her tiny skirt. "I don't know. Like I told you, one of the crew said her name was Annie." She started to walk away.

"Wait!" I reached for her arm, but she shook me off. "Listen, you have to tell the captain about this."

She stared at me for a minute with her dark eyes. I couldn't tell if I was seeing fear or loathing, but either way her gaze made me pause. "Now, I must dance." Her teeth glared brilliant white as she shot me a dazzling and somewhat disturbing smile before sashaying down the hallway. I couldn't help but wonder if she had made a move on Carlos when I left. Not that it was any of my business, and I knew I had no right to be jealous. I left, he didn't. But I could feel the heat in my cheeks and the pace of my breath quicken as I climbed the stairs. The thought of Carlos and Maria made me nauseous. She was notorious for breaking up relationships and flirting with every man on the ship.

I didn't like being jealous. Climbing the stairs two at a time, I tried to remind myself that this was my choice. I was the one who left Carlos, but I guess I had mistakenly believed him when he had said that he was committed to finding a way to make our relationship work. Finding solace in the arms of Maria wasn't exactly what I had pictured when he said that.

Stop feeling sorry for yourself, Jules, I told myself as I made it to the landing on deck two. I let out a long breath and squared my shoulders. I wasn't going to give Maria the satisfaction of knowing that she had rattled me. But I was going to find the Professor as soon as I could and tell him that I had learned that Jane Doe's name was Annie. I wasn't sure what to make of Maria's response or why she hadn't told the captain. What else wasn't she saying? Could she have known Annie? Or worse, could she have killed her?

Deck four was affectionately referred to by the crew as the fun deck. It housed a bowling alley, the main pool, arcade, spa, and tons of boutique shops. If it weren't for the wall of windows looking out onto the ocean you would never know that you were at sea. The deck resembled a high-end shopping mall with its glass atrium ceilings, rows of potted palms, and cute storefronts with seasonal displays.

The espresso bar, Anchor Coffee, embraced a nautical theme in every aspect of its design. Strings of sea floats hung from the coconut-husk ceiling. There were small bistro tables carved from driftwood and a row of bar stools inside and then a larger seating area that opened to the outdoor deck. Each drink was served with a signature shortbread cookie in the shape of an anchor. And the menu offered a lengthy list of beach-inspired drinks like the Mac-Nut Mocha, a mocha drizzled with dark chocolate and macadamia-nut syrup and the Lava Lava latte, a vanilla and Kahlúa-flavored latte.

There was a line in front of the espresso bar but the three baristas behind the counter were managing it well. "How's everything going?" I asked the manager, Henny, a British graduate student who had decided to put her studies on hold for a few years to see the world.

She pointed to the pastry case. "They are going through pastries like locusts." She wiped her hands on a yellow and blue striped apron that matched the beach towels. "I think it's because the sea is so calm. No one is seasick. Usually we lose at least a few potential customers on the first day or two." She winked.

"You're terrible." I laughed.

"True, but we're going to run out of coffee."

"Really? Are you already running low?" Each chef was responsible for ordering food and drink in advance. Pallets of coffee, wine, and meat were carted aboard.

Chefs had the ability to restock or purchase specialty items at port. Carlos loved bartering with local island vendors for the freshest catch of the day or exotic spices. The ship was loaded with a week's worth of extra food in the rare event that something like this happened. I was once on a ship that had a norovirus outbreak. We ended up quarantined at sea for five days. Not only were the guests miserable but I had to get creative with brown bananas and using oil in my baked goods when we ran out of butter.

"Not really. We should be fine, but this group of passengers is going to take the cake for coffee consumption."

"Funny." I checked her extra stock. "Let me know if you need anything."

"Will do! It's great to have you back, chef," she said as she handed a passenger a Lava Lave latte with an anchor out of foam on the top.

I started to tell her that I wasn't back, but decided against it. "Hey, can we chat for a minute? In private?" I nodded to an empty table on the sundeck.

"Sure." She untied her apron and came around to the front of the espresso bar.

Outside the water was eerily calm. "It's weird, isn't it?" Henny commented and stared ahead, where puffy white clouds touched the horizon. It was no wonder that our ancestors once believed the earth was flat. From our perspective the clouds appeared as an impenetrable barricade to the other side of the world.

"Yeah. I've never seen anything like this." There was no sound of the wind cutting over waves. I swallowed. Carlos might be right. A strange quietness surrounded the ship like an ominous halo.

Around us, passengers in bikinis and board shorts sipped iced coconut lattes and kids built towering sandcastles in a section of the sundeck designed to resemble a real beach with white sand, shady palm trees, and a spray park. A couple at the table next to us commented on how smooth the cruise had been. They reveled in the fact that their friends had warned them they might experience motion sickness.

"Please," the woman drinking a blended mocha from a straw said to her husband. "This ship is more solid than our apartment. Here's to the *Amour* of the steady seas." She clinked her glass to his.

I noticed Jeff the deckhand scrubbing a rubber foam mat from the spray park. He had never come to the kitchen for a cup of peppermint tea. I wondered if his stomach had settled now that the ship was so still. He didn't appear to be unsteady on his feet and I didn't see him running to the railing to throw up. That was one positive effect of the mystifyingly calm sea.

"Do you want a coffee or anything, chef?" Henny asked.

"No, thanks." I returned my focus to her.

She waved to one of her staff baristas who passed by our table with a tray of tasting samples in tiny plastic cups. "Want a mai chai?" she asked us. We both declined. Henny laughed. "Don't you love the coffee puns?"

Andy would appreciate Anchor Coffee's beachy island décor and whimsical coffee creations. "That's pretty funny. What's in a mai chai?"

"Spicy chai, pineapple juice, orange juice, fresh lime, a drop of almond extract, grenadine syrup, and coconut milk."

I would have to make a note for Andy. Maybe our next Sunday Supper at Torte could feature a tropical theme.

"We serve it on ice and finish each drink with a slice of pineapple, orange rind swirl, maraschino cherry, and tropical drink umbrella. They are delish. You should really try one." Henny waited for the barista to move on to the next table. "You wanted to talk to me about something?"

I nodded and lowered my voice. "I'll be quick because

I know you're busy. I was wondering if you've heard anything about the woman who died this morning. I heard her name was Annie."

"Well, there have been some rumors going around. I didn't hear a name. Annie, you say? I heard that she was dating a member of the crew, and that they were trying to keep things on the down low. There was another rumor floating around that one of the crew snuck her aboard."

"Really?" I tried to keep my face neutral. My thoughts immediately went to Grayson. What if he had lied about having a fling with Babs? Maybe it was a cover-up. Could he have been involved with Jane Doe and snuck her onto the ship? Or for that matter what about Maria or Rocky?

Henny paused as the barista passed back by our table. This time with an empty tray. "I have no idea whether any of it is true. You know how rumors go."

"Absolutely," I agreed. "Thanks for letting me know."

"Sure. Do you need anything else?"

I shook my head. Henny returned to the espresso bar and began foaming lattes. I took a minute to gather my thoughts and went to check in with Jeff before heading to the pastry kitchen. The air was stagnant and thick. In the short time that I'd been talking with Henny my cheeks had warmed and I had begun to sweat. Jeff appeared to be even worse. Sweat ran from his brow as he scrubbed a thick rubber mat shaped like a seahorse. The mats had all been cut in the shape of sea animals—white whales, blue dolphins, and pink starfish.

"How's it going?" I asked.

Jeff started and dropped the mat. Then he realized it was me. "Oh hey. Sorry, I didn't hear you."

"I didn't mean to spook you," I replied, bending over and handing him the orange rubber mat. "I just wanted to see if you were feeling better." The smell of bleach stung my nostrils.

"Huh?" He wrung a towel in a bucket of dirty water.

"You never came to the kitchen for a cup of my peppermint tea."

He picked at one of the acne scabs on his face. I had to resist yanking his hand away. I wanted to tell him that picking at it would only make it worse. "Right. I haven't had time. Some kid threw up and I got called to clean up."

I was surprised to hear disdain in his voice. Earlier Jeff had been sick. I would have expected him to have more empathy. Then again, I didn't have to clean up after the passengers.

"You're feeling better?" I asked.

He squeezed the rag and returned to scrubbing. "I'm not hurling anymore, but then again that was a rough morning. Have they said anything else about the girl in the pool?"

His skittish behavior made me wonder if he could have had anything to do with her death, but I couldn't picture the young woman with the gorgeous blond hair I'd found in the pool having a secret affair with him. And there was the issue of him being seen by his fellow deckhands.

"Not really," I lied. "They're still trying to figure out who she is."

Jeff didn't look up from his scrubbing. "I hope they do soon."

"Me too," I agreed, and left him to his scrubbing. I wound through a row of lounge chairs to the crew elevator. It wasn't a surprise that the effects of Jeff's motion sickness were lingering. It worked the other way around too. Sometimes it took days if not weeks to recover your "land legs" after time spent on the seas.

Was he a viable suspect? I considered the possibility. He was at the scene when I found Annie, but the question was, could he have snuck off, hit her, pushed her into the pool, and returned to his post without any of the other crew members noticing or hearing the commotion? I felt like with each thing I learned I had a hundred new questions.

My first order of business was to find the Professor. I checked his cabin, but no one answered when I knocked. One challenge of life at sea is communicating on the ship. Some passengers bring walkie-talkies to stay in touch since cell phones don't work. I wished I had an easy way to get in touch with the Professor instead of trying to hunt him down.

I stopped by the main galley on my way to the pastry kitchen to see if by chance he was there. Cruise ship kitchens look remarkably like commercial kitchens on land with one major exception—no open flames. Fire is the biggest safety threat at sea, so none of the kitchens are equipped with gas stoves. It's a drawback for chefs. New chefs will often complain and have to learn how to sauté on an electric burner.

My senses were greeted with the smell of succulent shrimp and seared teriyaki beef. If the pastry kitchen was busy, the main kitchen was a mob scene. Chefs shouted "on your right" and "move" as they carried pans of bubbling fish stew to the oven and chopped onions and garlic at a dizzying speed.

Everything about the kitchen was familiar, especially Carlos, who stood at the far end of the long stainless workspace in his white chef coat shouting orders and tasting sauces. "No, no, do not coat the sauce. It looks like you don't care. You must give it a gentle touch. You are an artist and this is your canvas." He wiped the edges of the plate with the towel tucked into his belt and demonstrated how to create dainty dots of the sherry sauce with a quick flick of his wrist. "See, this is beautiful, no?"

The chefs watching him plate nodded and attempted the same motion. One of them sent a splattering of sauce flying right at Carlos's face. He didn't get angry, instead he wiped his cheek with his finger and then proceeded to taste the sauce. "It is very good."

His team laughed. Carlos did too, then he wiped his hands on his towel and returned to teaching. "You must move your hand like—it is quick and light, see?"

He didn't notice me watching him until he had finished instructing each young chef on the technique. When he moved toward the salad plating station he caught my eye and smiled broadly. "Julieta, how are you?" He kissed my cheek. "What do you need?"

"Nothing. I had to check on the bakery so I just stopped by on my way back."

"You have been careful, *sí*?"

"*Sí*. As promised."

He looked over his shoulder. "They do not know yet? Has the captain said anything else?"

"Not as far as I know. I haven't heard anything. You haven't seen the Professor by chance?"

"*Sí*. He was looking for you earlier. I sent him to your kitchen. This was a while ago."

"Yeah, he came by. Actually, I guess there is some news. He told me that they haven't been able to identify the woman and think that she might have been a stowaway." I didn't tell him that I had learned her name.

Carlos's brow indented. "A stowaway. How?"

"That's what I said. It would be nearly impossible to get on the ship without help."

Someone dropped a vat of chicken stock on the floor. It landed with a thud and sprayed stock onto the stainless steel counters and half the plated salads. Carlos rolled his eyes. "I must go, but please, Julieta, you promise you will not be involved."

"Yep." I left, unable to trust that my face wouldn't reveal the lie. I couldn't tell Carlos that the Professor had asked me to get involved. Even if he believed me, he wouldn't approve and would probably march straight to the Professor and ban me from having any more to do with the case.

Is he your husband anymore? I asked myself as I headed to the pastry kitchen. Technically, yes. We weren't divorced and yet we weren't together. I was struggling with whether that was a good thing or a bad thing. For the moment it felt like both.

Chapter Sixteen

Lunch service was a breeze and knowing that the staff had things under control I took a twenty-minute break to go meet Mom. She was sitting at the same table where she had eaten breakfast. That didn't surprise me. People are creatures of habit; at Torte we had a number of customers who had their own tables. In order to manage the sheer number of passengers on the ship, the dining room opened for dinner in two shifts. Each guest was assigned a table and wait staff for the duration of the trip. Seating arrangements encouraged guests to mingle and were a great way to build a relationship with the crew.

Both breakfast and lunch were open seating, but true to our nature most guests sat at their assigned dinner tables. Grayson was warming up on stage as I squeezed through the packed room.

"How was your morning?" I asked Mom. Her cheeks were highlighted with color. She looked more relaxed than I'd seen her look in years.

Holding up her book, she pointed to the last chapter. "I'm almost done."

"That's impressive. Did you bring another?"

"I brought a stack. Doug keeps teasing me that I only packed books, but we're always so busy at Torte that I usually fall asleep with a book in my face. I intend to read every single title on this vacation."

"Looks like you're on your way."

Her eyes were bright. "Juliet, I can't thank you enough for inviting us along." She rubbed her shoulders. "This humid air and the heat have been so good for me. I haven't felt this limber in years."

"I'm so glad," I said, reaching for her hand. "But you know you should really thank Carlos. It was all his doing."

Her eyes twinkled. "Don't you worry, I know."

A waiter arrived to take our drink order. "I'd love one of your strawberry daiquiris," Mom said, giving me a sheepish grin.

"Just water for me," I added. "I'm on the clock." A bank of ominous gray clouds cast a shadow on the windows that looked out to the sea below.

"I can't believe I'm having a drink at lunch, but those daiquiris are so delicious and this is vacation after all."

Wait staff circulated the room with trays of garden-fresh salads and baskets of rolls and buttery croissants. Passengers had many options for lunch, including ordering from a prearranged three-course formal lunch menu or piling their plates at the buffet line.

"Yes, it is. Don't feel guilty. Go for it. We're not going anywhere, so you might as well enjoy yourself."

She unfolded her napkin. "Have you heard anything new?"

"Actually, yes. Have you seen the Professor?"

She shook her head. "Not for a while. He joined me at the pool for a few minutes earlier. In fact he said he was looking for you. You must be ships passing in the night."

I gave her a condensed update of my conversation with the Professor as well as the theory that Annie was a stowaway who had had help getting on board. I left out the piece about him asking me for my help, and that I knew her identity. I didn't want that to get back to the Professor without being able to explain how I learned that piece of information and to describe Maria's reaction. "What about you?" I asked when I finished my recap. "Have you heard anything or have you been in soaking-up-the-sun mode?"

"Soaking up the sun." She used the napkin to dab her forehead. "It's already hot. In fact with the clouds rolling in it's practically like a steam room outside. I might have to take a bit of a break and go curl up in the library this afternoon. It's air-conditioned, right?"

Rocky's booming voice interrupted our conversation. I nodded and we both turned toward the stage. His bald head glistened under the stage lights. "Hey, cruisers! How are we doing out there?"

A small scattering of applause and a couple of cheers sounded.

"Come on, this is your cruise director speaking, you can do better than that. Let me ask you again, how are you all doing out there?"

Louder cheers and a few whoops erupted from the crowd.

"That's better. I'm going to keep working on you, but I'll take it for now." He motioned to the side of the stage where Grayson sat on a stool with his guitar strung across his shoulder. "We have an amazing lunch show for you today! Now folks, I have to tell you, this doesn't happen very often so consider yourselves lucky."

"Lucky as in a brewing storm and a dead body on board," I whispered to Mom.

"You sound like Lance," Mom shot back with a wink.

Rocky moved a mic stand for Grayson. "If you came to last night's show then you already know that you're in for the performance of a lifetime with our resident singer-songwriter Grayson Allen."

People clapped and a table of older women wearing matching purple hats shouted, "We love you, Grayson."

"Ladies, you have good taste." Rocky made a shooting sign their way. "Without further ado I give you Grayson Allen."

Grayson strummed a few chords and then spoke so closely into the microphone that I worried he might swallow it. "Thanks for having me. I'm going to play a couple of new pieces. I've titled this set Coffeehouse. These songs just went up on iTunes so if you like what you hear give them a download. Let's get them trending."

"Is he allowed to do that?" Mom asked.

"What?"

"Self-promotion. I'm surprised that the cruise lets him do that."

I watched Rocky's mouth turn into a thin line. "I'm not sure he's supposed to," I said to Mom. "Look at Rocky."

While the lunchtime entertainment was in full swing I intended to use the opportunity to talk to Rocky and see if he would come clean on his interaction with Annie in the stairwell yesterday.

Grayson started to say something else, but he caught Rocky's glare and cleared his throat. "This first song is called 'Forbidden Kisses.'"

The music reminded me of a playlist that Sterling had created for Torte. It was composed of indie singer-songwriters with poetic lyrics. When the bakeshop was crowded we used the playlist for light background noise. There's nothing worse in my opinion than going to a coffee shop or bakery and having your ears assaulted by sound. Music should accompany whatever you're eating, but not overtake it. Grayson's music wasn't particularly unique or memorable, but I enjoyed it and the other passengers seemed to as well.

As his fingers gently strummed the strings and his haunting, soulful voice harmonized into the mic, I surveyed the dining room. Babs sat at a table to the left of the stage. By the way she was shielding her eyes from the stage lights with dark black sunglasses and sipping on a fizzy water, I suspected she was nursing a hangover. Twice Grayson looked her way and sang directly to her. Both times, she kept her sunglasses focused on her drink.

From that interaction I definitely got the sense that Babs didn't reciprocate Grayson's feelings. He reminded me of a puppy dog trying to please his master as he ended the song by closing his eyes, swaying from side to side, and then tapping his chest. Was it an act? From our earlier conversation I had gotten the distinct impression that Grayson was interested in Babs for her connections in the music world, but by the way he was serenading her now maybe he was actually smitten.

Babs swirled her drink with a red stir stick and couldn't appear more bored. All the more reason to wonder if he was lying. What if his "onboard" romance had actually been with Annie?

Once Grayson finished his second song Rocky jumped back on the stage and took over the mic. "Thanks, man. That was moving. Really moving, don't you think?" He placed his hand on his heart. "I felt that." In a flash his demeanor changed. "Okay, now who is ready to get their groove on?"

A few people shouted.

Rocky gyrated his hips. "That's right, baby. It's about to get sexy in here."

The group of women in purple cheered the loudest and one of them waved a dollar bill. Rocky winked. "I don't think you want me as your entertainment. I have someone much more enticing for you."

The woman waved her money higher in the air and shouted. "We want you!"

Mom caught my eye and shrugged.

Rocky grinned. "Consider it done, ladies. I'll come join your table in one minute but first let me introduce a woman who is going to rock your world. She has legs as high as the sky, a booty that can't stop shaking, and moves that are going to blow your mind. Our lead dancer . . . Maria!"

My back stiffened.

"What's wrong?" Mom whispered. One of the drawbacks to having such an empathetic and astute mom was that I could never successfully mask my emotions around her.

"Nothing." I shook my head.

She frowned. "Juliet."

"It's nothing. Maria has a thing for Carlos. That's all."

"I see." Mom retied the string on her cover-up and gave me a knowing look but dropped it.

Maria shimmied onto the stage in a sparkle of color and rhythmic pulsing moves. Salsa music blared from the speakers as she threw her hips into her performance. There was no debating that she was a talented dancer; Rocky wasn't exaggerating about her moves. She contorted her body in ways that defied the laws of physics. Everyone looked breathless when she stomped her platform shoe on the stage to the final tick of the beat. Then huge applause broke out. Maria took a bow and the music started up again.

Watching her twirl around the stage made me slightly dizzy.

"She's good," Mom commented.

"I know."

I must have scowled because Mom patted my hand. "Honey, you have nothing to worry about. I've seen the way Carlos looks at you. He only has eyes for you."

"Maybe." I pushed back my chair. "I should go check on the kitchen."

"Hmm." Mom wrinkled her brow. "Or you're trying to sneak out before things get serious."

"Me? Never." I blew her a kiss. "See you later."

I ignored Maria's shaking as I made my way to the side of the stage and caught Rocky's eye. He held up one finger for me to wait and finished making an adjustment to the sound system. "What's wrong?" he asked, hopping from the stage.

"Why does something have to be wrong?"

"I can see it in your face. You look stressed." He covered the mic on his lapel which I assumed was already off. "I can't have stressed pastries. Not today."

I almost laughed, but the veins visible on Rocky's head were bulging so much I thought they might burst. "The pastry is fine."

He wiped sweat from his brow. "Good. What do you need?"

"I have a couple of things I was hoping to ask you."

"Shoot." He folded his arms across his chest.

"Well, the first thing is about staffing. I'm not sure, maybe this is a question for the captain, but is there ever a time that the pool deck is empty?" From my recollection of early morning walks on the ship there always seemed to be a crew member around. If that was true it made it less likely that Jeff could have killed Annie.

"What do you mean?" He studied me.

"I was wondering about staffing. Is someone always up there?"

"Yeah, always. Why?"

"I wondered if any other deckhands could have seen something at the pool." I wasn't sure if I should mention Annie's name to see how he reacted. "I've been thinking a lot about the woman."

"What about her?" Rocky barked over the music.

"I feel responsible since I found her, you know?" I hoped that he would sympathize with me, but instead he gave me an exasperated look.

"Yeah, tell me about it. It's ruining this cruise. You feel responsible? Try being in my shoes. I am responsible. I'm responsible for keeping this ship upright and having a dead body is not helping."

That wasn't exactly the response I had been going for. Not to mention that Rocky was hardly responsible for keeping the ship upright. I tried a new tactic. "There are a ton of rumors floating around, and one of them is that someone snuck her on the ship." I folded my arms across my chest and gave him a knowing look.

The speaker squealed, causing everyone in the dining room to plug their ears. Maria whipped around in our direction and glared. Rocky shot her a look I couldn't decipher and then turned to me. "I've got to fix the sound. Here's my advice. Stay in the kitchen and leave it alone." He leaped onto the stage and began fiddling with the sound board. I could tell our conversation was done. I just wasn't sure if I should interpret his parting words as friendly or a warning.

Chapter Seventeen

I tried to be as discreet as possible and not interfere with any of the passengers' view of the stage while making my exit. As I squeezed past Babs's table she clasped my arm.

"Take a seat." It wasn't a question.

"Okay." I'm sure I must have sounded confused. "Is there something wrong with your meal?" Her salad looked like it hadn't been touched.

"No," she scoffed, and pushed the fresh salad away from her. "It's about him." She nodded toward the stage where Maria was still kicking up her legs and accentuating her well-endowed chest. "Who?"

Babs let out an exasperated sigh. "Him." She tilted her head to the side. I couldn't tell where she was looking because her eyes were completely hidden behind her sunglasses. The only other person who was nearby was Grayson who was standing to the left of the stage.

"Grayson?"

"Yes." She adjusted her sunglasses. "Obviously. I've seen him following you around too."

"I'm not sure I understand?" When had Babs seen Grayson and me together?

"Listen, let me warn you. I haven't been able to shake him." She tapped the red swizzle stick on the rim of her glass. "I think he's dangerous. Not only do you need to be warned, but you need to tell that cruise director to have his songwriter back off."

"Okay, I'm not sure this is exactly my domain. I can talk to Rocky, but if you're really concerned you might need to escalate this."

"I've already tried that." She tapped her black finger-nails on the tabletop. Like last night Babs was dressed in black leather. Although today she wore a tight leather miniskirt, ankle boots, and a black V-neck T-shirt with the word ROCKSTAR encrusted in rhinestones.

"You have?" I couldn't believe that Rocky wouldn't have immediately intervened or that if Babs had taken the issue up with the captain, he wouldn't have put a stop to any interactions with Grayson.

"Yes, and you know what that buffoon did? Nothing. Absolutely nothing. I thought passenger safety was valued aboard the ship, but obviously I've been mistaken."

"Are you worried about your safety?" I measured my words carefully. Grayson had told me that he and Babs had had a fling, but what if he was lying? Maybe he'd been stalking her. He didn't seem like the type, but in all hon-esty I didn't even know if there was a "type." Could Gray-son be dangerous?

"Why would I be speaking to you if I weren't worried about my personal well-being?" Her voice cracked slightly as she spoke.

"Wait, have you spoken with the captain?" I scanned the room to see if any other high-ranking crew members were around that I could call over.

"No." She folded her arms across her chest.

That was odd. If Babs was truly concerned for her safety—and warning me that I could be in danger too—why wouldn't she have sought out more help? I wasn't sure I fully believed her story, but given Jane Doe's death and Grayson's odd behavior, I couldn't take any chances.

"I think you should talk to the captain or the head of security if you don't feel comfortable around Grayson." She didn't strike me as meek. In fact, she came across as confident and sure of herself. I couldn't imagine why she hadn't gone to the captain.

"Fine." She sounded angry. I was about to leave, but she rubbed her temples and continued. "It was a stupid, stupid mistake on my part."

"What was?"

"Fooling around with Grayson." Babs snapped at a waiter walking past our table with a tray of empty glasses. "I need a martini, stat." The waiter gave her a thumbs-up and started to continue on. "Make it a double," Babs shouted after him. So Grayson had been telling the truth about his onboard romance. Of course, that didn't mean he couldn't have been involved with Annie too.

She turned to me. "What is it with watered-down drinks on this ship?"

"Have your drinks been watered down?"

Scowling from behind her oversized sunglasses, she pointed at her drink. "Taste this."

"I can't," I replied. "On the clock."

For a minute I didn't think she was going to say more. She swirled her drink with the stir stick and stared at Maria. As she twisted the straw in her drink I thought she might snap it in half, but she bent it and continued to focus on Maria. "Grayson was a moment of weakness. He's not a bad-looking guy and we are both consenting adults. I'm on vacation for the first time in ten years, I thought why not. But now he won't stop hounding me."

"You and Grayson hooked up and now he's following you around?" That part at least matched what Grayson had told me.

"Yes." She sucked the rest of her drink through the tiny straw and scanned the vast dining room for our waiter. "He thinks I'm going to get him a record deal. I'm not— *obviously.*"

The woman liked saying "obviously." I wasn't sure that was obvious to Grayson, especially if he thought they had a connection.

She twisted one of the half-dozen diamond studs circling her lobe. The sleek, modern earring that I found in the supply closet didn't seem to match Babs's rocker style. "I like your earrings, you're not missing one, are you?"

Babs scowled and pointed to a simple stud in her left ear. "I only wear studs. Why?"

"No reason. I found an earring and wanted to return it to its owner." Another strikeout when it came to figuring out who the missing earring belonged to. Neither Babs nor Maria were missing an earring, which made me wonder if maybe the earring had belonged to Annie. Then again on the first night that I'd met Babs she'd been wearing giant hoops. Was she lying?

Giving the stud one final twist, she reached for her drink again. "I don't do indie singer-songwriters. That trend is dead. I produce highly stylized shows. I told him that but he won't listen and now I can't shake him."

What she said made sense. Had he pursued Babs just to try and further his music career?

"You told Rocky this?" I asked as the waiter delivered Babs's refresher.

She snatched it out of his hand and began to guzzle it. "No. I told him to tell Grayson to leave me alone."

"And what did he say?" The way that Babs was drinking made me wonder if there was more to her story than she was letting on.

"He said he would, but *obviously* it isn't working."

I begged to differ. The lunch crowd began to thin out.

I heard a number of passengers comment on the fore-boding skies. From the looks of the menacing wall of gray clouds pushing our way and the fact that the windows were being pelted by rain, I had a feeling the fun deck was going to be packed this afternoon. Rainy days at sea can often be surprisingly enjoyable. The bowling alley and movie theater would be bustling and I knew from past experience there would be a group of adventurous passengers who would risk getting damp to watch the storm from the upper decks.

As if reading my mind the captain's voice came over the loudspeaker. "Ladies and gentlemen, as you can probably see from our diminishing view we've hit a bit of weather. I don't expect any trouble, but please be aware of your surroundings, and on the off chance we run into any choppy seas be sure to use hand railings as you pass through the ship. Our cruise director is going to offer some bonus activities on deck four—like popcorn, hot chocolate, and movies for the kids and penny poker and trivia for adults in the lounge. We'll do our best to navigate through this and have you back to sunny skies in no time."

Babs wasn't fazed by the captain's update. She pushed her sunglasses to the tip of her nose and watched Grayson sling his guitar around his shoulder and leave the stage. "He's going to be waiting right outside the doors for me. Just watch."

"Were you and Grayson together this morning?"

I thought her face flinched. It could have been the lights flickering from the gusty winds outside. She folded her hands on her lap. "Why?"

"I thought I saw you after I found the . . ." I trailed off.

"The body?" Babs finished my thought.

"Yeah. How did you know?"

"I was there."

"You were?" I knew it. Her words confirmed that it had been her that I'd seen fleeing down the crew stairwell.

"Grayson and I took a bottle of champagne to the pool deck late last night or early this morning. We both ended up passing out."

"Did you know the woman—I heard her name was Annie? Had you seen her before?"

Babs shook her head. "No, but there was something familiar about her. I can't place it, but I see so many faces in my line of work. I have a stack of headshots thicker than a book on my desk. Plus I see a lot of young girls trying to get their break—singers, dancers."

"Have you told the captain this?"

"I've been sleeping off a splitting headache for the last three hours. I haven't left my cabin."

Her comment surprised me. If she had been sleeping off a headache why was she drinking like a fish? "You should tell the captain. He and the Professor—the detective—are asking passengers for any information they have on the missing woman."

"I don't think this is information. There was something familiar about her. Annie, hmmm. All I know is that she was young. Really young."

"You have to tell the captain," I insisted. "Any lead is critical right now."

She rested her sunglasses on the tip of her nose and focused her bloodshot eyes on me. "Is that right?"

"Yeah, why?"

"I do have a lead that they should follow up on if they are trying to figure out who the girl was."

"What's that?"

She glanced to the table of purple-hatted women. "Him."

"Rocky?"

"That's right. I saw him fighting with the girl last night."

"You saw Rocky and Annie fighting? When?" I flashed back to seeing them arguing in the stairwell yesterday. Was that why Rocky told me to leave it alone?

She shrugged and stared into the darkness outside. "I don't remember exactly. After dinner. I went to my cabin to slip into something more comfortable before I met Grayson for a drink. He told me to use the employee stairwell. I saw Rocky yelling at the girl. I didn't want to get Grayson into trouble so I left and used the guest elevator to get to the pool deck instead. Now I regret that. I should have made a scene and let him get caught."

"You're sure it was Rocky?" Despite the captain's assurances the storm was building. I wasn't worried. I'd been through much worse weather, but there was no denying that the sea was swelling below us as the chandelier flickered and the dining room began to tilt ever so slightly from side to side.

"I'd recognize that shiny bald head anywhere."

My mind felt heavy and my body began to sway. Rocky and Annie were fighting again after I'd seen them? He had definitely lied to me. He told me that she was drunk and he was sending her to her cabin to sleep it off.

To Babs, I said, "Be sure to tell the captain."

She returned her sunglasses to the bridge of her nose. "Will do. And if you see Grayson tell him to stop bugging me."

I told her that I would and encouraged her to talk to the captain about that too. He couldn't harass passengers. That wasn't professional. And I kept flashing back to the earring. What if it belonged to Annie? Had Grayson killed her and been trying to stash the evidence in the supply closet? I had no idea whose story to believe.

Babs's hard exterior had cracked. I almost felt sorry for her. Could it be that she was lying about Grayson because she thought he was really interested in her at first? Was she really sounding a valid warning, or was she a woman scorned?

As I returned to the kitchen I couldn't stop thoughts from assaulting my brain. Not only Grayson's and Babs's possible involvement with Annie's death, but also Rocky's. He knew Annie and had intentionally lied about it. Why? Maybe he had a good reason, but the only reason I could think of was because he had killed her.

Chapter Eighteen

My staff was cranking out cookies and cakes at a break-neck pace. I hadn't been gone for more than thirty minutes, but in that time they had churned out trays and trays of sweets ready to be devoured by the guests. After watching Maria shake it on the stage people were probably going to be even hungrier.

"Someone was looking for you," one of the cake decorators said as I checked on his piping. He had the painstaking task of piping hundreds of star patterns onto the top of the individual Bundt cakes.

"How's your arm holding up?" Delicate pastry work like piping can really take a toll on your arms and hands. I showed him how to support the pastry bag better.

"Not too bad." His white coat looked as if it had been spray-painted with frosting. Splotches of blueberry buttercream and pastel pink French cream were splattered on his sleeves and navy and yellow royal icing (the *Amour of the Sea*'s signature colors) was smeared on the middle section of his chef's whites.

"Who stopped by?" I picked up a Bundt cake and examined it. The banana-coconut cake had a lovely even browning and springy center. It smelled like breakfast. I tore off a chunk and tasted it.

The decorator steadied his hand and continued piping. "Some guy wearing a Hawaiian shirt and wire-rimmed glasses. We thought he was a guest who took a wrong turn, but he said he was a detective or something."

"The Professor. Did he say anything else?" Tracking down the Professor was taking hours. Unless he had left specific instructions about where and when to meet him, my best bet was to stay put and wait for him to come back. I had to tell him about learning Annie's name and about my conversations with Babs and Rocky.

"He said he would come back in an hour." The decorator moved on to the next tray and began drizzling yellow royal icing on lemon shortbread cookies. "He said there's a message for you from home. He left it on your desk."

"Thanks. Keep up the good work." I wondered who would have contacted me through the Professor and went to my office to check. There was a printed e-mail sitting on my desk. I picked it up to read it.

Dear Juliet,

I'm helping the Professor with some details from the case and he asked me how things were going at Torte. He figured that you and your mom might want an update, so I stopped to check in on my way to the flower shop this morning and everything seems to be running well. There is one piece of news. The construction crew has finished work at Trickster and Torte is next on the list. Sterling told me that they are going to start excavating the basement tomorrow.

It's a big step, Jules. Congratulations. Torte is going to take over the plaza before you know it. I can tell you one person who won't be happy about that—Richard Lord. He's been sending in complaints and trying to get me to stop progress. He's claiming that the tent and scaffolding they've put up on the Calle Guanajuato is impeding the sidewalk and illegal. They have to reroute pedestrian traffic on the walkway while they excavate. But don't worry—everyone knows this is how he operates. I've been in talks with Rosalind and the city code inspector. I'm sure we'll get it taken care of, but I wanted you to hear it from me first.

I hope that you can relax and enjoy your trip. You deserve it. Just don't forget about all of your friends in Ashland who love you and want you to come home.

~Thomas

It was thoughtful of Thomas to check in, but his last line rattled me. Maybe I was reading into things, but Thomas had professed his feelings for me a few weeks ago. In all honesty I wasn't sure that he really did still love me. I think that he loved the idea of me—the girl I used to be. But I had grown up, seen the world, changed. I didn't want to go backward. I was focused on the future, and had told Thomas as much. He had been kind and hadn't pushed it any further. I just hoped that we could keep things as they were. I didn't want our relationship to be awkward. Thomas was a dear friend, and I needed friends like him.

The good news was that it sounded like construction was progressing faster than we had expected with the basement remodel. The bad news was that Richard Lord was at it again. Why did he always have to have it in for me and Torte? I'd have to find Mom later and let her know, and cross my fingers that he wouldn't be successful in his attempts to hinder our forward motion.

For the next few hours I lost myself in baking. As I melted butter and whisked in copious amounts of heavy cream and a touch of coconut extract for a custard that I would layer with a flambéed fruit puree, I couldn't stop thinking about why Rocky had lied. Had I misinterpreted what he had said? I played back the scene on the pool deck. No, Rocky had denied knowing Annie. Why would he lie? Between thoughts of the murder, the distraction of knowing that Carlos was nearby, and trying to multitask so many desserts and remember new faces the room started to feel like it was spinning. Was the ship rocking, or was it me?

I clutched the counter and tried to steady myself. One of the sous chefs noticed. "Hey, are you okay, chef?"

In a professional kitchen of this size everyone addressed me as "chef." I held on tighter and said, "That was a big wave."

He nodded his head in agreement and stopped and squinted at his workstation where his paring knives were sliding slightly to the left and then back to the right. "We're rocking, for sure."

"We are, aren't we?" I felt relieved that it wasn't in my head. "Seas must be picking up." Immediately I thought of the deckhand Jeff. If he had struggled on flat water he was really going to be in trouble. And what about Jeff? I kept coming back to him as a suspect in Annie's murder. Surely one of the other deckhands would have seen him slip away, that morning. There were two other crew members on deck but maybe he was more spry than he appeared. People had surprised me in the past.

"Yeah. Hopefully the captain will steer out of the storm soon. It won't be fun if we get stuck in choppy waters."

He was right. Cruising on a vessel our size meant that even in moderate seas there was the potential for disruption. Even the outer edge of the storm would pack a punch. We were going to start feeling every swell, and if the waves continued to build it was going to get more than a little bumpy.

I put on a brave face and finished assembling my custard parfaits. The layers of creamy pudding and colorful fruit puree made a striking presentation. They reminded me of candy sticks I used to get in my Christmas stocking when I was a kid. My stockings always contained oranges and clementines, homemade chocolate and caramel-coated marshmallows, and an assortment of old-fashioned striped candy sticks. I carried trays of the parfaits into the walk-in fridge. They would set for the next few hours and be nicely chilled for the late afternoon snack buffet.

The task list in the pastry kitchen was never-ending. I had probably already logged miles going back and forth between workstations to make sure that everyone was on task and that desserts were being plated to our high standards.

Seeing my colorful parfaits reminded me of two things. First, that I had promised the captain a lemon jelly roll. I could bet that he would appreciate a slice of some sweet comfort right now. I also realized that I had never asked Carlos about a dessert pairing for dinner service. It wasn't always feasible but I usually tried to pair at least one of the evening desserts with something from the main kitchen. If Carlos was serving a particularly hearty dinner then I would make sure my staff prepared at least one lighter dessert offering like an elegant fruit and cheese tray, or a lemon jelly roll dusted with powdered sugar. The reality was that most passengers appreciated food in excess while on board. It was the rare occasion that we got special dietary requests, although we always offered a few low-sugar options for diabetics and those passengers trying to be calorie conscious. But there weren't many cruisers who came for diet fare.

I got to work on the lemon roll by whipping eggs, sugar, and fresh lemon juice together. Once the mixture had been beaten into a frothy opaque yellow color I added baking soda, a dash of salt, and flour. Then I lined a jelly roll pan with tinfoil and poured the batter in a thin one-inch layer. The sponge cake wouldn't take more than ten minutes to bake. After I slid it into the oven I began mixing the filling. I'd made many variations of jelly rolls over the years, but for the captain I stuck with my standard fare of lemon curd whipped with heavy cream and powdered sugar.

Once the cake had cooled I spread a generous layer of the creamy mixture over its surface, sprinkled it with powdered sugar, and gently rolled it into a log. Then I dusted the top of the roll with more powdered sugar and garnished it with lemon zest. I cut the log into thick slices and plated them for the captain and his crew. After one more walk-through of the kitchen I took the tray and headed for the bridge.

The bridge was the command center for the ship. Most of the time the bridge was manned by the OOW (officer of the watch) or one of the able seamen, but I knew that given the squall we were sailing through, the captain would definitely be at the ship's helm. I steadied the tray of lemon rolls while navigating the crew stairwell that led to the bridge. Twice I had to stop and hang on as waves rocked the ship.

When I finally made it to the top I was greeted with sounds of beeping computer equipment and the captain barking out orders to the crew. Rain slammed into the bridge's front-facing windows. The interior of the bridge always reminded me of a scene from *Star Trek* with its massive computer arsenal, high-tech compasses and sonar, and captain's chair front and center. Usually visits to the bridge involved the captain explaining technology and the modern navigational system to passengers lucky enough to get an insider's view, but today it looked like a war room.

"Lemon roll delivery," I called out above the noise of the computer equipment and crew.

The captain noticed me and left his post momentarily. "Chef, you have no idea how happy I am to see you with that platter." He took a slice of lemon roll from the tray and handed it off to one of his crew members to pass around to the rest of the staff.

"It's pretty dark out there," I said, nodding to the thunderous sky. Waves that reminded me of whitewater rapids slammed into the hull.

The captain stuck his fork into the jelly roll, took a bite, and then closed his eyes. After savoring my cake for a minute, he opened his eyes and steadied them on me. "This is worse than I was expecting. I don't have a choice though. With a dead body on board I'm under strict orders to steer her directly to the nearest port. It just happens that the port is in the path of this storm."

"Is it bad?"

"I'm not sure. When we charted a new course we figured the storm would track west. We planned to stay two hundred and twenty nautical miles to the northeast of it, but it has shifted closer than we expected." He frowned as an alarm sounded on one the computers. "I've got to get back to work. Be careful. It could get worse." He took another bite of the lemon roll. "Thanks again, and tell your crew to stay away from the aft deck. It's blowing pretty hard out there."

"Have you talked to the Professor?" I asked on my way out.

He shook his head. "No. Unfortunately I've had my hands full here. Never have I been so glad to have a detective on board."

I left with a feeling of dread. What kind of a storm were we in for?

Chapter Nineteen

I tried to push images of big waves and fierce winds from my head. I had to find the Professor. I had so much to tell him.

For the time being I returned to the main kitchen to check in on Carlos's menu. He was a chef who led with his heart when it came to cooking. He was made for life at sea, with one exception. As head chef he had to plan ahead—way ahead. His personal style was much more fluid and organic. When we were at port he would spend an afternoon perusing the local markets and return home with a small basket of vibrant vegetables and herbs, briny shellfish, and uncommon fruits. With a glass of wine in hand and Latin music blaring from the stereo he would fillet the fish and let the flavors of wherever we had landed guide him. His dishes were always unique and bursting with flavor.

He added touches of spontaneity whenever he could in the ship's kitchen, both through his ongoing pranks and by picking up produce and seafood to incorporate into the menu at every port. But otherwise he was bound by the limits of the ship's pantries and freezers. He used to complain endlessly about being at the mercy of island fishermen and tied to a menu he had to prepare weeks in advance.

"Julieta, the food, it suffers. Menus have no life. Food it should be fluid. It should be free."

"Right, but you can't exactly run to the grocery store or market when we're hundreds of miles away from land."

He would laugh because he knew that I was right, but it never stopped his lament. "How can I give our guests food that is inviting, seductive for the senses, and filled with life if I have to order my supplies weeks ahead? Food is where I live and my mood it strikes my creativity. What happens when I buy a rack of beef but my heart, it calls to me to make a lovely sea bass?"

"I guess you'll have to tell your heart that it's wrong."

"But the heart it is never wrong." He looked injured.

I understood his struggle. Chefs, like painters or writers, were artists at heart. Food was a form of expression and Carlos felt like he was being stifled when it came to expressing a particular whim. He eventually learned to compromise by adding local flourishes and ordering as much variety as he could. It was a delicate balance because passengers expected familiar food like hand-carved honey hams and steak and lobster, while Carlos believed it was his duty to introduce them to new tastes and flavor combinations. He had earned a reputation for pushing food boundaries on the ship, like the night that he served an entirely white dinner—white appetizers, white sides, and white fish. Guests were asked by special white invitations to dress in white attire and were treated to white linens and lavish white floral bouquets.

A dinner in white might have sounded bland, but Carlos's meal permeated every taste bud on the tongue. He served cod with a tangy white pepper and vinegar sauce, and jasmine rice with bamboo shoots. His halibut showcased his Latin roots with its crisp sear and creamy garlic and cumin sauce. For those who didn't like fish he basted whole chickens in butter and transformed them into a spicy

Indian white curry dish. The chicken swam in a sauce of coconut milk, star anise, coriander, cloves, cinnamon, and fresh ginger.

Guests talked about the dinner in white for the remainder of the cruise. It was so popular that it became a tradition. Passengers would receive invitations sometime during the duration of their trip inviting them to a dinner in black or red. Carlos knew no limits when it came to color and passengers were introduced to regional specialties and exotic delicacies from all over the world. Return guests would eagerly await the arrival of their invitation and run to the boutiques to buy a purple scarf or a blue sundress for the occasion. In the pastry kitchen we would produce desserts in accordance to Carlos's theme. Raspberry mousse and cherry trifle for a dinner in red or coconut meringues and white chocolate mousse for a dinner in white. The bar staff made custom cocktails and the wait staff wore color-coordinated boutonnieres and ties.

I couldn't believe that I'd forgotten about the dinner-in-color night, but I'd only had a few days' notice. Hopefully Carlos wasn't planning something that would be tricky to match in dessert, like dinner in black. As I neared the main kitchen I heard the sound of laughter and Spanish conversation.

A new wave of dizziness assaulted me as I stepped into the kitchen to see Maria with her long arms draped over Carlos.

Carlos tossed Maria's arm off his shoulder and ran over to me as I started to back out of the door. Maria shot me a look of disdain and then turned her attention to a line cook. Her sequined miniskirt and six-inch stilettos looked completely out of place among a throng of chefs in white coats.

"Julieta, how are you?"

"I'm fine. I'm still looking for the Professor, but didn't mean to interrupt."

"What would you be interrupting?" Carlos looked confused.

I motioned toward Maria.

He threw his head back and laughed. "Julieta, you are too much." Kissing the top of my head he pulled me into the kitchen. "It is nothing. She came to give me an update from the captain."

I doubted that Maria had any information to share from the captain, especially since I'd been on the bridge minutes ago and there had been no sign of her sparkly costume in sight. As much as I wanted to comment on Maria's behavior, like why did she have to have her scantily clad body pressed next to Carlos's, I kept quiet. "Really? What's the update?"

"The storm is picking up. You noticed, no?"

"Yeah." A row of stainless steel pots hanging on a pot rack above the prep station rattled together, sending a clang reverberating through the galley. "I've noticed." For some reason I didn't bother telling him that I had just spoken with the captain.

"*Sí,* the captain, I think he might be worried, Julieta. This storm it feels different, no?" Carlos's dark eyes met mine. The look of uncertainty was unfamiliar. "I do not have a good feeling about this."

"You said that."

Carlos nodded toward Maria who seductively licked tomato sauce from a wooden spoon. "Ask Maria. She spoke to him. I have not seen him since this morning."

She wasn't first on my list of people I wanted to spend extra time with, but I was curious to know if the captain had actually given her an update. It didn't make any sense for him to share critical information about the ship's well-being with a salsa dancer, but maybe she knew something

I didn't. The captain had just informed me that he didn't know anything more about the investigation. Was Maria lying? Or was she hanging out in the kitchen for another reason? And I had to admit I wanted to ask her about Annie.

"How is the pastry kitchen? It is good, yes?" Carlos steadied himself on the wall as a gust rocked the kitchen. It must be getting nasty outside because the kitchens were situated midship. The interior sections of the ship were the most stable. So much so that it wasn't rare to have passengers who had booked staterooms with balconies downgrade their guest rooms to a viewless room in mid-ship because the odds of experiencing seasickness were much less in the interior. Of course there was also a theory that having a sightline to the horizon helped reduce the effects of motion sickness as well.

"It's good. They're a great staff. Why did the chef leave?"

"He was—how do you say?" Carlos paused and tried to find the word. "Pompous."

"A pompous pastry chef." I laughed.

"*Sí*, he was terrible to the staff and the crew. If the captain had not fired him I think we would have had mutiny on the ship. The entire pastry kitchen staff were going to walk off the ship."

"They're amazing. I've been very impressed and have been praising their work every chance I get."

"*Sí*, this is why I knew it must be you to come. I knew that you would give them a boost."

"I don't know about a boost, but like I've said they've got it under control. Sometimes I feel like I'm in the way." Behind us pans clanked together as line cooks muscled through the turbulent motion. Tomato sauce splattered out of massive vats and tubs of chicken breasts marinating in teriyaki sauce splashed on the counter. If things kept up like this, cleanup was going to be a major undertaking once the storm passed.

Now Carlos laughed. "Julieta, you could never be in the way in the kitchen. Never."

"Mom might disagree with that." I smiled. "Actually I came to check on the dinner in color. Are you doing one this cruise?"

"*Sí, sí.* I should have mentioned this when we spoke on the phone. It will be tomorrow night. Dinner in green. Is this okay?"

Green. Hmm. Why couldn't he have picked something easier like orange or yellow? Green would be a stretch but I was up to the challenge. "I think so," I said to Carlos. "I'll go check our stock and see what I can come up with." I began mentally running through every green fruit—kiwi, honeydew melon, green apples, limes, and grapes. As long as we had enough product I should be able to come up with something creative. I might even try something radical and incorporate avocado in a dessert.

Back in Ashland the Green Goblin, a bar with an "old-English forest" vibe, made an avocado daiquiri that had quickly become one of my favorite drinks. With that as my inspiration I could make an avocado whip with cream, sugar, blended avocado, lemon, lime, and fresh mint. It definitely wouldn't be a flavor profile that many of the guests would be familiar with.

"Julieta." Carlos was staring at me. "You are blanking into space."

"Sorry. I got swept up in the green idea. What do you think about an avocado whip?"

Carlos's dark eyes gleamed. "See, this is why we work so perfectly. Yes. *Sí.* You must make this."

"I don't know yet. Let me go experiment." Carlos was used to me getting lost in my thoughts when I was baking or creating new recipes. I registered the fact that he was chuckling as I backed out of the kitchen. I also registered that Maria swept right over to pick up where they had left off. The old saying of "having your cake and eating it too" rang through my head as I walked down the stairwell. Leaving Carlos meant that I had to give up my claim to him. Still, it stung to see Maria flirting with him. And I had to find the Professor—stat!

Chapter Twenty

A dinner in green might be more challenging than other colors but I needed something besides Carlos and Annie to occupy the afternoon. I checked our fruit supply. We had plenty of kiwis, apples, and a few melons. We were well stocked with limes, but I would have to check with the other kitchens to see if I could beg them for some avocados and grapes. Neither grapes nor avocados were something we typically used in pastry preparation. The green menu was going to require some planning in order to ensure that I didn't deplete our supplies.

I sent one of the young chefs upstairs with a heaping platter of cookies to try and sweet-talk some grapes and avocados from one of the other kitchens. What other pastries were green? I mentally went through my recipe files back at Torte. Then it hit me—pistachios. They were green and decadent. I could make a pistachio cake with a dark chocolate ganache filling and pistachio buttercream. My mouth salivated at the thought. In addition to the pistachio cake, we would do an avocado whip (assuming we could scrounge up enough avocados), kiwi tarts, a melon and grape fruit salad with a creamy lime sauce, and lime cheesecake. There was a ton of prep work to do.

My staff jumped to attention. "Aye, aye, chef," one of

them joked as I explained our plan of attack and assigned everyone tasks.

It had been a while since I had made a pistachio cake. I knew I had a recipe for one at Torte, and I wanted to make sure that I got the proportions right, especially because I would have to adjust my recipe to a massive scale for the ship. With a frenzy of frosting and kneading going on around me, I scooted out to see if I could get a hold of someone at Torte for the recipe. The employee lounge was much more crowded than it had been earlier. Talk was of the storm. An air of uncertainty hung in the room.

I found a computer and sent off an e-mail to Sterling to check on progress and ask if he could e-mail me the recipe. Then I checked my messages. There was a new message from Lance.

Darling,

What's the news on June Dough? I'm simply dying for details. Had a little tête-à-tête with your former leading man and apparently he's already spoken with the Professor. Thanks to modern technology you may be halfway around the world, but rest assured I'm doing my own digging here.

In other news your staff is doing just beautifully without you. I'm thinking of poaching all of them for the stage. Sterling with those steel-blue eyes would make some of my older ladies swoon, and all-American Andy is so sincere. Who wouldn't fall for him as Huck Finn? I can picture it now. But I really have my sights set on Stephanie—that pouty upper lip and purple hair! I want a scene with her as a badass fairy. What do you think? You can spare them for your dear pal Lance, can't you?

Richard Lord has been sniffing around. The excavating equipment arrived an hour ago and he's been pacing back and forth in front of the Merry Windsor trying to sneak a peek at what's going on here. Have you heard that he's claiming that Torte is in violation of a municipal code? Some nonsense about blocking sidewalks and access for emergency vehicles. It's ridiculous. Thankfully Richard's villainous attempts to thwart progress have been met at every turn by your Thomas. Don't you worry, we've got it under control and won't let Mr. Lord anywhere near the premises.

You won't believe what I've had to suffer through. A tasting! A tasting of his deconstructed menu. It started with what he claimed to be an aperitif, but in reality was a gelatinous glob of warm champagne with a scoop of cheap caviar on the top. To say it was the worst thing I've ever eaten would be too high praise. I'll spare you the details of the other course. Good Lord, please come back soon and rescue me from Ashland's resident Lord.

Lastly, your puppy-dog police officer, when he's not fighting off Lord, has been pacing back and forth like an expectant father. He's caught wind of a killer in close quarters as well as some tiny storm which he has blown out of proportion. Suddenly he's sure that you're sailing through The Tempest—*you know? Apparently he's convinced that you're in harm's way. The man is watching the Weather Channel ad nauseam on his iPad and giving us minute-by-minute updates. Do send him a note to assure him that every fine hair on your head is fine, won't you?*

I hear my pastry cast calling. Must run.

Ta-ta,
Lance

How much time was Lance spending at Torte? By asking him to check in I never imagined that he would completely take over. Poor Sterling, Andy, and Stephanie. I had a feeling that Stephanie's pouty upper lip had nothing to do with trying to be cast in one of Lance's productions and everything to do with wanting Lance out of the bakeshop.

I shot Sterling another apologetic e-mail asking for another update specifically about Lance. I wasn't above telling Lance to leave my staff alone, not that he would listen, but if he was impeding work at Torte I was going to have to intervene. A new message sounded in my in-box—it was from Sterling.

Hey Jules,

Things are great here. Don't worry. I hope that you and Helen are enjoying the trip. Thomas is freaking out about a storm. We're all pretty sure that he's worrying for nothing. Ships have to steer well clear of storms like that, right?

Steph found the recipe. It's attached. Let us know if you need anything else and how you're doing.

Sterling.

His e-mail was short and sweet and there was no mention of Lance. While I printed out the recipe I clicked send and receive a few times to see if he would respond to my second e-mail. Just as I was about to log out a new message beeped.

Jules,

You're supposed to be on vacation, remember? Stop e-mailing and stop worrying. Everything's cool. Thomas has Richard Lord in check. Lance is hanging around, but he's fine. Usually he parades around the dining room with a pot of coffee. The customers are loving it. You know Lance. He's in his element, but honestly he's been leaving us alone. Although he is giving Steph the hard sell to audition for a part in an upcoming production. He wants her to be a fairy or something. I'm sure you can imagine how she feels about that. She may have said a few words under her breath that I can't repeat. I hate to admit it but having Lance here has been good for business, especially with the out-of-towners.

They can't believe that OSF's artistic director is actually talking to them and refilling their coffee. It's nuts.

Yes, the crew arrived a while ago to start demo. Steph is going to take pictures of the process. She's going to use them for her art class. We'll send them so that you and Helen can see progress.

Really, don't sweat it. Bethany's been great. She's pretty cool actually and shockingly she and Steph have been getting along. You'd think they were besties or something. Every time I turn around they're laughing about something. Her brownies have been selling like mad. We just went through two pans of her sweet-and-salty pretzel brownies and orange-kiss brownies. I think you might need to put her on the permanent payroll when you get home.

Andy's yelling at me to ask you to bring back some new coffee blends if you can. He's making tropical drinks in your honor, and wants me to tell you that you better be ready for some mind-blowing mixology when you get back.

Hope that helps. We've got this. Hey, and you didn't mention anything about a storm or a murder. Is everything cool?

~Sterling.

His e-mail made my heart slow. I felt better knowing that Sterling and the team were doing fine without us and that Lance wasn't interfering with their work too much. The thought of Lance trying to convince Stephanie to audition made me laugh out loud. I'd come to know Stephanie better in the last few months and to appreciate her introverted style, but I couldn't imagine anyone more inclined to shun the limelight. Good luck with that, Lance. I was also happy to hear that Bethany had blended in with the team. Mom and I hadn't talked about more staff, but Sterling might have a point. With the expansion we could use more hands, and Bethany's baking skills were undeniable. I'd have to mull it over.

Before I logged off, I sent Sterling a final thanks and assured him that while the ship was rocking a bit there was nothing to worry about. I didn't want to worry my staff, but in reality the ship was getting thrashed and I wasn't sure how bad it was going to get. For the moment the only thing I could do was grin and bear it.

Returning to the kitchen, I headed straight for the pantry and pulled out a ten-pound bag of pistachios. I wanted to make a test cake this afternoon in order to give myself time to make any necessary adjustments to the recipe. Thankfully the pistachios had already been shelled so I grabbed a handful and dumped them into a Cuisinart and pulsed them into a fine green powder. Then I mixed butter, eggs, sugar, almond extract, and buttermilk. Once I sifted in the dry ingredients and pistachio powder I tested the batter for taste and color. The nutty flavor came through perfectly but the ground pistachios weren't enough to give the cake the dense green color I was looking for. I added a few drops of food coloring to enhance the green. That did the trick. The batter was a luscious green that reminded me of freshly cut grass.

Baking in choppy seas took patience and every muscle in my body. I could feel my core fire as I tried to maintain my balance and stay upright. The noise in the kitchen became almost deafening as pots and pans slammed into each other and mixers whirled.

I clutched the counter for support as I spread the batter into eight-inch round pans and slid them into the oven to bake for thirty minutes. Then I started on my buttercream. For this cake I opted for a classic French buttercream made with egg yolks, which gave the frosting a velvety smooth finish. French buttercream is more involved than a typical everyday frosting, but worth the extra effort. I started by heating sugar and water on medium heat in order to create a simple syrup. While I waited for the syrup to come to a boil I beat egg yolks on high speed until they began to foam and turn creamy. Once the syrup registered at two hundred and thirty degrees I slowly incorporated it into the egg mixture.

Then I let it cool and checked on my cakes. They had baked to a gorgeous golden green. I placed them on racks and returned to the frosting. The key to a silky French buttercream was adding butter in cubes one at a time. I dropped the first cube into the mixer and whipped it, adding cube after cube until all the butter had been added. I finished it with a touch of salt, a dash of almond flavoring, and more green food coloring. Finally I folded in pistachio chunks. They should give the smooth buttercream an unexpected crunch.

I sliced my cakes into four layers and spread chocolate ganache and more pistachios between each layer. Then I frosted the entire cake with the French buttercream. "Anyone want to be a taste tester?" I called to my team.

Within seconds I was surrounded by volunteers. Someone handed me a stack of plates, so I sliced my creation into tastes and passed them around the room. Before I took a bite I studied my plate. Our eyes taste everything we eat or drink first, which is why presentation is so important to professional chefs. Just like judging a book by its cover, people judge the taste of food based on how it looks on the plate. A messy or crumbly cake slice, uneven layers, too much frosting—all can throw off the tasting experience. I was pleased with how my pistachio cake had turned out. Each layer had a thin coat of ganache followed by a fluffy amount of the green buttercream. The cake itself looked moist and springy.

I bit into my piece and was treated to delightful flavors

of the salty pistachios and sweet cake. The buttercream was like silk in my mouth, and with the texture of the nuts it met my criteria for a balanced dessert.

"This is amazing." One of the chefs held his plate out for more. "Can we have seconds?"

"You can polish it off. We're going to be baking many more of these beauties tomorrow."

"Sweet." He gave me a goofy grin and sliced himself another piece.

In a matter of minutes my cake had disappeared. Although that wasn't necessarily a sign that the cake was a keeper. Kitchen staff were notorious for gobbling up anything put in front of them. I sent everyone back to their workstations and then returned to the office to begin adjusting my recipe for mass production. When modifying a recipe it doesn't always work to do a straight swap of proportions. After sketching out math in a spiral notebook I figured out how many vats of butter and pounds of cake flour it was going to take to magnify the pistachio cake. With that task complete I felt confident that the rest of the afternoon and evening would be a breeze, except for the fact that a steady blowing *breeze* was beginning to rock the ship even more.

Chapter Twenty-one

By the time I finished dessert prep the light wind had blown into a full storm. I'd forgotten how difficult it was to maintain balance while the ship lurched from side to side, sending rolling pins circling down the counter like a bowling ball and rattling the stainless pans hanging above my head. The noise in the pastry kitchen reached an ear-splitting pitch as everyone shouted over the sound of the banging pots and whirling mixers. The palms of my hands developed deep indents from clutching the bottom of the countertop every time the ship tilted to one side.

No one was more relieved than me when we sent the last round of tortes and iced tea cakes up to the dessert buffet. A new round of kitchen crew would come in to relieve the day shift. They would keep the late-night buffets stocked and handle any midnight room-service calls. I was done for the evening and was more than happy to hang up my chef's coat and leave the pastry kitchen in the capable hands of the night manager.

Before I met Mom and the Professor for dinner I wanted to change and take a quick shower, and see if I could find even a few minutes to speak to the Professor alone. Mom and the Professor had opted for the late seating so that I could join them. I was eager for a break and to share my news.

After a quick scalding shower I changed into an ivory halter dress. It fell to my knees and brought out the honey highlights in my hair, which I wore loose. I dusted my cheeks with powder, added a touch of gold shadow to my eyes and rose gloss to my lips. The dress had tiny pearl beading on the bodice and a silky ivory ribbon around the waist. Observing myself in the foggy mirror I was pleased with the fit and thought it flattered my lanky figure by accentuating my waist. I finished the look with a pair of tangerine sandals and matching shawl. Carlos had purchased the silk wrap with a warm tangerine weave and light creamy paisley flower pattern in the Indian holy city of Banaras. It was elegant and simple—exactly my style— but I hadn't had many occasions to wear it.

Wrapping it around my bare shoulders, I gave myself one final glance and headed for the dining room. The hall-way appeared tilted like something out of *Alice's Adventures in Wonderland* as I used the railing as my guide. All of the art work was bolted to the wall, but the potted plants near the elevator looked like they were about to topple.

I kept one hand on the railing as I put one foot in front of the other. Guests passing me on the other side looked like they were moonwalking.

"We're riding the rails!" a guest in a suit and tie called. "Get it? Handrails!"

I laughed. "Be careful. It's getting worse."

He seemed to be enjoying the ride and smiled broadly as he rode the handrail down the hall. Inside the dining room the chandeliers swung overhead. The wait staff weren't taking any pleasure in the rough seas. They strug-gled to balance drinks and stay upright.

Mom and the Professor waved from their table. I swayed

and had to stop twice and grab one of the columns in the large room to steady myself.

"It's a wild ride," Mom noted as I took a seat. "Have you ever been in a storm like this?"

I nodded. "Yeah. This is a bad one though." I thought back to a storm that I had weathered with Carlos a few years ago. We hit a patch of rough sea off the coast of Greece. Carlos had wrapped me in his strong arms, stroked my hair, and sung silly Spanish songs in my ear. His equally romantic but goofy gesture had made the storm feel like it passed in an instant. I felt a momentary sense of longing for his tender touch, but shook myself back into reality.

The Professor tapped his upper lip and stared into the black night sky. "I believe we may have met a tempest. This likely won't come as a surprise but one of my favorite quotes of all times is about a storm. Any guesses?"

Mom and I shook our heads.

" 'I'm not afraid of storms for I am learning how to sail my ship.' "

"That's Shakespeare?" I asked.

He tapped his fingers on his beard. "No. The one and only Louisa May Alcott."

"I hope the captain isn't still learning how to sail this ship," Mom replied. She didn't look contented by the Professor's words. Neither was I.

Then the Professor removed a folded white handkerchief from his jacket pocket. For a moment I thought he was going to be sick, but instead he laid it across his dinner plate. Then he made a quick motion with his wrist and yanked the handkerchief away. Two single-stemmed red roses appeared on the plate.

Mom clapped and gave him a look of amazement. "Doug, how did you do that?"

He handed us each a rose. "I always find it pays to have

a few tricks up my sleeve. Did I ever tell you about the summer I spent working at a magic camp in college?"

"Magic camp?" Mom and I asked in unison.

"Certainly you jest," he said with a pained expression. "Every self-respecting student of the Bard's works must know a touch of magic."

"I had no idea." Mom smelled her rose.

The Professor caught my eye and winked. "Exactly as I intend."

I was about to ask more about magic camp, but the captain's voice came over the loudspeaker. It gave me time to weigh my options. I'd spent the entire afternoon trying to track down the Professor; now he was in front of me but I didn't want to worry Mom.

"Ladies and gentlemen, I have a weather update. Our current weather is stormy."

Everyone in the dining room chuckled, including the three of us.

"It's good that he's trying to lighten the mood," Mom said, scrunching her face to listen. She needed hearing aids. When we were back in Ashland I was going to have to force the issue.

The captain continued. "We're expecting some occasional gusts and heavy seas. Please use extra precaution when you're moving throughout the ship."

"That sounds serious." Mom's tone changed.

The Professor placed his arm around the back of her chair. "Ah yes, the winds they may blow." He paused and then smiled. "As the Bard said, 'A little gale will soon disperse that cloud. And blow it to the source from whence it came: The very beams will dry those vapors up, for every cloud engenders not a storm.' "

It never ceased to amaze me that the Professor had a quote by Shakespeare at the ready for every occasion. How did he retain that much information?

Mom's jaw relaxed a little, but it was temporary because the next thing we knew a wave slammed into the side of the ship, sending plates and chairs flying. Glass shattered onto the floor and a woman seated at the table next to us fell backward and bumped her head on a column.

The Professor moved to help her. I grasped the table as hard as I could. "Are you okay?" I shouted to Mom over the commotion.

"I'm fine." She exhaled. "How big was that?"

"Big. Really big." On the *Amour* decks were numbered from bottom to top. That meant the wave had made it five decks up. The windows were splattered with water and a few of them had broken with the impact.

The woman the Professor was attending to sat up and told the crowd who had gathered around her that she was okay. Silverware, napkins, and broken chunks of ceramic plates littered the floor. Once the initial shock of the jolt had passed, passengers began to quiet and return their chairs to upright positions.

"Sorry about that." The captain's voice sounded again. "We're going to do everything we can to try to navigate out of this, but in the meantime I'm canceling the late evening shows. I've spoken with Rocky, your cruise director, and he's going to provide some dinner entertainment for you, but I'll be updating you throughout the rest of the night. We're anticipating hitting some heavy swells in the next hour or two. I'll be asking all of you to return to your staterooms at that point. Very sorry for any inconvenience this may cause you."

The captain's update sent another round of chatter through the dining room. Passengers were visibly shaken by the recent megawave and the news that it wasn't safe for the show to go on or maybe even to leave their staterooms.

"Has that ever happened?" Mom asked.

"A few times. It tends to happen more on small ships like this. You might not feel more than a gentle rocking if you were on a huge ship. One summer we were in a storm for about twelve hours off the coast of England and the captain ordered everyone to their staterooms. I'm sure he's being overly cautious."

Mom's brow furrowed. "I hope so."

The Professor seconded my input. "Juliet is right, dear. The captain is trained to err on the side of safety. We can retreat to our stateroom with a cup of tea and watch the storm rage outside."

"Sure." Mom's face had lost some of its color. "Let me make a stop in the ladies' room first."

She excused herself and the Professor and I watched her inch her way to the bathroom, grabbing the back of chairs every so often as the ship pitched from side to side.

I seized the opportunity. "I've been looking for you all day. Every place I ended up you had just left."

He smiled. "Yes. I know that you claim our vessel is small, but conducting an investigation on a ship this size has proved a daunting challenge."

"I have so much to fill you in on, but first the most important piece of information. I learned her name. It's Annie."

Water sloshed in his glass as he attempted to take a sip. "Annie. Indeed. I heard that name come up twice in my questioning as well."

I felt slightly dejected after holding on to my news all day, but I quickly filled him in on my conversations with Maria, Rocky, and Babs. He jotted down notes on a pad of paper from his cabin.

"Do you have a theory on whether she was just trying to sneak on the ship or trying to escape a bad situation?"

I couldn't remember if I had mentioned what Henny had told me earlier about the gossip that Annie was dating a crew member.

The Professor frowned. "She was so young. It seems quite plausible that she could have simply been seeking adventure and unencumbered by the perils of age. Ah to be twenty again."

His words struck me. She was young. Who had mentioned that fact to me recently? Rocky? I racked my brain, trying to think through everyone I had talked to about Annie. Then it hit me—Babs. Babs had mentioned more than once that Annie was young. How did she know? She had mentioned seeing Annie and Rocky arguing, but how did she know that Annie was young?

"Yet I can't discount the crime scene," the Professor continued. "I don't believe that her death was premeditated. This was a crime of passion. And crimes of passion typically revolve around *passion*."

Mom returned from the bathroom and she and the Professor agreed it would be time to retreat to their cabins as soon as they finished their after-dinner drinks. I felt terrible for both of them. First, I had had to wrap the Professor into a murder investigation and now we were in the middle of a looming storm. Weather like this in March was rare. Ships are outfitted with state-of-the-art navigational systems, and weather forecasts are analyzed days ahead of leaving port. We had hit a stretch of bad luck and from the sound of the captain's warning it was about to get worse.

Chapter Twenty-two

"Well, I don't know about you, but that certainly puts a damper on our vacation, doesn't it?" A woman's voice interrupted my thoughts. I turned to see Babs standing behind the empty seat at our table. She was wearing a skintight black leather skirt and a leopard-print shirt.

"Sit, sit." Mom pointed to the chair as Babs almost lost her balance. The Professor leaped to her rescue and pulled out a chair for her.

"Thanks." She shot him a severe look. I couldn't tell if she was grateful for his help or irritated. I got the sense that Babs liked to come across as strong and self-sufficient.

The Professor bowed his head in acknowledgment, but Babs flipped her chair around to face the stage. "They are performing now, is that the deal?" she asked me.

"It sounds like it. Did you hear the captain's announcement?"

Babs tapped her manicured nails on the table. Each nail was painted jet black, except for her ring fingers, which had a leopard design. I thought about having my nails designed like that and chuckled to myself. They would be coated in flour and bread dough in about a minute. The kitchen and fashion don't mix.

"Is the dancer performing?" Babs asked. "Or just Grayson?"

"I'm not sure. Why?"

"No reason." She yawned as if intentionally trying to appear uninterested, but I watched her scan the stage and her eyes linger on Grayson who was warming up off to the side.

Mom tried to engage her in conversation. "Did you already eat?"

Babs answered with short one-or two-word responses. She clearly wasn't in the mood to make small talk. Her eyes never left the stage. It seemed like a strange reaction compared with what she'd told me earlier. If she was really scared of Grayson or concerned that he had been stalking her, why would she focus her attention on him? Maybe I was misreading the situation. Could she be worried about the weather? People responded to stress in different ways. She didn't strike me as the anxious type, but there was always the possibility that she was nervous about the storm and not in the mood for conversation.

Rocky took the stage. His Hollywood smile was still plastered on but it didn't reach his eyes. As cruise director he was sure to take the brunt of guest complaints. Organizing shows, lectures, and the slew of onboard entertainment took as much planning as my menus, so it wasn't a surprise that he was feeling the effects of canceling the rest of the evening. Or, could it be that he was nervous about Annie's death? Had Babs told the captain or the Professor that Rocky had been fighting with the stowaway the night before her murder? I couldn't exactly ask the Professor now.

"Good evening, cruisers, how's everyone enjoying this rocky weather brought to you by yours truly?" He intentionally swayed from side to side. "Rocky is rocking. Who wants to join me?"

A handful of people responded.

"No, come on, you can do better. I told you we were going to get ship faced, remember? This isn't what I planned, but we can get this ship really rocking, can't we?" He held out his hands to form a T with his body. "When I wave my left hand I want all of you on this side of the room to start rocking. When I wave my right hand it's your turn," he said, pointing to our table.

I didn't get the sense that many passengers were excited about Rocky's game, but when he waved his left arm half of the dining room acquiesced and waved their arms in the air. Then it was our turn. I shot Mom a look.

"It's like doing the wave at a Southern Oregon football game," she said, raising her thin arms. "Andy would love this." Her empty ceramic coffee cup went flying through the air and broke into a dozen pieces.

"True." I followed suit, not wanting to look like a poor sport. Babs didn't appear worried about not fitting in. She sat with her arms folded across her chest. After three or four rounds Rocky could sense that the energy was waning. "Okay, now that we've had a little fun, how do you all feel about some tunes?" This was met with more generous applause. He motioned to Grayson, who strolled onto the stage keeping his eyes glued on Babs the entire way. Babs folded her arms tighter across her chest. The Professor caught me staring at her. He met my eye and gave me a knowing nod. My curiosity bubbled inside. If only Babs wasn't at our table, I could ask him if he had any more news.

The lights flashed off, sending a collective gasp through the dining room. Plunged into darkness the ship felt like it lurched hard to starboard. A few passengers screamed and I heard a woman at a table nearby begin to whimper. My mind started running through emergency protocol. I had been trained to respond in situations like this. Just as I started to get to my feet the lights flickered back on.

Mom's face had lost all trace of color. The Professor placed his arm securely around her shoulder and gave me a nod. The constant swaying was taking its toll.

Rocky tried to shift the tone. "How's that for a show?" He pointed to the twenty-foot-wide chandelier above his head, then continued on as if nothing had happened. "As you heard, the captain is asking us to close the entertainment venues early. We didn't want to leave you with nothing, so I've asked Grayson to perform a couple of numbers and then our dancers will do a short show. After that you will be asked to return to your staterooms. It sounds like the captain is trying to find calmer waters and as soon as we get the all clear the show—or shows—will go on." He was trying to sound relaxed but his rigid body language showed otherwise.

"All right then, without further ado, I give you Grayson Allen." Rocky clapped and exited the stage.

Grayson played two of the songs he had performed earlier as well as three new songs, or at least songs that I hadn't heard. His style was intimate and soothing. It was exactly what we needed. I barely noticed that the salt and pepper shakers were sliding around the table like ice skaters on a pond as Grayson's lilting voice dissipated the negative tone in the room. I glanced in Babs's direction. She was staring directly at me and giving me a look that made the tiny hairs on my arms stand at attention.

"We should get his CD for Torte," Mom commented. She pushed around her rosemary and garlic smashed potatoes and barely touched her slice of beef burgundy.

Babs, who hadn't said more than two words since she sat down, snapped, "He's not with a label."

"Does that matter?" Mom looked confused.

"It should." Babs flipped her attention back to the stage.

Mom mouthed "What?" to me.

I shrugged. For as disinterested in Grayson as Babs was trying to appear, she was protesting too much in my opinion. I felt like the Professor as the phrase "The lady doth protest too much" ran through my head. I couldn't remember which of Shakespeare's plays the line was from. Maybe *Macbeth*? Or was it *Hamlet*? I would have to ask the Professor.

Grayson finished with a ballad that he dedicated to a "special woman" in the house. His eyes pierced through Babs, who continued to appear unmoved. The lyrics didn't leave much to the imagination. It was a song about passion and unrequited love.

Mom fanned her face when Grayson strummed the final chord and took a bow. "Whew, is it hot in here, or is it just me?" She winked at the Professor.

"The young man certainly does have a way with words." The Professor smiled.

Rocky returned to the stage to introduce Maria and her shake-your-booty dance team. Pulsing Latin music blasted overhead. It was in stark contrast to Grayson's slow and easy tunes. The sound startled me so much that I almost tipped back in my chair. Soon a blur of color whirled around the dining room as twenty dancers shimmied between tables. Tassels and sequins swayed from their hips as they jiggled and stomped to the beat. The flash of color from their bright neon yellow and green feather boas made me dizzy.

I had to give Maria and the other dancers credit. Staying upright in turbulent seas was hard enough without dancing in platform heels. They were true professionals. I couldn't help but feel glad that Carlos wasn't here to watch Maria shake and shimmy. Men drooled as she strutted past them, dragging a hand along their backs as wives looked on with daggers.

Each move was choreographed and the first number ended with the dancers spinning simultaneously and posing with one arm stretched to the ceiling on the final drumbeat. Thunderous applause broke out. The dancers flipped their hair and promenaded in a conga line back to the stage. They performed three more numbers. Maria's body glistened with sweat, making her skin dewy. When I sweated I turned red and clammy, but Maria glowed.

Rocky appeared by my side as Maria shimmied off stage. He knelt next to me and clutched the table for support. I could smell rum on his breath and he slurred his words slightly. "We need to talk. Tonight."

"Okay." I wondered if he had taken his own advice and gotten "ship faced."

"Meet me in the kitchen. Ten minutes. Got it?"

I agreed, but thought of Carlos's warnings. Was it a good idea to meet Rocky? The night crew would be working so we wouldn't be alone, but I didn't want to do anything stupid either. The truth was that there was a killer on board. Whoever killed Annie had done it once, what would stop them from doing it again?

Right after the dancers sashayed out of the dining room the captain came over the loudspeaker with another update. "Okay, folks, the winds are picking up. I need everyone to calmly begin to return to your staterooms. Please take your time and use hand railings as you're walking. If you need assistance, ask any member of my crew. They will gladly assist. I have good news and bad news." He paused for a moment. "The good news is that we have navigated a course out of the storm's path. The bad news is that it's going to get worse before it gets better. I'm asking the crew to return to their bunks as well. There will be no midnight buffet or room service. I ask that you only call the crew if it's an emergency. Otherwise, return to your staterooms, relax, and we'll have you out of this as soon as we can."

I had no problem with calling it a night, but I didn't like the sound of things getting worse before they got better. That meant my meeting with Rocky would have to wait.

Chapter Twenty-three

Thank goodness the captain had sounded the warning and sequestered everyone to their staterooms. As the evening wore on the winds began to gust and scream. The ship was tossed about in the giant swells. Anything that wasn't bolted down in my cabin flew around the tiny room. My window, which had provided a view of the calm sea earlier, now looked as if I was on a submarine. Waves crashed into the side of the ship and sent my stomach churning. The ship creaked and rattled. It was unnerving. This rivaled some of the storms I had ridden out during my decade at sea.

"Folks, another update for you." The captain's voice was direct and concise. "The weather we've encountered is more intense than anticipated, so again a reminder to stay where you are. Please do not move about the ship."

A knock sounded on my door. Who was out and about? Rocky?

My heart thumped. Should I answer it?

What if he was dangerous?

Another thud sounded on the door.

I had to clutch the wall in order to keep from toppling over. I peered through the peephole and let out a sigh of relief when I saw Carlos was standing in the hallway with a death grip on the door frame.

"Julieta, how are you?" He reached for my arm but a wave sent him backward and slammed him into the wall.

"Carlos!" I ran to make sure he was okay.

He laughed and tried to push himself to standing. "I am fine," he insisted, but I had to help tug him to his feet. He struggled to get his bearings as we both inched toward my cabin. I braced myself for the impact of another wave. They were unrelenting, crashing one right after the other.

Once in my cabin we both fell on the bed as another wave assaulted the ship.

"This is bad," I said, sitting up.

"*Sí*." Carlos held on to the headboard. He had changed into a pair of relaxed jeans and a brilliant white T-shirt that made his skin look four shades darker than mine. "It is one of the worst that I can remember. Are you sick?"

"My stomach isn't loving this, but I'm not too bad. What about you?"

He pushed his shoulders back and flexed his abs. "I have, how do you say? A stomach of steel."

"Right." I punched him in his rock-hard stomach. "That's what all the chefs say."

"It is true, *mi querida*. To be a chef you must be able to eat anything."

I had to agree with him on that. When I had been in culinary school the head chef had a policy that his students had to eat everything put in front of them. He didn't care if one of us didn't like fish or cilantro. His philosophy was that in order to develop a refined and professional palate you had to expose it to every taste and flavor combination possible. I had a friend who refused to eat shellfish, not because of an allergy, but because she didn't like the briny taste and chewy texture. The chef berated her, and she fought back. "Why do I have to develop my palate when I'm training to be a pastry chef?" This sent him into a rage.

"A chef is a chef. You will taste the shellfish or you can pack up your knives."

To her credit she stuck with the program and tried the shellfish. I don't think she would ever order clams at a restaurant, but she did begrudgingly admit that his method worked. By the time we finished our seafood rotation she was able to discern quality and spice profiles after weeks of tasting mussels, clams, and lobster.

"Would you like a cup of tea?" Carlos asked. "It might help relax your stomach."

I laughed. "How do you propose we drink tea in conditions like this?"

He brushed me off. "It is nothing." Keeping one arm on the wall he moved to the dresser and warmed up the coffee maker. "Lemon or mint?"

"Mint."

I watched as he steadied himself with one arm and warmed hot water with the other. Once the water had boiled he poured it into a paper mug and opened the tea bag. I was impressed that he was able to make tea while being bounced in an onslaught of waves, but I still questioned how we were going to drink the tea.

He caught my eye and must have seen the skepticism on my face. Then he reached into his back pocket and removed two plastic travel lids. "See, I told you, it is nothing."

The minty scent of the tea brought an instant calm to me. I clutched the paper mug with both hands and tried to time each sip with the waves. The travel lid helped, but I still managed to splash tea on my shirt as I drank. Carlos was right—the tea did settle my stomach.

"Would you like me to stay with you tonight?" Carlos asked, returning to a corner of the bed with his tea.

There was a huskiness in his voice and a look in his eyes that made me think that his offer wasn't just about reassuring me. I hesitated. There was no denying the attraction I felt for him. It had been instantaneous when I met him and never dissipated. We had had many happy and blissful years together on the ship. At first I was completely captivated by his charm, easy wit, and seductive eyes. He was older than me, and unlike some of my earlier boy-friends, he wasn't afraid to express his feelings. He tucked love notes under my pillow and delivered spicy chorizo omelets and tangy fruit salads to bed. He showered me with romance and professed his love every day. I had been lucky. We were inseparable. Life at sea could be lonely, but not with Carlos.

As our relationship grew, I grew too. Because of him I had learned to trust my instincts and expand my creativity as a chef. In many ways our years together had been perfect, but with the gift of distance I realized now that maybe they were a little too perfect. Yes, our attraction and connection had been real but our daily life was more of a fantasy. We weren't tied to permanency. We traveled from port to port and ventured into rain forests and untouched villages. I cherished the memory of our time together, but I had changed and now I wanted more. I wanted roots and a place to call home. I had found that in Ashland, and as much as it hurt to leave Carlos, I couldn't ask him to give up a life I knew that he loved.

Why did it have to be so complicated? It would have been so much easier if I could have hated him. I had be-gun to wonder what might have happened with us if I hadn't found out about Ramiro.

When I had learned that Carlos had a son and had kept that from me I had been blinded with hurt and left without looking back. Now that I had had time and space to process what went wrong with us, I was beginning to understand my role in our separation. I hadn't even given Carlos a chance to explain. Why? Had I really been happy on the ship, or was Carlos's lie of omission an excuse to leave?

Looking back I knew that I was at least partially to blame. That didn't mean that Carlos was absolved from lying to me about something so important, but he had made amends and I understood his reasons. Had I lied too? Had I lied to myself? Carlos and I used to dream about finding a plot of land on the Italian coast or on an island in the warm Caribbean waters. We would start our own restaurant with a small farm. Carlos would prepare daily feasts inspired by whatever was fresh in our organic garden or the catch of the day, while I would bake pastries and cakes. It sounded idyllic, but we could never come to an agreement on where we should land.

I had suggested places like Portland and Seattle, which were closer to home but alive with vibrant and cutting-edge food trends. Carlos was drawn to more exotic and tropical locales. We never fought about it. It was a faraway dream. Could we have made it a reality? Could we have landed on the same plot of land? I wasn't sure, and I wasn't sure I had been entirely honest with myself or with Carlos.

In truth I had been homesick for a while. Ten years at sea had allowed me experiences that I had never imagined, but my heart had been missing something. It wasn't until I returned to Ashland that I realized what it was—home. I had been longing for home, and as much as I loved Carlos he wasn't home.

That reality hit me harder than the waves thrashing the ship. How could I love someone and someplace? Was one more important than the other? Or did I really love Carlos, deeply and passionately, if I was willing to give him up for the promise of a place to call my own?

I felt equally confused and clear at the same time. I knew exactly what I had to do. I had to tell Carlos goodbye and the thought of actually speaking those words made every cell in my body ache.

Chapter Twenty-four

"Carlos, listen, we need to talk," I started.

His eyes flinched, but he held my gaze. "What is it, *mi querida*?"

"It's us." I wished I could will the words back inside, but once I started they spilled from my body. "I love you, I really do, but this isn't going to work. Being back on the ship has made it so real and so clear for me." I paused for a quick breath, but didn't want to give him a chance to respond before I finished what I had to say. I'd been holding the words—the thoughts—inside of me for months now and it was time to say what I needed to say.

The hurt was evident on his face.

"It's not you. I promise. I'm fine. I understand why you did what you did. I still wish you would have done it differently, but I'm not holding a grudge. I forgive you."

His eyes misted. "Julieta."

"Wait." I held out my teacup and didn't even bother to wipe up the drop of tea that splashed onto my finger. "I have to get this out. I've been thinking about it for a long time now. Part of what happened between us is on me. I don't think I was honest either. I think I was done with this life a while ago, but held on for you. You gave me an excuse to leave and when I walked out I realized what I've been missing. I missed home. I missed Mom. I missed the familiar streets of Ashland and its funky people. I missed it all."

"And do you miss me?" he asked quietly. Then he caressed my scarf and wrapped it tighter around my shoulders.

I was afraid of my answer. "I do, but . . ."

"But not enough to leave." His hands traced my collarbone. The gentleness of his touch made my throat squeeze shut. Tears poured out of my eyes. I didn't trust myself to speak, and I wasn't even sure I could speak so I answered with a nod.

He sighed. "*Sí,* this is what I thought." His tone was stoic yet resolved. Reaching for a towel hanging from the nightstand, he handed it to me.

I dabbed my eyes and tried to stop the sobs. I couldn't. It was as if I had opened a floodgate. Once I spoke the words aloud I couldn't take them back and for the first time I understood their meaning.

"And if I come to you?" Carlos asked.

"I don't know."

"I see."

"Why does it have to be this hard? It hurts so much."

"This is love," he said, and then pulled me into a hard embrace. "If it does not hurt it is not real," he whispered into my ear.

His words made me cry harder. Why did he have to be so nice?

After I spilled tears and the rest of my tea, I finally pulled away from him and wiped my eyes and the comforter with the towel. He had always been my shelter in the storm. How could I let him go? "I'm sorry."

"I know, *mi querida.* I know." He stood and kissed the top of my head. "It is late. I will leave you, but I must also promise that I will not give you up without a fight."

I forced a smile. "You don't need to fight for me."

"No. I fight for me." He winked and walked out the door.

What had just happened? Had I ended things with us for good? And how did he plan to fight for himself? I threw myself on the bed and burst into another round of tears. For the duration of the night I faced my own internal storm. As painful as the realization had been, I knew it was also the breakthrough I'd been waiting for. No matter where things went from here, I had been honest—brutally honest—with Carlos and more importantly with myself.

Sometime late in the night, or early in the morning, I finally fell asleep. When I woke the next morning the seas had mellowed, as had my emotions. Was last night the beginning of the end for Carlos and me? I was pretty sure I knew the answer and as painful it was to face I knew that everything that had spilled out of me had needed to be said. Not only for him, but for me.

I showered, downed three cups of coffee, and went to assess the damage. The pastry kitchen had taken a beating in the storm. Pots and pans had been flung around the room, leaving dents in the stainless steel countertops. Plates and ceramic coffee mugs had been shattered. Flour, sugar, and cornmeal dusted the floor and countertops. What a mess.

"Morning, chef," one of the crew greeted me, holding a broom and dustpan. "What a night."

"You can say that again." I surveyed the kitchen. Cleanup was going to take at least an hour with all hands on deck. Picking up half of a broken plate, I tossed it into the trash bin with hundreds of other shards. "That's the worst storm I've ever been through."

"That's what everyone said. You should have seen the bunk rooms last night. It was like being at some kind of international prayer convention. People were stringing through their prayer beads, chanting, and singing."

"Well, it worked. We survived, didn't we?" I reached for a pair of latex gloves. "Now the cleanup."

"The captain has called for all hands on deck this morning. We should have reinforcements soon."

"Good. We're going to need it." I gathered pieces of broken glass.

For the next thirty minutes crew poured into the kitchen armed with mops, rags, and extra garbage cans. I kept them motivated with strong steaming coffee and pans of cherry and almond coffee cake. Cleanup went much faster than I anticipated. The kitchen was gleaming and ready for pastry production less than an hour later.

I gave my staff tasks and inventoried what we had lost in the storm. There were cases of broken coffee mugs and dessert plates. The ship was overstocked when it came to dinnerware and flatware, but losing so many essentials was going to mean that the dishwashing team was going to have to work at a steady pace to keep the dining room supplied with clean plates and cups.

"Morning, morning, what a morning this is!" Rocky's voice boomed.

How was he so enthused this early and after such a horrific night? And why was his demeanor so different?

He headed straight to me. I stacked my inventory sheets and rested my pencil on the countertop. It was a relief to see it stay in place and not go rolling away from me. "Just who I was looking for." Rocky reached for the pencil and tapped it on the countertop twice. "We never had a chance to talk last night."

"I know. We had orders from the captain, remember?" Rocky shrugged. "I've been through worse."

"What can I do for you? We've got coffee and maybe a

slice of cherry cake, but as you can see we're right in the middle of breakfast prep." I had to admit that I was interested in knowing what he wanted to talk to me about, especially if it was connected to Annie, but I wanted to stay firmly planted in the crowded kitchen.

"Excellent. That's what I wanted to talk to you about." The stainless steel pans hanging above us reflected on his bald head.

"Breakfast?"

"Yeah. We need a showstopper this morning. I want you to floor the guests with this meal."

"A showstopper?" Was this what he wanted to talk to me about last night?

"Yeah." He scanned the room. "I'm thinking chocolate sculptures, a chocolate fountain, maybe a couple of ice sculptures. Tons and tons of pastries. Can you do some tiered breakfast cakes or something?"

"Well." I hesitated. "We don't have much time, and you'll have to talk to the chocolatier team about sculpting. That's not my area of expertise." Many of the bigger luxury lines like ours employed sculptors who specialized in creating magnificent chocolate works of art and ice sculptures that would rival Michelangelo's *David*.

"Where is he? I've been looking everywhere for him."

"No idea." I shrugged. "Probably recovering from the brutal night."

"I'll find him, but I want you to work on showstopping sweets, got it?"

Rocky didn't have any authority over the kitchens or my menu. He was solely responsible for entertainment on the ship. I thought about telling him as much, but I didn't have the energy to battle. "I'm not promising anything showstopping. We just got the kitchen back in working order so my goal is to deliver breakfast at the moment."

"But we *have to* dazzle the guests. You said it yourself, they had a horrific night last night and I need them happy this morning."

"Trust me, everything we put out is going to be delicious, but I don't have time to bake layered cakes or design sculptures. And I'm pretty sure that no amount of showstopping food is going to erase the memory of last night."

"It has to!" He raised his voice and snapped my pencil in half.

"Relax." I held out my hands in a calming motion.

"Sorry." He placed the pencil on the counter and patted his bald head. "I didn't mean to yell."

"It's okay. I know that our nerves are frayed after last night. Don't worry about breakfast. We'll make sure that the passengers have fabulous coffee and an assortment of delicious pastries to wash down last night's wild ride."

His cheeks were splotched with color. "Right. Sorry. I've never lost a cruise like this."

"Lost one?"

"Yeah. That was insane last night and I bet you anything that my return booking numbers are going to hit an all-time low."

Was that why Rocky was so upset? Maybe he was feeling the pressure of having passengers rebook.

"That's not your fault. We sailed through a major storm last night. You can't control the weather."

"Tell that to the unhappy guests." He grabbed half the pencil again and tapped it on the counter repeatedly.

Was it just the storm and Rocky's concern that passengers would be less likely to book another vacation, or was he upset about something else? I checked the kitchen. My staff was consumed with rolling cinnamon roll dough and filling muffin tins. I lowered my voice. "Is something else bothering you?"

Rocky's blotchy face turned cherry red. "No, why?"

I pushed on. "Look, I know that you were fighting with Annie."

"Annie?" He played dumb.

"You know, the stowaway?"

He cleared his throat and chewed on the broken pencil. "What about her?"

"Did you know her?"

"No! Why would you say that?"

"Well, first of all I saw you after Annie swiped food from the send-off party, and then someone else saw you fighting with her later that night."

Rocky dropped the pencil. The color drained from his face. It wasn't particularly warm in the kitchen, but sweat dripped from his shiny head. "Who told you that?"

"I heard it secondhand." I didn't want to tell him that Babs had spilled his secret.

He swallowed and glanced around the kitchen. Nodding toward the door, he whispered, "Not here."

So he did know her. I couldn't believe it. As I followed him to the hall, his posture changed. He slunk against the wall. "Who told you?"

"Honestly I don't know. I heard a few members of the crew talking. I don't know where they heard it."

He rubbed his bald head and banged it against the wall. "Oh no. No, no, no."

"Rocky, what's going on? If you have any information about Annie, you have to go to the captain."

"Yeah and lose my job?"

"What are you talking about?"

He looked like he was about to cry or explode. I couldn't tell. I wasn't worried about my safety. There were crew members everywhere, rushing around to put the ship back together before the passengers awoke and emerged from their cabins, but Rocky was unstable to say the least.

He pounded the wall. "I knew this was going to happen. I should have dragged her body off the ship."

My heart pulsed. What did he mean by that?

"I'm not sure I understand," I said as calmly as possible.

"Look, she begged me for a job, okay?"

"Okay. I still don't understand why you lied about not knowing her, especially since she's dead."

He let out an audible groan. "Look, I didn't kill her. I barely knew the girl."

For a minute I thought he wasn't going to say anything more, but then he continued. "She was a dancer and begged me to give her a chance. I mean like down on her knees begged me and pleaded for a job. I didn't have one open and I told her that. I was crystal clear. I told her that I would keep her headshot on file, but that she needed to get off the ship."

"Why didn't you tell the captain or the Professor?"

He gulped. "Someone else asked me not to."

"What?"

He looked around. The artery was surprisingly empty. The vast majority of the crew was likely still scattered throughout the ship on cleanup duty. "Look, she had a friend on the ship. That's how she got on in the first place, and I'm sure she was stowing away with her friend."

"Who?"

Rocky pursed his lips and scratched his head. "Another dancer. The girl, Annie—her full name was Annie Lundy—she claimed that she and this dancer worked together in Miami."

"Another dancer?" I had a pretty good guess who he was referring to, but I wanted to keep him talking.

He nodded.

"You have to tell the captain."

"I guess. I'm probably getting fired after last night's disaster anyway."

"Rocky, I'm trying to understand why you kept this from everyone. You've worked on the ship for decades. Why would you risk your career?"

He groaned again. "I know. It was stupid. Stupid!" He banged his head into the wall.

I reached to rub the back of my head in response to the hit he'd taken. Ouch.

"Let's just say that I had a good reason I didn't want the captain to find out."

Now it was my turn to scowl. "You're going to have to give me more than that."

He sighed. "Some of my dancers padded their resumes, if you know what I mean."

"I don't."

"The ship runs background checks, and let's just say that some of my dancers came from less than reputable working environments."

Suddenly I began connecting the dots. "Oh."

"Yeah." He gave me a knowing look. "Some of my best dancers got their 'break' working in nightclubs and in the adult entertainment industry."

"Oh," I repeated.

"The cruise line isn't willing to take risks with some of them, but I know talent. I can tell you within two minutes of watching a performance whether someone has the 'it' factor. The dancers I recruited had the 'it' factor, who cares where they worked before."

"So you helped get them work?"

His shiny bald head glowed red. "I might have fudged a resume or two or found some people to vouch for them as references."

No wonder Rocky hadn't wanted to tell the captain. I

couldn't imagine that any of those hiring practices were approved.

"I swear I told Annie to beat it. I didn't have room for another dancer, and I didn't have time to scrounge up references. She showed up the day we were setting sail."

"Because she knew someone on the ship?"

Rocky nodded.

"Who?"

He frowned. "Take a guess."

"Maria?" I asked, but I knew the answer. Of course it was Maria.

Nodding, he confirmed my suspicion. "My star."

Chapter Twenty-five

"Rocky, you have to tell the captain—now!" I couldn't believe that he had kept Annie's identity a secret, regardless of whether he was worried about losing his job.

He punched the wall again. "I'm going to get fired."

That was likely. If he had gone to the captain right away, the captain might have understood, but keeping quiet about information critical to the case—like Annie's identity—was going to make it much worse for him. "Look, you don't have a choice. Annie is dead and someone killed her. If you don't go to the captain right now, I will," I warned him in my most authoritative chef voice.

"I know. Fine, I'm going, but you have to put together a showstopper for me. I need it now more than ever." He turned and plodded down the hallway. I had little sympathy for him. He'd gotten himself in this position.

Before I returned to the kitchen I took a moment to center my thoughts. Rocky was right about one thing and that was that the passengers were going to be in need of some extra TLC this morning. There was nothing more comforting than food, and it was my job to provide them with a touch of happiness and warmth on the plate. Rocky and I differed in our approach. After such a tumultuous night I doubted that any of the passengers would care about being dazzled by a chocolate centerpiece. The way to re-store calm was through buttery, flaky bear claws and warm, gooey dark caramel bread pudding. As much as I wanted to run and find the Professor, I knew I had a job to do and I wanted to do it well.

At Torte we often say that we serve comfort on a plate, and that's what I intended to do this morning. In addition to the bear claws, bread pudding, and our already estab-lished menu I wanted to make a breakfast classic—the Monte Cristo. The decadent sandwich is like grown-up grilled cheese, with thick layers of honey ham, smoked tur-key, and gooey melted Swiss cheese served with a side of spicy red currant jelly.

I started by slicing brioche bread into one-inch slices. Next I spread a thin coat of Dijon mustard on both slices of bread. Then I layered my meat and cheese, stacked the sandwiches, and secured them with toothpicks. Some chefs deep-fry the Monte Cristo but I preferred to panfry the sandwich to give it a crispy golden crust but cut the grease. There was already plenty of fatty goodness with the meat and cheese.

I whisked eggs and heavy cream together. My secret is to add a dash of salt and pepper and a healthy dose of nut-meg to the egg wash. Next I submerged the sandwiches into the egg wash, being sure that each side of the bread absorbed the moisture. With a sizzling hot pan of butter I browned one side for two minutes. Then I flipped the sand-wich and browned the other side. Once it was a gorgeous golden color, I turned the heat to low and covered the pan with a lid. The steam would keep the Monte Cristo moist and help melt the cheese.

It smelled heavenly. I knew that the passengers would appreciate the deluxe French toast/grilled cheese mashup. When the cheese had melted completely I finished the sandwich by dusting both sides with confectioners' sugar and setting out ramekins of currant, strawberry, and raspberry jam, as well as one with hot maple syrup.

"Come have a taste, everyone," I called as I cut the sandwiches into tasting bites.

The taste did not disappoint. It was the ideal balance of sweet and savory with steamy melted Swiss and a hint of sour from the currant jam. I nearly groaned out loud as I polished off my tasting bite.

"What do you think?" I asked the team.

None of them spoke as they savored the comforting sandwich. "It's like hangover food," one of them commented. "Everyone needs one of these this morning."

"My thoughts exactly." Rocky could worry about wowing the passengers with showy entertainment. This was my style. I wanted to give everyone a touch of home and a warm start to what was hopefully going to be a new day on the ship.

I assigned staff to brioche cutting and egg wash stations and then checked progress on the remainder of the menu. The kitchen was fully functioning and everything was staying put. I felt a sense of relief knowing that we had weathered the storm and hopefully would be making our way to port soon.

There wasn't time to dwell on Rocky or what he had revealed about Maria. As soon as I had a break I was going to check in with the Professor. My hands worked at lightning pace as I flipped Monte Cristo sandwiches, dusted, and plated them. Soon platters of my comfort offering along with nutty and spicy bear claws the size of my head, and steaming dishes of caramel bread pudding, were complete and ready to be delivered to the dining room.

I wiped sweat from my brow. "How are we doing on croissants and pineapple coffee cake?"

"We're all set, chef," one of the pastry crew replied with a salute.

"Great. Good work this morning." I shook off my chef's coat that was splattered with butter and egg wash. No one wanted to see the reality of working in a commercial kitchen. When I made my rounds in the dining room, I always made sure I was wearing a pristine white chef coat, and that there was no trace of the chaos of the kitchen on my face. Diners had a perception of chefs that it was my responsibility to uphold. I checked my appearance in the mirror in the office. I needed a little work to look presentable at breakfast service.

My hair looked stringy and my face glistened with sweat. I dabbed it dry with a kitchen towel, then I grabbed the hairbrush and toiletry set I kept in the top drawer of the desk. It was a chef's secret that I'd learned in culinary school. You never knew when a VIP customer would ask to meet the chef or a food critic would show up in the dining room. I untied my ponytail, gave my hair a quick brush, and twisted it in a low braid. In order to mask my dewy skin I patted my cheeks with powder and applied pink lip gloss. That was better. I looked more like a professional chef and less like I had been coated in the Monte Cristo batter.

I grabbed a tray of cinnamon rolls that were smothered in vanilla buttercream and headed for the dining room. The place was packed. Every table and chair was occupied. People were swapping war stories of how they had survived the storm. The tone was upbeat and the air filled with an undercurrent of relief.

By the looks of the empty platters on the buffet, Rocky might not have to worry about his rebooking stats. As I expected, our pastries and creamy lattes were working their magic. I wondered if more people would rebook a trip, not just because of our breakfast display but because now they had a story to tell. There was a level of comradery not often found on a four-day cruise because the passengers had a shared experience. Watching strangers show off their bumps and bruises and speak with animated gestures as they noshed on mango sweet bread and guzzled Americanos brought a smile to my face.

The ship's grand dining room felt like Torte this morning. If nothing else, last night's storm had brought the guests together. It made my heart happy to see that passengers had embraced the harrowing and frightful evening. Instead of complaining about the gale-force winds and lack of sleep they joked about which deck took the brunt of the monsoon and compared video of the storm on their phones.

"The tempest has brought out the best in humanity, has it not?" The Professor's voice sounded behind me.

I turned to see him wearing another Hawaiian-style shirt, this one with a pattern of bright yellow pineapples and green palm trees. He held a plate with fruit salad, yogurt, and one of my Monte Cristos. "I was just thinking the same thing. I half expected to be fielding complaints about why there wasn't double chocolate cake at midnight."

"But you have outdone yourself this morning, haven't you?" He held up his plate. "How could anyone complain? A wise move, Juliet. I'm not surprised at your foresight."

"Thank Mom. You know what she always says, 'Never underestimate the power of pastry.' "

"True, and we might also add 'the power of people.' " He nodded to the buzzing dining room. "In my line of work it can be disheartening. I appreciate this reminder that we as humans can rise to any occasion."

I spotted a table open up and headed in that direction. The Professor followed. While he sat, I cleared the empty plates and gave the table a quick wipe down. "How did you and Mom do last night?"

He savored the Monte Cristo. "This is otherworldly."

"Thanks." My cheeks warmed at the compliment.

"My goodness. How have you managed such a feast? The cleanup must have been horrendous this morning." He closed his eyes and took another bite of the sandwich. "Divine. No wonder the mood in here is so upbeat. You're a pastry goddess."

"You sound like Lance," I kidded.

The Professor's eye twinkled. "Oh dear. Do not tell your mother that. She'll never let me live it down."

"I have more news for you. Rocky just told me Annie's last name. It's Laundy."

"Annie Lundy." The Professor frowned. "That does highlight some things very clearly, doesn't it?"

I wanted to shout no, but the Professor cleared his throat. "I believe that your dear mother is behind you." He raised his hand in the air. I turned around to see Mom carrying a heaping plate and coming toward us.

She set her plate down and wrapped me in a tight hug. "How are you, honey? That was a rough night."

I returned the hug. She smelled like lavender and coffee. "I was just asking the Professor the same thing," I said after we pulled away.

"Doug was a rock. A monolith." She sat and winked at the Professor. "I don't know what I would have done without you."

He reached out and placed his hand over hers. Her small hand disappeared under his large, weathered fingers. " 'You drown not by falling into a river, but by staying submerged in it.' "

"Is that Shakespeare?" Mom asked.

"No, Brazilian writer Paulo Coelho," the Professor replied. "I believe he said something else along the lines of 'the more violent the storm, the quicker it passes.' I knew that we would sail through fast. We wouldn't stay in the eye long enough to drown."

His words hit me like a punch in the gut. It was as if he

was speaking directly to my heart. If I stayed in the same river with Carlos, would I drown? Is that why I had left? Had I returned to Ashland to find my own stream?

"Juliet, are you okay?" Mom asked with concern.

"Huh?" I gave my head a slight shake.

"You look spacey," Mom said.

"I'm fine. Just a lot on my mind with the storm and Annie."

Mom frowned. I sensed that she could tell I was holding back. The Professor finished his Monte Cristo. "I might have to get seconds," he said to Mom. "Your daughter has a gift."

"I know." Mom beamed.

I wished I had the gift of mind reading. The Professor obviously knew much more about Annie's murder than he was telling me.

Chapter Twenty-six

I excused myself to check in on the kitchen. Mom gave me a parting hug and I promised to find her at the pool later. As much as I wanted closure about what had happened to Annie, I felt lighter knowing that the Professor was in the loop and would follow up with Rocky. It was out of my hands now.

As expected, the kitchen staff continued to churn out platter after platter of pastries and baked goods.

"Rough seas make people hungry," one of the chefs commented as she balanced heavy trays in both arms. "This is my fourth trip in twenty minutes."

"It's crazy up there," I agreed. "That's a compliment to your hard work and talent," I said louder so that everyone could hear. The Monte Cristo station was fast at work grilling the eggy brioche sandwiches. "How are we doing on supplies?" I asked.

The line cook pointed to a two-foot tray that was stacked with sandwiches. "That's the last of them. As soon as I finish what's in the pan we're out."

"Okay." I checked the clock. We had thirty minutes left in breakfast service. Any passengers who straggled in late might be out of luck. I swapped my focus to the espresso cart and making sure everyone knew their lunch service responsibilities. How were we already shifting into lunch prep?

"Once you deliver the last of the breakfast platters, everyone take a ten-minute break," I told my staff. "We need as much room in here as possible for cleanup." I had called for extra help as we transitioned from breakfast to lunch. Since so many dishes had broken in the turbulent seas, I asked the head of the cleaning department for additional staff to wash by hand. My staff could take a brief break to refuel, grab a snack or coffee, and then we would dive right into lunch prep. This was life on a floating luxury hotel. No rest for the weary.

The last trays were loaded with bagels, cake doughnuts, and Monte Cristo sandwiches and delivered to the dining room. I shooed everyone out of the kitchen and instructed the cleaning crew on what needed to be done. With that task completed and the kitchen taken over by a crew of mad dish scrubbers, I took advantage of the break time too.

I knew exactly what I was going to do with my ten minutes—see if I could find Maria. I checked the employee lounge and then the crew decks. There was no sign of the leggy dancer, and I was about to give up when I passed the nightclub and spotted Maria stretching on the stage. She wore black leggings that looked like they had been painted on and a skimpy black tank top.

"You're up early," I said, walking into the dimly lit room. The cleaning crew must have already picked up the lounge. The tables and chairs were arranged throughout the room, but I noticed a stack of broken chairs and candleholders piled near the stage. As well as a huge potted plant that had shattered and scattered dirt everywhere.

"I must stay limber. Rocky has asked for another lunch show as well as our evening shows." She lifted one leg behind her back and stood like a crane.

"I was hoping to talk to you for a minute." I came closer

to the stage. Rows of empty theater seats reminded me of the Angus Bowmer at OSF. There was something about the dark, vacant auditorium that gave me the creeps.

Maria untwisted her leg, lifted her hands above her head in a stretch, then she leaped off the stage in one graceful move. "Sit." She chose a two-person table in front of the stage and sat with perfect posture.

I joined her, but then wondered how to approach asking her about Annie. There was no denying that Maria was gorgeous. This morning her face was clear and free of her stage makeup. Without the heavy makeup I could make out faint lines on the corners of her eyes. She wasn't the youngest dancer in the show, and I wondered if there was any chance she had been envious of Annie. The Professor had said that he guessed that Annie was barely twenty. What if Maria was worried about a younger dancer swooping in and taking over the stage? She had the height and a dancer's strength to have killed Annie.

Maria gave me a challenging stare with her dark eyes. "Is this about Carlos?"

"What?" The question threw me.

"*Sí*, I have seen how you look at him and me."

"I don't understand."

"I think you do. We are competing for the same man, no?"

"Uh, no." I wasn't sure how to respond. "Carlos is my husband."

"*Sí*, but you left him. He has been heartbroken since you went away. I have been here for him."

My words jumbled together as I spoke. "I'm not really sure what to say."

"What is your relationship? Are you here to take your husband back? Because I do not think you are."

She was more astute than I had thought. "I don't think

that my relationship with my husband is any of your business."

"*Sí*, but it is. If you tell me you are here to take your husband back then I will let go." She raised both of her hands in surrender. "But if you are setting him free then it is fair for me to comfort him, no?"

I wanted to scream, but instead I sighed and said nothing.

Maria scooted her chair closer to me. "I see the way that he looks at you, but I don't see you look at him the same. Am I wrong?"

"I don't know." I shook my head. Maria had flustered me. As much as I didn't want to admit that she might be right, I knew that she was. "Is it obvious?"

She gave me a kind smile and shook her head. "No. Only to us. We women know the look of love, *sí*?"

"Do we?"

"Carlos loves you. He will not let you go, unless you set him free."

Her words took my breath away. She was right. Could she see through me? Was that why I had agreed to come on the ship? Part of me knew that it was time to set him free.

She nodded. "It is for you to decide."

This wasn't how I had intended our conversation to go. I had come in to confront her about her relationship with Annie, not have my relationship dissected.

We sat in silence for a moment. I hadn't expected this kind of a reaction or understanding from her. In a few succinct sentences she had summed up what had been fermenting in my mind for months. I had to let Carlos go. I had to set him free.

"Are you okay?" She finally broke the silence.

"Yeah." I nodded. "I'm fine." I wasn't sure I was, but I brushed off the thought of setting Carlos free and sat up straighter. "I appreciate your honesty. Can I ask you something?"

"*Sí.*"

"It's about Annie."

Maria's face tightened. Her eyes narrowed and she clutched the side of the table. "You know?"

"Not really. I'm hoping that you can fill me in."

"What do you know?"

"Not enough. Rocky told me that she snuck on board and begged him for a job, but that he turned her down and told her to get off the ship. He said that he thought she must have stowed away with you."

Maria arched her back in a graceful stretch. "*Sí*, I let her sleep in my cabin. I couldn't refuse. She was desperate. I couldn't let her go back to that life."

"What life?"

Tears formed in Maria's eyes. Maybe it was our conversation about Carlos that opened her up because she spoke in rapid English, slipping in an occasional Spanish word. "Annie worked at a club where I got my start. It is a terrible place and not something I am proud of. When I came to America I dreamed of the stage. Of Broadway or a real show, but I could not get a job. My English was no good, and the directors, they only want dancers who have come from professional training and academies."

Now it was my turn to stay silent and let her speak.

Her hands shook as she continued. "*Mi mamá* would be so disappointed in me. I did not want to dance at a place like that but I must eat. What can I do? When I met Rocky there he gave me a break. I get this job on the ship as a real dancer where I do not have to take off my clothes. It is such a good life and I do not want to give it up or go back to my old life in Miami. Now I can send *mi familia* money and I can be proud of how I have earned it for them."

I could tell that talking about her former life was distressing.

She took in a breath. "No one on the ship can know. That's what Rocky told me when he gave me this job. If the bosses or the captain find out they can fire me and send me back to the dance club. I cannot let that happen."

"How did you meet Annie? At the club? Isn't she a lot younger?"

"*Sí, sí.*" Maria nodded. Her hands continued to tremble. "I did not know her, but she knows of me. It is from Rocky. He finds girls at these clubs and makes a new life for us. He is like an angel on this planet."

I wasn't sure I would describe Rocky as an angel, but I let her go on.

"He saved me. I owe him everything."

"So he asked you to help Annie?"

"No." She shook her head. "Annie came to me first. I did not know her, but she knew one of my old dancing friends. Annie was in trouble. Someone at the club was stalking her. She took out a restraining order and tried to leave the club but she had no place to go. My friend told her to come find me. She thought that I could help Annie get a job. Before we left port I got an emergency call asking me to come meet her. The girl was so upset. I couldn't leave her there and not help, so I snuck her on the ship and introduced her to Rocky."

"But Rocky wouldn't give her a job?"

Maria frowned. "No, he refused. He said he didn't need another dancer, and that he could not make papers for her in time for us to depart."

That lined up with everything Rocky had said to me.

"I begged him. I could see that Annie was scared. She had to get away."

"Did she tell you who was stalking her?"

Maria rubbed her temples. "No. She did not say, but I

knew that it must be bad. Some girls want the glamour of the ship, but not the work. You make good money at the clubs in Miami. When they come to the ship they realize they must work much harder for their money, but it is a better life, no?"

I nodded.

"Annie said she would do anything to be on the ship. I heard her tell Rocky that she would scrub toilets. She did not care. She had to be away from Miami." Maria's shoulders began to convulse. She broke down, letting giant tears pour from her dewy eyes.

"Wait here," I told her, getting up to find a napkin. There was a stack of folded linens near the pile of broken chairs. I tried to console her by handing her the napkin. She barely looked up as she dabbed at her eyes and continued to cry.

"It is my fault," she managed to say between sobs. "She came to me for help and now she is dead."

"No," I said, putting my hand on her knee. "It's not your fault. You tried to help her."

"But she is dead," Maria wailed.

So much for hating her. Maria obviously had a kind heart and was devastated about what had happened to Annie. I had been convinced that she was the killer, but her reaction showed me that she really cared. There was no way she could have killed Annie. I was stumped. Who could have done it? Annie's stalker had to be on the ship.

Maria blew her nose into the napkin. Her glamorous façade disappeared. "It is so terrible. Who could have done this?"

"I don't know. That's what the captain and police are trying to figure out." I handed her another napkin. "Did you tell them all of this?"

Maria wiped her tears away with such force it made my face hurt. "No, how could I? The captain will tell me I must go. I could not let that happen. Rocky made me swear we would tell no one."

Now her reaction to Annie's death made even more sense. She'd been holding in guilt over not telling the captain what she knew.

"Listen, Maria." I kept my voice calm but firm. "You have to tell the captain. He has to know everything you've just told me. I'll go with you if you want."

"You would do this for me?"

"Yes, and for Annie."

She sniffled. "*Sí,* for Annie."

I held out my hand. "Let's go find him or the Professor—the detective in charge—together."

"Okay." She folded her tearstained napkins on the table and let me lead her out of the nightclub.

Chapter Twenty-seven

I knew that Mom and the Professor were planning to be by the pool so I opted to start with the Professor. He had a naturally calming presence that should put Maria at ease, and she wouldn't be in fear of losing her job by talking to him first. She continued to sob as we climbed the back stairs to the pool deck. "It's going to be okay," I assured her.

She wiped her face with the back of her hand. "I know. I feel terrible for keeping this secret. Will they put me in jail, do you think?"

"No. I don't think so. Just explain everything you did to me to the Professor. He'll understand." I hoped that was true. The Professor was cerebral and understanding, and I couldn't fathom him arresting Maria for withholding information. But then, this was a murder investigation. Maybe she had reason to worry.

The sound of heavy, fast footsteps thudding on the metal stairs made us both stop. Jeff, and two other deckhands, came crashing around the stairwell, taking the stairs three at a time. When they saw us they stopped. One of the deckhands nudged the other. "Hi, Maria."

Jeff shot Maria a weird look then turned beet red and raced down the stairs.

"What was that about?" I asked, climbing up the stairs.

"All the young ones fall for me." She looked calmer and the tears had stopped, at least for the moment.

On the pool deck the crew was still cleaning up from the storm. Deckhands swept water off the sides of the ship and crews were stacking lounge chairs and rearranging umbrellas. There was no sign of the storm's aftermath on the horizon. Cloudless blue skies stretched as far as I could see and the water beneath me looked like glass.

I spotted the Professor talking with two crew members near the bar. "Over here," I said to Maria.

The Professor excused himself from his conversation when he saw us. "Juliet, long time no see." He raised one eyebrow in Maria's direction.

"Professor, you've met Maria, right?"

He gave her a half bow. "I have had the pleasure. Your performances have all been captivating."

Maria smiled. "Thank you."

"She has some information about the case that you need to hear," I said.

"I see." The Professor slid a bar stool close to Maria. "Shall we sit?"

Dabbing her eyes with the back of her hand again, Maria agreed.

The Professor caught my eye and gave me a questioning look. "Maria has been holding on to some important information that may help your investigation. She feels terrible about it. I'll let her explain," I said. Then I glanced at the far deck where the pool chairs had been lined up. "There's Mom. I'll be over with her if you need me."

I left them to talk alone. The Professor would know what to do about Maria's situation.

Mom was lathering her skin with coconut-scented sunscreen. Her floppy hat covered her face and she had three books resting on the side table. "Are you going for a reading record today?" I asked.

She adjusted her hat. "Why not! I have all day. The captain said we wouldn't be to port until dinnertime. Do you think I can read a book an hour?"

I kicked off my shoes and sat on the lounge chair next to her. "If anyone can, it's you."

"What are you doing up here?" Mom asked, sitting up. "I thought you would be in the middle of lunch prep."

"I should be, but I got sidetracked."

Mom placed her sunglasses on the tip of her nose. "Juliet." She gave me a hard stare.

"It wasn't my fault. I went to check on Maria and she opened up. I didn't expect it to happen, but she has some information that the Professor has to hear."

"What's that?"

I filled Mom in on everything that Maria had told me. When I finished Mom clicked the lid on her tube of sunscreen shut and handed it to me. "Here, you should put some on your face."

"That's it?" I laughed, taking the tube and squeezing a dollop of sunscreen into my hand.

Mom touched her smooth cheek. "You can't be too careful when it comes to the sun."

"Or leggy dancers."

She chuckled. "Or leggy dancers. Hmmm. It makes sense though, doesn't it?"

"Which part?"

"All of it. Wanting a better life. Trying to escape the world of exotic dancing."

"I know. I keep wondering who killed Annie though. Do you think that her stalker could have followed her on to the ship?"

Mom shifted her chair so it faced the sun. "It's possible. But how?"

"My thoughts exactly. If Annie reached out to Maria how would he have known? Unless he literally followed her onto the ship, but he would have had to have a passport and a ticket. You can't just walk on to a cruise ship."

"Right." Mom frowned. "Unless he was part of the crew."

"True, but again, there's an entire hiring process. It takes time."

"Then maybe someone is lying."

I couldn't stop running through the possibilities and the crew members.

"Honey, Juliet?" Mom's voice broke through my thoughts.

"Yeah, sorry." I blinked twice.

"You're a million miles away."

"I know. I can't stop thinking about who might have killed her." I didn't tell her but I was just struck by an idea, but I needed confirmation from the Professor.

"You don't need to solve this, you know." Mom's voice was gentle but her gaze was solid.

I sighed. "You're right. I know. I just get stuck in this loop sometimes."

She pushed her sunglasses back onto the bridge of her nose. "I know. We both do, especially when we're not coated in flour or bread dough, right?"

"Right."

"Your father used to say that working with his hands, kneading dough or crimping a pie crust, was the only therapy he needed."

"I believe that."

"Can I ask you something, honey?" Her eyes became soft.

"Of course."

"Could it be that you're wrapped up in this again because you're coming to terms about what's next for you?"

"Is it that obvious?" I couldn't believe she'd completely captured my feelings.

"No." Then she wavered. "Well, maybe to me. I see how you've changed. You're so confident and strong. It's amazing to watch your transformation. You've stepped into yourself and I'm so proud of you. So proud."

My throat closed in. "Thanks."

"But stepping into yourself means that you're leaving something behind, doesn't it?"

I swallowed. "Yeah."

"Carlos?"

"How do you know?"

She reached for my hand. "I've known for a while, honey."

"You have? Why didn't you say anything?"

"There are some things we have to figure out on our own."

I placed my head in my hands. "It's so complicated. I love him, you know?"

"I know."

"But I love Torte and my life in Ashland." I paused. "Maybe more."

She nodded. "I understand. Sometimes love is hard."

"I never thought it would be like this. I wish it was black-and-white. I keep telling myself that if I hated him it would be so much easier."

"I know."

"But I can't go back. Being here has shown me that. I don't want this life anymore and as hard as I try I can't see Carlos in Ashland."

"Have you considered letting him decide?"

"Yes, but I know that if I open that door he will try. He'll come to Ashland for me—for us—but then what? His heart longs for adventure. It's why I fell in love with him. I can't force him to give that up for me. Can you really picture him in Ashland? It's so small. It's so remote and so far from the sea." I stared out into the azure waters.

"True." She fiddled with the strings on her sunhat. "You might consider letting him decide instead of deciding that for him. People can surprise us, you know."

"Are you saying that I should try to make it work with him?"

"No, not at all. I'm saying that you have to follow your heart. It knows what to do. It won't lead you wrong. But I'm also saying that if you love Carlos and want to try, don't write him off. You never know how the heart might open to new possibilities."

"But can you imagine Carlos in Ashland?"

"He was in Ashland, and he seemed to fit right in."

That was true, but he'd only been in Ashland for a few days. It wasn't long enough for him to get a sense of what life in a small town was really like or to be bored.

She patted my hand. "Listen, I'm not forcing anything. This decision is yours. I would hate for you to give up someone you love because you're not sure you're worth the risk."

Worth the risk. Did I not believe that I was worth the risk? Was I being honest with myself? Could it be that I wasn't inviting Carlos to come to Ashland with me to protect my heart? Was I worried that he would say no? Or that he would come and quickly tire of the life that I loved? I had never thought of that before. How was it that Mom could read me so clearly?

The Professor was heading our way. Mom stood, kissed the top of my head, and said, "Think about it."

Chapter Twenty-eight

Mom's words pulled me out of the loop about Annie's murder, but now I couldn't stop thinking about Carlos. I had been telling myself that I was doing this for me, but what if I was protecting my heart? Was it fair not to at least give us a chance?

The Professor cleared his throat. "Many thanks for bringing Maria to me, Juliet."

"Did she tell you everything?"

He nodded. "Yes, and I've instructed her to go share this information with the captain."

"What do you think the captain will say?"

"I've found your captain to be a reasonable and thoughtful man. I'm sure he'll find a suitable response for the situation."

"Is she in trouble?"

"Withholding critical information is indeed a serious offense, but I tend to believe her sincerity. We'll have to see how the case shakes out."

"What about Annie's stalker?" I asked.

I caught him giving Mom the eye. "We've created a monster, haven't we?" the Professor joked.

"We?" Mom pointed at him. "Don't look at me. This is on you."

"Perhaps." He smiled. "I must bid you both adieu and go find an Internet connection. I do believe we are quite close to solving this case."

"Good," Mom said. "That means we can relax and read this afternoon."

"One can only hope, Helen."

"I'll take you to the computer room," I said to the Professor. "Thanks for the chat." I gave Mom a wave. "See you at lunch."

She blew me a kiss. "I love you, honey. Think about what I said."

I promised that I would and led the Professor to the staff lounge. "I have an idea about who the killer is," I told him as we made our way down the crew corridor.

"Juliet, let me stop you there. I too have a theory and I suspect we may have come to the same conclusion, but alas I must check in with Thomas," he said. "Would you consider waiting for a moment?"

"Of course." I busied myself with checking e-mail to give the Professor privacy.

There were three e-mails waiting in my in-box. The first was an update from Sterling.

Hey Jules,

Glad to hear that the storm is no big deal. I had to pass that on to Thomas. Man, I thought the guy was going to hire a private jet and fly down to save you or something.

Wanted to give you an update on the basement. Things are moving—literally. The entire kitchen is vibrating. It's like we're in an earthquake here. Richard Lord has mounted a protest. He's a one-man protest show. He keeps marching up and down the Calle Guanajuato trying to rally support. Here's a shocker: no one has joined him.

Andy says to tell you it's keeping him on his game. He also wants me to remind you that he's dying for tropical coffee. He's working on a seafoam honeycomb latte for you. Steph is doing well. She and Bethany are testing a new brownie loaded with marshmallow fluff and Cocoa Puffs. It sounds like a gut bomb, I know, but it's pretty amazing. Customers are losing their minds over them.

Lance is Lance. I'm sure you'll get an e-mail from him. The customers are having fun with all the shaking going on around here. We started a pool for a free coffee if the floor caves in. I'm kidding. Sort of. Hope you're having a good time. Hopefully by the time you're back the trucks will have cleared out and the floor will stop vibrating.

Cheers,
Sterling

PS—Andy is yelling at me to tell you to bring him anything you can. He wants beans, beans, and more beans!

The next e-mail was from Thomas.

Hey Jules,

I've been tracking that storm and it looks like she hit you square in the jaw. I've been trying to get updates from the National Weather Service without much luck. From what I can tell you should be out of her path by now. There was brief mention on the national news this morning that the Amour of the Seas *was in some pretty big waves. I really hope you, your mom, and the Professor are all okay. We've been super worried here.*

Richard hasn't been successful in trying to lobby the city. It turns out that Torte is not in violation of the sidewalk code, so now he's decided to start picketing. It's pretty funny to watch. Honestly, I don't think he really cares. He's eating up the attention and handing out flyers for the launch of his new menu to any poor passerby who happens to catch his eye.

Speaking of the Professor, he tells me that you're help-ing with the murder investigation. Be safe. I know how you can get. Don't do anything crazy.

Thomas

The last e-mail was from Lance.

Juliet,

Darling, I feel like you've been at sea for ages. This must be how the poor souls in ancient times felt when their betrothed departed on a maiden voyage. You're missing all the fun. Torte is the place to be right now. I mean the entire town has come out—at my encouraging—to see the spectacle. Don't distress. It will all come together, but let's just say that Torte looks like a Mesopotamian dig site at the moment. Maybe we'll unearth a priceless piece of pottery, or better yet—a body!

I must have an update on your *body. How is our little Jane Dough? Oh, I know that her name is Annie, but she'll always be Jane Dough to me. Do tell, what's the latest?*

There's more news from the Richard Lord front. He tried to lasso my Lothario into picketing along the Calle Guana-juato with him. As if! Please. I told my bloated actor that if he joined in Richard's dastardly quest that he can pack his bags and schlep over to the community theater. I do hope you'll be back in time for the launch. I simply cannot stom-ach a meal at the Merry Windsor without you. Plus, just think of the fun we'll have deconstructing Richard's menu together.

Wait, wait, the sweaty construction crew has come in for refreshments. Must run.

Ta ta,
Lance

The three e-mail accounts of what was happening at Torte couldn't be more different. I guessed that the reality was probably something in the middle of Lance's dramatic tale and Sterling's "don't freak out" e-mail. A wave of homesickness hit me. I wanted to be back in the mix, especially the excavation. Two more days and I would be home.

I closed my e-mail without sending any replies because the Professor had finished his phone call and was giving me a look of shock.

"What is it?"

"I do believe we know who our killer is and he is on the ship."

"It's definitely a 'he'?"

"Indeed." The Professor was already heading for the hallway. "If I might beg your assistance one final time?"

"Anything. What can I do?"

"Follow me."

Chapter Twenty-nine

The next few minutes passed in a blur. I raced to keep up with the Professor as he moved with agility and speed between the crew and passenger decks. He asked me to meet him at the pool in ten minutes and went to discuss his plan with the captain. I still wasn't sure if my theory was true.

I was breathless when I reached the pool deck. The Professor had instructed me to wait by the pool. I felt weird standing by myself in my chef coat, so I took it and my shoes off and found an empty bar stool in front of the Top Shelf.

Mom was asleep on her deck chair. Her book had fallen on her chest. I didn't bother to wake her, not only because I didn't want to disturb her sleep but also because I wasn't sure what the Professor was planning.

The captain's voice came over the loudspeaker as the emergency warning sounded. "Passengers, this is an emergency drill. Report to your lifeboat stations immediately."

Muster drills were mandatory. Everyone had to participate in the lifeboat drill before embarking on a voyage. Passengers are instructed on how to use their life vests, where the closest escape routes were, and assigned a life-boat. I'd never heard of a muster drill while at sea. I wondered if it had something do with the storm or if this was part of the Professor's plan.

The passengers looked as confused as I felt as they headed for the exits to the sound of blaring alarms.

"There is no need to panic. Please move in a calm and orderly fashion to your muster stations," the captain repeated three times. "This is a drill."

I debated whether I should report to my muster station or stay put. My gut told me this was part of the Professor's plan, but the captain and crew take safety seriously. I didn't want to set a bad example for the guests.

Mom woke with the noise and commotion and hurried over to me. "Are you sure this a drill, honey? It seems odd given what we went through last night." Her eyes were wide and I could see her heart pulsing through her periwinkle cover-up.

"I'm sure it's just a drill," I assured her. "The captain may have received orders from the Coast Guard to run passengers through emergency protocol because of last night."

"Oh, that makes sense." She looked relieved. "Are you coming?"

I stood and pushed back the bar stool. "In a minute. I want to make sure the pool deck is clear first."

"Okay, see you in a few." She joined the crowd lining up in front of the elevators.

I felt guilty letting her go, but the crew checked each passenger in at their muster stations. If Mom didn't show a new round of alarms would sound.

The pool deck cleared. An eerie feeling came over me as I waited on the abandoned deck. If the Professor didn't show up in five minutes, I told myself that I would go to my muster station. As the thought passed through my mind, the sound of heavy footsteps broke through the empty silence. Jeff burst through the back stairwell door and ran to the middle of the deck.

Jeff, I knew it was Jeff. But I didn't know what to do next. The Professor had failed to give me further directions about how I was to help with his plan.

I inched behind the bar. He hadn't seen me and I wanted to keep it that way. Then he ran toward the pool. I ducked below the bar. What was he doing? I watched through a crack in the wooden slats. He scanned the pool area, walked to one of the deck chairs, and flipped it over.

The alarms continued to sound as Jeff flipped over another chair and then another. He was looking for something. What? The murder weapon?

I could feel my pulse throbbing in my neck. Where was the Professor? He should be here by now. Was this part of his plan? Jeff was obviously looking for something. What?

He became more agitated, throwing chair after chair aside. He slammed one onto the teak deck so hard that it shattered in four pieces and caused me to duck down under the bar.

"Where is it?" he yelled to the deserted deck.

He was like a different person. Gone was the weak and nervous young deckhand who'd been seasick. He had been replaced by a raging storm of energy. I didn't want to be anywhere in his wake.

Time seemed to slow. I wondered how long the alarms had been going off. Maybe five minutes? Ten? Had Jeff taken advantage of the fact that the passengers and crew were distracted by the muster drill and come in search of something he'd stashed on the pool deck when he killed Annie? I stared at rows of fancy bottles of gin and tropical syrups.

Should I continue to hide or should I make a run for the crew stairway? Neither option sounded wise. Jeff was making the pool deck look like it had been hit by a hurricane.

If he didn't find what he was looking for under the lounge chairs, the odds were probably good that he'd come search the bar. However, the stairwell was on the opposite side of the bar. In order to make an escape I would have to run out in the open.

Think, Jules,

I scanned the bar. The shelves were lined with bottles of tequila and rum. There were shot glasses, paper umbrellas, and bowls of lemons and limes. None of them would provide me any protection. Slowly I moved toward the cupboards and reached for the heaviest bottle I could find. I removed it as carefully as I could. The last thing I needed was for bottles of alcohol to come crashing down around me. I clutched the bottle of spiced rum to my chest and crouched back down.

Jeff had moved to the opposite side of the pool. He neared the chair that Mom had been sitting on. When he got to it I watched as he tossed her books aside and yanked up her chair. There were only about ten chairs left that he hadn't overturned. If he didn't find what he was looking for in the rows of lounge chairs would he search the bar next?

I took in a deep breath and closed my eyes. In the distance I heard the lonely call of a bird above the sound of the continuing alarms. The bar smelled of wood polish and the ocean air felt warm on my skin. I clutched the cool bottle of rum to my chest. Where was the Professor? This was a stupid idea. What was I thinking? I should have just gone to my muster station.

The sound of chairs thrashing on the deck stopped. My heart felt like it stopped too. Jeff must have turned over the last chair. I held my breath as his footsteps stomped toward me. I scanned the bar one more time for anything else I could use to protect myself. My eyes landed on a corkscrew. I grabbed it like a sword with one hand and held the bottle of rum with the other.

Then the footsteps stopped abruptly.

I was too scared to move. Why had Jeff stopped? I froze and tried to listen. Was he heading toward me?

He was. Or a herd of elephants had invaded the pool deck. The floor began to shake as the sound of multiple feet hitting the deck reverberated everywhere. I dropped the corkscrew and let out a long exhale.

I heard the sound of the captain's voice and wondered for a moment if I was imagining it over the PA. But he said, "Stop right there, Jeff. We have you surrounded."

More footsteps pounded on the other side of the bar. Had the captain sent the entire crew? Thank goodness. Relief surged through my body. I pushed myself to standing, still holding the bottle of rum.

The next thing I knew Jeff leaped over the bar, knocking off lemons and paper umbrellas. In a flash his hands were around my neck. "Back away!" he yelled to the captain and the twenty-plus crew members surrounding us. "Back away!" he repeated. "Back away or she goes overboard."

Chapter Thirty

Everything happened so fast I didn't have time to think, which in hindsight was probably a good thing. Jeff's fingers dug into my neck. I gasped for air as he dragged me toward the side of the ship. He was serious. He was really going to throw me overboard.

I couldn't believe how strong he was. The seasickness must have all been an act. How had I felt sorry for him?

The Professor and the captain both motioned for the crew to hold their positions. The captain took two steps forward. "Listen, there's nowhere to go, son. This is over. Let her go, and we'll sit down and talk about this."

Jeff threw his head back. "Talk, yeah right. I know how that goes. You'll cuff me and throw me in a Mexican jail. That's not going to happen."

"We're long past Mexico," the captain said. He looked authoritative in his crisp white uniform and hat. Maybe Jeff would realize that and release me.

"Wherever we are!" Jeff shouted back. "You know what I mean. You couldn't care less about me. Just like Annie."

"Let's talk about Annie." The Professor stepped next to the captain. "Why don't you tell us about Annie?"

Sweat poured from Jeff's palms. I could feel his entire body shudder. He might be putting on a tough-guy act, but he was nervous. "What do you want to know? That she hated me. I didn't do anything to her. I loved her. I would have died for her. But she took out a restraining order. A restraining order. Like she needed that. I would never hurt her. I would never do anything to her."

I wasn't sure if it was just my imagination but it felt like his grip was loosening a little. I didn't have to struggle as hard to get air.

The Professor stepped closer. His Hawaiian shirt billowed in the breeze. I had noticed that the wind had picked up again. When I glanced above me the sun glared back at me, making tiny dancing lights cloud my vision. "I know that. It was an accident, wasn't it?"

Jeff relaxed for a brief second, but then tightened his grasp. "It was. I didn't hurt her. I would never hurt her. I loved her. She wouldn't listen."

"I know. That's what you said," the Professor repeated and took two more small steps forward. Jeff didn't notice as the Professor carefully kicked a broken chair to the side and made eye contact with a crew member. "Why don't you tell us about the accident?"

Jeff's body lurched. He yanked my neck to the left so hard for a second I thought it was going to snap. Pain shot down my side. I winced.

The Professor caught my eye and gave me a hard look. He was trying to tell me something, but what?

"I can't help you if you don't tell me what happened," the Professor said to Jeff. "Trust me, I want to help you. We all do." He turned to the captain who stood rigid in his crisp uniform.

"That's right." The captain gave the Professor a salute. I wondered if it was an intentional show of his power. "We can end this now and no one gets hurt."

Jeff tugged me closer to him. "Yeah, you're smart. I could tell from the first day. It was an accident, but the captain doesn't believe me and I'm not going to jail." He pulled me toward the railing.

The Professor gave me another look and motioned his eyes toward the ground. Suddenly I realized what he was getting at. The rum bottle! I'd been holding it the entire time, but had been so taken aback by Jeff grabbing me that I hadn't even realized it.

Holding three fingers next to his shorts the Professor started counting. When he got to the number one he nodded at me. "Jeff, we are here to help you." He gave me a nod and without hesitation I lifted the bottle and smacked Jeff on the head.

Unlike in the movies Jeff didn't fall to the ground. The shock of being hit startled him enough to release his grip on me. I used the opportunity to slip from his hands and run toward the Professor. I couldn't see what was happening behind me, but the Professor yelled "Move!" and the entire crew sprang into action.

I heard a scuffle and shouting as I ran toward the Professor, but I didn't look back. I landed in the Professor's arms. "Good work, Juliet," he said, squeezing me tight. "I do believe our ordeal is over. You are most safe and secure now."

The captain handcuffed Jeff who had made it halfway over the railing in the time it had taken me to run to the Professor. I guess I hadn't hit him as hard as I thought I had.

"Do you need to sit?" the Professor asked.

"No, I'm okay." I pulled away from his comforting arms. It surprised me how attached I had grown to him. My father had been gone for over a decade and I had forgotten how nice it was to have an older and wiser man around.

"Take him to the bridge," the captain ordered two crew members. "Everyone else back to your stations."

"What happened?" I asked the Professor. "Was this your plan?"

He chuckled and shook his head. "Oh dear, no, I'm afraid it wasn't. If this was my plan then it would be time to throw in the towel as they say."

The captain clapped the Professor on the back and shook my hand. "Nice work, both of you. I must go inform the authorities. If you would both please join me for dinner tonight, I would be most grateful."

We agreed. A few members of the crew started the task of rearranging the chairs that Jeff had overturned. The Professor walked to the bar. "Shall we?"

I was still holding the bottle of rum. "Yeah, maybe I should crack this open."

"This sort of occasion calls for a drink, I believe." He took the bottle from my hand. The bar was still standing despite Jeff's hurling lounge chairs at it. I could smell the citrusy lemons and limes. The Professor reached for two shot glasses and poured us each a bottom full of rum. I'm not usually a rum drinker and certainly not used to taking shots in the middle of the day, but I drank it in one gulp. It burned the roof of my mouth and sent a warm feeling up my spine.

"Ah yes, that's better, isn't it?" The Professor knocked back his shot too.

"What happened? I don't understand what your plan was."

"Yes, yes. I know that you have many questions." He removed a folded square of paper from his shirt pocket and handed it to me. It matched his tropical shirt. Had he color-coordinated his outfit intentionally? That was something I would expect from Lance, but not from the Professor. "To answer your first question, any investigation requires three things—motive, opportunity, and means. In this case we had a number of suspects with some thin motives, a few with the means and opportunity, but none with all three."

"Except Jeff." I looked at the paper he handed me.

"Except Jeff. Thanks to modern technology and the magic of fingerprint dust, we were able to find our stowaway's identity, which was confirmed by Maria and Rocky. What's more," he continued, nodding at the paper, "Thomas discovered that Annie had taken out a restraining order on Jeff. It all came together quickly once we had a last name."

"So he was stalking her?" I wanted to kick myself for taking so long to put the clues together. When Maria had said that all the young ones fell for her something had clicked. I'd been operating under the assumption that Annie had dated her stalker and then things went terribly wrong. I never thought about the fact that the feelings could have been one-sided.

"Indeed, it appears that way. And Maria's story corroborates that. Alas, it seems that Annie sought refuge in the wrong place."

"How did Jeff get on the ship?"

"The captain and FBI agents who will meet us at port will have to determine that. The captain's initial paperwork shows that Jeff applied for the job weeks ago. We can only surmise that he must have learned what Annie was planning and was one step ahead of her."

"That's terrible."

He frowned. "Love is merely a madness, as the Bard would say."

"Poor Annie." I wondered if she had mentioned that she knew Maria or if Jeff had overheard a conversation. The thought of Annie plotting her escape while Jeff was planning to follow her gave me the creeps. I put my hand to my neck. I had a feeling his fingers had left a mark on me.

The Professor noticed me touch my neck. "Do you need ice for that?"

"No, I'm fine." I took my hand away. "What was your plan though?"

"Ah well, the best laid plans sometimes go awry. The captain and I concurred that if we could clear the deck perhaps Jeff would try something. I suspected that he had stashed something from the victim here, so the crew had already combed this entire deck. Alas, lady luck was not on our side. That is until you discovered a critical clue.

"The earring?"

He nodded and winked. "Like I reminded you and your mother at dinner the other night, I still have a few tricks up my sleeve." Then he reached into his pocket and removed the earring that I had found in the supply closet.

"So it was Annie's?"

The Professor laid the earring in his palm. "Indeed."

"But how did it get in the supply closet?"

"Our best guess is that Jeff accidentally dropped it in his utility cart. He's been looking for it ever since. Although remember, this is a crime of passion. The earring isn't proof of anything. I believe he was desperately in love with Annie. He took the earring as a token. It might have been the only thing of hers that he had and he was frantic to get it back."

I thought back to seeing Annie sneaking out of the supply closet on my first day on the ship. Could she have been hiding from Jeff? Or had Jeff discovered her hiding spot? "So you thought Jeff would search the deck for the earring?"

"We hoped, but we weren't sure. You were our backup, but alas things didn't quite go according to plan."

"I don't understand."

"If Jeff didn't out himself, then we intended to call him

to the pool deck. We were going to stage the murder over again and see how he reacted."

"You mean with me?"

"Yes, you my dear were going to be cast in the role of Annie. I know that our friend Lance has been eager to get you on the stage. This might have been your chance. We only would have needed you to float in the pool for a minute or two, just to see what Jeff would do."

"Are you serious?"

A smile tugged at his cheeks. "Of course not. We wanted you to drop the earring in front of him and see his reaction."

I laughed. "That sounds more like it. But what took you so long?"

"Poor execution. We didn't anticipate the fact that passengers and crew would clog the stairways and elevators. It was the captain's brilliant idea to call a mandatory muster drill, but we were swimming upstream so to speak. It took us nearly twenty minutes to get from the bridge to the pool deck. I was afraid that Jeff would have been long gone by the time we arrived. Fortunately for us, although not so fortunately for your neck, he was bent on his mission. Little did he know that I had been in possession of this since you found it." He clasped his hand around the earring. "We'll be sure to return this to Annie's family."

"What about the weapon? Did you ever figure out how he killed her? And how did he do it with the other deckhands around?" I was glad to hear that Annie's family would get her earring.

"That's another question we'll have to sort out. The ship's doctor called the time of death a half hour before you found Annie's body. My guess is that Jeff killed her before anyone was around and awake on the pool deck. Time of death is an estimate and I'm hoping we'll get a full confession out of him once we're on shore. As to the murder weapon, that is easy. A broom handle. Can you believe that? Not exactly a weapon from the pages of *Hamlet*. Quite an unexpected weapon in this new millennium. However, this was a crime of passion so he likely took advantage of whatever was close at hand."

"Do you think he was even sick?"

The Professor raised one brow. "I'm not sure I understand."

"Jeff was seasick the morning that I discovered Annie. Or maybe he wasn't. Maybe he realized what he'd done." I shuddered at the thought and the memory.

"Yes, that could be true. As the Bard said, 'When to the sessions of sweet silent thought I summon up remembrance of things past, I sigh the lack of many a thing I sought, and with old woes new wail my dear times' waste.'" The Professor sighed. "What do you say, shall we go find your mother and fill her in?" He pushed back his stool.

"Absolutely." I did the same. My mind felt clear, even though my neck burned with the memory of Jeff's painful grasp. A crime of passion. Suddenly my hurt over leaving Carlos seemed trivial compared with what Annie must have gone through.

Chapter Thirty-one

We didn't have to search for long. The elevator doors dinged and Mom hurried out and threw her arms around both of us. "I was so worried about you." Then she stepped back and scolded. "You two are in so much trouble."

The Professor looked at me and shrugged. "We deserve that, don't we?"

I left them to their happy reunion and returned to the kitchen. "Did you think I deserted you?" I asked the sous chef.

"Not at all. Things are going great in here."

They were. Lunch had been prepped and was ready, but put on hold thanks to the captain's muster drill. I needed to bake and I craved the stability of my kitchen routine. I helped put the finishing touches on the desserts and sent them up to the dining room. Once the lunch rush was complete I turned my attention to the dinner in green. First I mashed avocados and blended them with fresh lime juice, a hint of sugar, and a splash of cream until they whipped into a light and airy foam. To showcase their satiny green color I layered the whip in parfait glasses with vanilla custard and topped them with sprigs of mint and a slice of sugared lime.

Soon everything was vibrant and alive with green. I felt a new sense of purpose and energy. I would dedicate tonight's dessert to Annie's memory. She deserved to be remembered in brilliant color.

I dined at the captain's table with Carlos, Mom, the Professor, Babs, Maria, and Grayson. The captain looked regal in his dress whites with a green swatch of silk pinned to his chest. He stood and addressed the guests. "Ladies and gentlemen, first I want to extend my thanks to you and our amazing crew. I realize that the last eighteen to twenty-four hours have been extremely uncomfortable, but the vessel handled it beautifully as did all of you. I know that it's a disappointment to have had to cancel a port, but we have made special arrangements to dock tonight. You'll have a chance to explore a tiny island. I encourage those of you who choose to disembark to take a walk on its sandy beaches. You may even see phosphorescent sea life on the shores. I've been assured that shops and bars will be open for our arrival. We'll only have three hours, but I'm sure that after last night you'll enjoy a chance to stretch your legs."

Once the captain finished his address he raised his glass and asked for a moment of silence in Annie's honor. My throat felt tight as I thought of Annie's family receiving the news. Carlos squeezed my hand and offered me his napkin to dry my eyes.

Carlos's dinner in green was a testament to her memory as well. The first course was a grilled green chili salad. The chilies had a lovely, smoky char that mingled perfectly with the bright and tangy citrus cilantro dressing. For the main course he had seared skirt steak and smothered it with a green chimichurri sauce and served it with asparagus and green beans sautéed in olive oil and a gorgeous green poblano rice, a specialty in Mexico.

"Carlos, you have outdone yourself," Mom said, placing her hand on her heart. "I never knew green could taste so good."

"*Sí*, I'm so glad that you enjoy, Helen. It is a festive treat for our senses to eat in color, no?"

Everyone at the table agreed. The dining room was alive with color. Green linens had been draped over each table. The floral staff had created cascading centerpieces with palm leaves, pale green roses, delicate daylilies, and fragrant bunches of jasmine. Mom looked resplendent in a shimmery green strapless dress. She had tied her hair back with a silky green ribbon and dusted her lids with green shadow.

I had opted for a seafoam-green cocktail dress that I had worn when I first met Carlos. It hit just above the knee and fell from my waist in layers of tulle. I always felt a bit like a princess when I wore the dress, which wasn't very often. Like Mom, I wore my hair in a loose bun and had borrowed a pair of dangling rhinestone earrings from one of the cake decorators.

Carlos and the Professor both embraced the green theme with ties. The Professor's tie was emerald green and had almost an iridescent glow. Carlos's tie was the color of a freshly picked lime and he had tucked a sprig of thyme into his breast pocket.

Grayson was seated next to me. His homage to the evening was a pale green strap around his guitar. Babs was on his other side. She wore a black leather dress with an evergreen scarf and emerald studded earrings. I leaned close to Grayson. "How's everything going with you two?" They looked pretty cozy with their chairs pushed close together.

"Good. I think Babs finally believes that I'm not just into her because of her connections."

"Really?" I was surprised by this news. Grayson had made it sound like that was the only reason he was interested in Babs. Then again I thought about how many times he had serenaded her and tried to capture her attention. Maybe he was legitimately in love. "Can I ask you something?" I whispered.

"Shoot." Grayson leaned back in his chair. His guitar was propped up against one of the legs and almost slipped.

"Were you looking for an earring when I bumped into you in the supply closet that day?"

He returned the chair to the floor and repositioned his guitar. "Earring?"

"Yeah, I found an earring in there that belonged to Annie."

"Woah." He shook his head. "I didn't see an earring."

"What were you doing in there?"

A blush crept up his baby face. "Uh." He motioned his head toward Babs. "We kind of snuck away for a minute."

I caught his meaning and dropped the subject. He hadn't been trying to stash Annie's earring. He had been making out with Babs and didn't want any of the crew to find them.

Wait staff arrived with trays of green sweets. My desserts were met with effusive praise. The favorite was my pistachio cake, but the lime tarts came in a close second. By the time we had finished our meal everyone was groaning in satiated delight.

After a round of espressos the captain excused himself. We were due to make port later in the evening and he had to make sure his crew was ready for our first stop. The rest of our tablemates went to prepare for the evening show. I noticed Maria let her eyes linger on Carlos when she invited us backstage later.

Once it was just the four of us, the Professor stood, cleared his throat, and extended his hand to Mom. "I'm hoping for the pleasure of your company, on the pool deck, Helen. I have it on good authority that tonight's sunset will be spectacular."

"I would love to." Mom grinned.

"Juliet, Carlos, will you join us?" The Professor and Carlos shared a brief look that I couldn't decipher.

"Oh, I don't know . . ." I started to say, but Carlos grabbed my knee under the table and gave it a squeeze.

"*Sí,* we would love to."

I shot him a look that made him squeeze my knee harder. "Let me go get a sweater," I said.

The Professor looped his arm through Mom's. "Excellent. We'll see you in a few."

"What was that about?" I whispered to Carlos as we walked to my cabin.

"You will see." His eyes twinkled.

"Carlos, look, I hope that you're not planning something. I don't think it's a good idea. I'm so confused right now."

"Do not worry, *mi querida.*" He laced his fingers through mine. The gesture felt so familiar.

"Carlos, I don't know what to do next."

"*Sí,* it is not to think about now."

"But I love Ashland," I protested. "Being back here has been great, but now I know for sure that Ashland is where I want to be."

"*Sí,*" he said softly. His eyes lost their sparkle, but he kept his tone light. "That is for another day."

"But I can't leave you hanging. It's not fair. If you want to move on I understand."

He shook his head. "Julieta, it is fine. I understand. I do not want to move on as you say. Not now. You are in my heart—always—even if you are far away."

"But . . ."

He placed his finger over my lips. "No, do not say more.

We will see each other soon." His eyes brightened. What did he mean by that?

We arrived at my cabin before I could ask. I grabbed a cashmere sweater and wrapped it around my shoulders.

"You are so beautiful tonight." Carlos reached for my hand again and we walked arm in arm up to the pool deck.

The Professor was right. Golden orange light danced on the water. In the distance the sun was sinking on the horizon, making the ocean look alive with light.

"Wow."

"You know what they say about the sky after a storm," Carlos said, staring into my eyes and making me feel off balance. "If you can make it through the rough seas the sun will always reward you."

I knew that he wasn't talking about the sunset. He leaned close and kissed me. I wasn't sure if it was the beauty of the evening, the relief of knowing that Annie's murder had been solved, or the ever-present attraction between Carlos and me, but I allowed myself to be consumed by his kiss. I got lost in the moment. We might have stayed that way for hours but the sound of seagulls flying above forced me to pull away. The sun sank lower as the purple sky faded into darkness.

"*Sí, mi querida*, our love it is strong. You do not need to worry." He pointed to the far end of the deck. "Come with me."

There a two-person table had been dressed with a huge bouquet of daisies and yellow sunflowers, Mom's favorite flowers, a bottle of champagne, and two lit votive candles. Grayson appeared out of nowhere strumming his guitar.

"What's going on?" I whispered to Carlos.

"Watch, you will see." He wrapped his arm around me.

For a brief moment I was worried that Carlos had done this for me, but the daisies and sunflowers made me think otherwise. At that moment the Professor and Mom stepped off the elevator and Grayson strummed an old English ballad. Leading Mom to the table the Professor knelt on one knee. "Helen, I find myself calling on the Bard's poetry tonight. Will you allow me to use his words to express myself?"

Mom bit her bottom lip and nodded.

He cupped her hand in his. " 'Love comforteth like sunshine after rain. Doubt the stars are fire.' " He paused and raised his eyes. Stars flooded every inch of the sky. They glinted and shined down as if awakening in response to his words. " 'Doubt that the sun doth move; doubt truth to be a liar; but never doubt that I love you. I love thee, I love thee with a love that shall not die. Till the sun grows cold and the stars grow old.' "

He removed a small black velvet box from his pocket and opened it. "Would you do me the grand honor of becoming my wife?"

Mom gasped. She was oblivious to the flowers, music, candlelight, and sunset. She only had eyes for the Professor. I felt my eyes begin to well with happy tears as she shouted, "Yes," and he slipped the ring on her finger.

Carlos released me with a kiss on the cheek. He grinned and began snapping photos. I hadn't even noticed that he had a camera. "Were you in on this?"

"*Sí*, it is love." His eyes enveloped me. They held a familiar hunger. I had to look away.

Mom realized that we were there and clapped with delight, waving me closer. She threw her hand over her mouth as Grayson serenaded her and the Professor popped open the bubbly bottle of champagne. We embraced. "Can you believe it, honey?" she asked, showing me the antique platinum ring. It looked perfect on her dainty fingers.

"I can." Her ring shimmered in the starlight. "Are you happy?"

"So happy. Did you know?"

"Let's just say I might have had an idea." I took a glass of champagne from the Professor who gave me a conspiratory wink.

Her face turned serious. "And you're sure you're okay with us?"

"Mom!" I held her arm as tight as I could. "I've never been happier."

It was true. Mom had found love again. I wasn't sure where my love life was headed, but I knew that I was heading for home soon. I couldn't wait for the captain to chart a course that would take me back to Ashland and Torte. So many exciting things lay ahead—a basement renovation, expanding our bakeshop, and now a wedding.

I was ready for all of it.

Chapter Thirty-two

We made it to port in the late hours of the evening. Mom and the Professor opted to celebrate their engagement with a moonlight walk on the beach after the Professor finished handing off Annie's case to the port authorities and Coast Guard.

I watched them leave the pool deck arm in arm. Mom was engaged. I couldn't believe it. After so many years of managing Torte on her own she had the Professor now. Her steps were lighter as they strolled toward the elevators. My eyes welled with salty tears again.

Carlos took notice. "You are happy for her, no?"

"Yeah." I brushed tears from cheeks with my fingers. "So happy."

"*Sí.* They belong to one another. Like you and me." His eyes reflected the stars. "I will come for the wedding. Would it be okay if I bring Ramiro?"

My heart skipped a beat. I hadn't met Carlos's son. I hadn't known that Carlos had a son until a year ago. The idea of finally getting to meet Ramiro filled me with excitement and nerves. What if he didn't like me? What if he was different from what I imagined? I pushed those thoughts aside. Regardless of whether Carlos and I stayed together I loved him and I already knew that I loved Ramiro.

"Yes, yes. That would be wonderful," I said, blinking back the last of my tears. "Mom would love it too."

"It is done, then. You tell me when the wedding will happen and Ramiro and I will be there." He reached for my hand and pulled me to standing. "I told you, I will not give up on us. And now I know that I will see you again soon, which is how I will survive without you."

We walked to my cabin in silence where we parted with a lingering kiss. Carlos was making it nearly impossible to leave, yet like a siren's song Ashland was calling me home.

The rest of the cruise was relatively uneventful aside from the usual stress of running such a massive kitchen, but nothing compared to Annie's murder and sailing straight into a storm. With Annie's case out of his hands the Professor and Mom soaked up the sun and celebrated their impending nuptials by joining in the conga line on the pool deck, securing front-row seats at Maria and the Salsa Sisters' final performance, and lingering over late-night bottles of wine with the wind to their backs and a stunning show of stars above.

By the time we arrived back in Miami, I could almost smell Torte's signature orange-cardamom rolls and Andy's biscuity coffee. There was so much waiting for me in Ashland. And one ache I was leaving behind. Fortunately, in the frenzy of disembarking and preparing for a new round of passengers to come on board, Carlos and I only had a moment to say good-bye.

He found me in the galley turning in my uniform and reviewing my checklist for the permanent pastry chef. "Come with me," he said with a glint in his eyes.

"I don't have much time," I said, glancing at the clock. Our plane was due to depart in two and a half hours.

"*Sí, sí.*" He ignored my protests and dragged me to the same supply closet where I caught Grayson and Babs and found Annie's earring.

The tight space smelled of chlorine. He pushed aside a plastic cart and two buckets. "*Mi querida,* I have something for you before you go."

"No." I started to protest again but he put his fingers to my lips.

"Ssshhh. It is nothing. Only a token for you to remember that my love is bigger than the sea. I will be with you again soon." He kissed the top of my forehead. My knees buckled. I didn't trust myself to speak.

He pressed something into my hand. It was a small box wrapped in pale blue tissue and tied with a silky ribbon.

"What is it?" I looked down at the package, which wasn't more than four inches in diameter.

"You will see, but you must promise me that you won't open it until you get to Ashland." Carlos's face lit up with delight.

"Why?"

"I cannot say." He closed my hand around the package. It wasn't heavy. I wanted to shake it but resisted.

"What are you up to?"

"You will see." He grinned. Then an announcement sounded on the PA system warning passengers that final disembarkation had begun. "You must go, Julieta." He kissed me softly on the lips. "I will see you soon."

With that Carlos left me standing in the supply closet and staring at the box in my hands. I tucked the box in my carry-on bag and made my way to the gangway. I guessed I would find out soon enough. Ashland, Torte, OSF, and everyone else I loved most in this world were only a plane ride away from me. Even with the sting of leaving Carlos, my feet felt light as I traversed the steep ramp and headed for home.

Chapter Thirty-three

I knew I was home by the crisp morning air and the peaceful early quiet that greeted me as I walked along the plaza. Tiny pink and yellow buds were beginning to bloom on the tree-lined street. The smell of evergreens and the refreshing Siskiyou Mountain air filled my senses. Announcements touting the new season at the Oregon Shakespeare Festival hung in every shop window. But otherwise the plaza's sleepy sidewalks looked unchanged after my brief absence. That was—until I spotted Torte. Sterling and Lance hadn't exaggerated.

Twenty-foot scaffolding had been erected on the side of the brick building and a massive canvas tent stretched from the bakeshop's front awning around the corner to the Calle Guanajuato. A mound of dirt and broken bricks that reminded me of a miniature Mount Ashland had been piled to the right of Torte, blocking access to the walking path.

I watched my footing as I tried to get a better glimpse of the basement property. An excavator and backhoe blocked any view. The only thing I could see was dirt and more dirt. What a mess. I was confident that the construction crew knew what they were doing, but from the massive amounts of dirt they had untethered, a fleeting image of the bakeshop collapsing into the ground flashed through my mind.

Don't even think about it, Jules, I cautioned myself as I shifted a grocery bag containing coffee I had brought for Andy in one hand and unlocking the front door with the other.

Torte sat in a hallowed slumber. I breathed in its cheery dining room, pastry case, espresso bar, and the lingering scent of baking bread. I was *home*.

Taking in a calming breath, I flipped on the lights and got to work. My first order of business was dropping off Andy's bag of coffee. As promised I had purchased an assortment of nutty, spicy, and chocolaty beans from each port of call. The beans smelled heavenly as I unpacked them and stacked them in front of the espresso machine. A cup of a medium-bodied roast sounded divine, but I wanted to wait for Andy to arrive before I fired up the machine.

Then I continued into the kitchen. The island and countertops were spotless. A stack of neatly organized orders and inventory sheets awaited me. The whiteboard spelled out the morning's task list and what had already been prepped and stored in the walk-in. Wow. I couldn't help but smile. Our team had done an incredible job while we were away. Everything was in its place and ready to go.

I washed my hands with an organic honey-lavender soap and tied on a Torte apron. It felt much freer and less constricting than the formal chef coat I had worn on the *Amour of the Seas*. Within a matter of minutes I had cranked on the ovens, begun melting butter on the stove, and had yeast rising. I didn't have time to lose myself in the meditation of baking the first batches of bread because Stephanie, Sterling, and Andy arrived all at once.

"You're here early," I said, brushing flour from my hands and hurrying to greet them in the front.

"We knew you couldn't stay away, boss," Andy said. He yanked off his baseball hat and gave me a half hug.

Sterling unzipped his hoodie and wrapped me in a hug. "Good to have you back, Jules."

Even Stephanie smiled and nodded in agreement. Mom appeared behind them at the front with an armful of tropical shopping bags. Sterling opened the door for her and she bustled in glowing from her time in the sun and her news.

"You're all here!" She kissed each of them on the cheek. "We brought you gifts. Come, come see."

We moved into the dining room where Mom started opening bags and handing out trinkets from our stops at sea. She held up plastic flower leis and shell necklaces. "I know these are cheesy, but I had to get them. Jules and I were thinking we could theme our next Sunday Supper after the cruise. What do you say?"

Andy hung a strand of shells around his neck. "You got it, Mrs. C." Then he noticed the stack of coffee on the espresso machine. "Beans!" Giving me a fist pump in thanks he ran behind the counter and started ripping open each bag. "Get ready, you guys, I'm going to have to try every single one of these. We're going to be buzzing by noon."

A timid knock sounded on the door. We turned to see Bethany standing outside holding a basket of brownies. Mom waved her in.

Bethany wore her UNBEATABLE BROWNIE T-shirt but had one of our Torte fire-engine-red aprons draped over one arm. "I wasn't sure if I should come this morning or not?" she said with a touch of nervousness in her voice.

"Of course, of course." Mom swept over to welcome Bethany with a hug. "We have presents for you too."

While Mom continued to pass around gifts Andy appeared with his first creation. "These beans are killer, boss," he said to me. "Give this a try. I used the single-estate beans. They have a nice light flavor and cherry finish." Andy handed out tasting samples of the black coffee.

The team caught us up on everything that had happened while we were gone, including Richard Lord's continued protests and Lance's daily visits. The energy was vibrant as we caught up happily while kneading bread dough and sipping coffee varietals.

There was one piece of news that hadn't come up yet—Mom's engagement. Stephanie brushed loaves of sourdough with butter, Bethany jumped in and expertly whipped pastry cream, and Sterling started on the daily soup, French onion, by thinly slicing sweet Walla Walla onions. Mom reviewed the orders and inventory sheets. I wondered why she hadn't said anything yet, and if any of our team had noticed her sparkling antique ring.

About twenty minutes before we were due to open the Professor arrived. He was back in his Ashland attire in a tweed jacket and casual jeans.

"Good morning," he said with a half bow. "I see the merry team is at it as usual."

Mom placed the stack of papers on the island and went to the dining room. She looped her arm through the Professor's and cleared her throat. "Everyone, I want to make a little announcement before it's time to greet the masses." She looked up at the Professor and smiled. "Doug and I are engaged."

Andy let out a whoop of delight. Sterling, Steph, and Bethany all looked genuinely surprised and happy as they offered congratulations.

The Professor took a ceramic mug that Andy offered him and raised it in a toast. "You are all Helen's family. I am humbled by you and promise she will be loved and adored in our years ahead." His voice became husky. He had to pause for a minute to compose himself. "We want each of you to be part of the celebrations that are to come."

Andy tapped a spoon to his coffee mug. "Kiss. Kiss."

Mom blushed as the Professor nodded acknowledgment and planted a kiss on her lips. She swatted him playfully and clapped her hands. "Enough. Let's get back to work."

The Professor excused himself and invited everyone to a celebratory dinner once we had settled back in. With a renewed sense of energy and excitement over Mom's news we all returned to our stations. I wanted to re-create my pistachio cake and went to check the pantry to see if we had enough pistachios on hand. Bethany followed after me.

"Hey, Jules, do you have a second?" She tugged at her shirt as she spoke.

"Yeah, of course."

"I just feel sort of weird being here now. Should I take off? I don't want to be in the way."

"No, no, not at all." I reached for her arm to reassure her. "In fact Mom and I want to talk to you about a more permanent position here. We're going to need more help with the expansion and Mom and the Professor want to travel more. You could continue the brownie business too—or we could even officially partner on it—the Unbeatable Brownie by Torte or something. It's up to you."

Bethany's butterscotch eyes brightened. "Really? I would love that. I have had a blast working here the past few days. I've been dreading the thought of going back to my lonely kitchen."

"See, it was meant to be." I patted her arm. "The three of us can sit down later and work out the details and compensation. You've been a lifesaver and we would be thrilled to officially have you on the team."

Bethany gave me a hug. "Can I tell everyone?"

"Please do. It's that kind of morning. Celebrations all around." I continued into the pantry and found a bag of pistachios. When I returned to the kitchen everyone was cheering over the news that Bethany was joining the staff.

What a homecoming, I thought as I whipped butter and sugar. As I slid the first round of gorgeous pale green pistachio cakes into the oven the doorbell jingled with the arrival of customers.

For the next few hours Mom and I balanced baking with catching everyone in town up on our trip. Word of Mom's engagement spread faster than frosting. Thomas appeared after ten with an oversized bouquet of lilacs, daisies, lavender roses, and greenery. He handed them to Mom. "A gift from my mom, Mrs. Capshaw. Congratulations from A Rose By Any Other Name. Mom says she'll be over once she closes up shop to hear the details."

Mom took the heavy bouquet and placed it in the center of the pastry case. "These are gorgeous, Thomas. Tell your mom thanks."

Thomas stepped to the side as I brought a tray of pistachio cake slices to place in the pastry case. "Good to have you home, Jules." He tapped the gold deputy badge pinned to his blue police uniform. "I had to flash this a couple times to keep Richard Lord in check."

"Thanks." I held out a plate and offered him a slice of cake.

He grinned, reached for a plastic fork, and took a bite before asking, "What is this?"

"Shouldn't you ask first, and then taste?" I joked.

"Nah. If you made it I know I'll like it," he said with a mouthful of cake.

"I'm glad you have such faith in me."

The easygoing look in his blue eyes shifted. "I always have faith in you, Jules."

My body tensed slightly. I decided the best idea was to change the topic. "So Richard has been at it again?" I knelt and lined slices of the green cake on the top shelf.

"You almost have to give him credit for being persistent."

I looked up at him and scowled.

"Almost. I said almost." Thomas finished the cake. "Don't worry. I think he's finally given it up. He's getting ready for the big launch party this weekend and has been distracted by that."

"Let's hope you're right."

"Jules, I'm always right." He laughed. "However, I'm also late. The Professor and I have an important meeting. Can't imagine what that might be about." He winked. "See you at the launch dinner this weekend?"

"Yeah, right." I stood and took his empty plate.

Thomas strolled away and I watched him interact with people on the plaza. He stopped to answer a tourist's question about parking and passed out stickers to a group of preschoolers on their way to Lithia Park.

I was lucky to have a friend like Thomas watching out for me. I just hoped that we could keep things the way they were. Is that ever possible, Jules? I asked myself as I returned with the empty tray to the kitchen. Wasn't change the only thing that was constant?

Change and baking. Baking was the constant in my life and I was perfectly content to push up my sleeves and immerse myself in pie dough.

Chapter Thirty-four

The construction crew arrived at lunchtime, so I left the bakeshop in my team's capable hands to go outside and have them walk me through their progress. They assured me that the pile of rubble would be gone soon, and that Torte was structurally solid. There was no danger of the bakeshop collapsing and they were on track to finish excavating and begin laying new drainage pipe by the end of the week.

It sounded like a major undertaking to me, but they didn't appear frazzled which I decided was a hopeful sign.

"Darling!" Lance's voice sang out as I stretched over a stack of broken bricks. "There you are."

He crossed the street from the Lithia fountains, holding a picnic basket and dressed in an iridescent gray suit. When he reached me he kissed me on both cheeks and then stood back to appraise me.

"You look exactly the same. Your porcelain skin is untouched. Well done, darling. You must have shunned the sun."

"I was working, Lance. I didn't even pack a swimsuit."

"And your skin thanks you." He held up the basket. "Come with me. I've brought lunch."

I glanced in Torte's front window where customers were

munching on chicken-almond sandwiches on crusty baguettes and double-chocolate brownies drizzled with caramel cream. "I should probably get back to work."

"Nonsense." Lance grabbed my arm. "You need lunch and we need to talk."

There was no point in trying to argue with him, so I let him link his arm through mine and head in the direction of Lithia Park. Signs of spring sprouted around us. The park's enormous lawns were a brilliant green. Lance stopped at a bench next to the duck pond where a mama duck and her babies dipped their necks into the cold water. Stately trees surrounded the pond and wood-framed timbers of the Elizabethan theater peeked out from the hill above.

Lance unpacked a bottle of sparkling white wine, cheese, crackers, salami, and grapes. "Eat, eat," he insisted, handing me a plate and glass of bubbling wine.

"What's the occasion?" I placed a slice of sharp white cheddar and salami on a cracker.

"Is it a crime to want to have lunch with your best friend?"

I was touched by Lance calling me his best friend, but there was something off about his demeanor. He kept glancing up at the OSF complex and tapping the pine needles on the ground with his expensive leather dress shoe.

"Well, do tell," Lance said, returning his attention to me. "I must have all the gossip. We have so much to discuss: Jane Dough, your mother, and of course that delicious Spanish husband of yours."

Lance sipped his wine but didn't touch his plate while I recounted the confrontation with Jeff and the Professor's romantic proposal.

"How's everything with you? You seem distracted." I asked when I finished.

He stared at OSF and sighed. "You think I kid, but I am ready to murder that untalented air bag."

"The young actor you hired?"

"Yes, who else? Did you not read my e-mails? He is driving me to drink." Lance held up his nearly full glass of sparkling wine as if providing proof. "What's worse is that the board is not listening to anything I suggest. Nothing. Not a single word, do you hear me?"

I nodded.

"The board won't let me cut him loose, and we're having the company launch at the Merry Windsor. If this keeps up, I'm out."

"Out?"

"Out." Lance folded his arms across his chest.

I'd never heard Lance talk like this. Lance *was* OSF. He couldn't really be considering leaving, could he? "But you can't leave," I protested.

"Look, this isn't the only theater company, you know. I've had offers. Quite generous offers, I might add."

"You have?" I almost choked on a cracker. Had Lance actively been seeking a new position? I couldn't believe it.

"Chin up, darling." He tapped the bottom of my chin. "Don't look so glum. I'm not doing anything drastic—at least not yet."

"Have you met with the board? They love you. Everyone does."

"That's why I adore you, Juliet. You still have a trace of such innocence." He broke a cracker in half. "In any event, you are coming with me to Richard's disastrous launch. Don't even think about saying no. I need you there."

I could tell that Lance was serious.

"Okay, I'll go." I folded my paper plate in half and discarded my wine in a nearby garbage can, aptly designed to blend in with the park's natural surroundings.

"We'll suffer through it together, but then I have something fabulous planned." He pointed up the hill to the back of the theater. "I'm going to throw the most wicked cocktail party the theater has ever seen, and you, my darling, are going to cater it."

"You're going to throw two parties? One at Richard's and one here?"

"Exactly. We'll just see whose party is better received." He clapped his hands together and packed up the remains of our lunch. "You didn't spill any details about that succulent chef of yours."

I shrugged and tossed his plate in the trash can. "There's nothing to tell," I lied.

Lance lasered his eyes on me and frowned. "Please. My five-year-old extras are better actors than that. You don't have to tell me now, but I will get it out of you, darling."

We walked to the park entrance together. He kissed my cheeks. "Ta-ta. I'll be in touch." He started up the Shakespeare stairs and I returned to Torte. I was worried about him. Despite his steely exterior I could tell that he was upset by not having the board's support. That was a first. Lance had always been OSF's darling. I also wasn't ready to dissect what had happened with Carlos. I wasn't even sure what had happened between us. There was no way I could articulate my complicated feelings to someone else.

The rest of the afternoon was a blur of baking and chatting with friends and fellow business owners. By the time we closed the bakeshop I practically crawled home. I was exhausted, jet-lagged, and blissfully happy to back in my small apartment.

I made myself a bowl of soup and curled up on the couch with my favorite cookbook. I had the pages memorized. There was something so comforting about flipping through familiar recipes and studying photos of stylized food. With a long list of tasks waiting for me tomorrow, I decided to make it an early night and headed for bed as soon as I had finished my soup.

My suitcase and carry-on bag sat on my bed. I hadn't bothered to unpack last night, so I took a minute to reorganize my things. When I unzipped my carry-on the first thing I saw was the box that Carlos had given me. For a minute I thought I might not open it, but then I changed my mind and untied the silky ribbon.

I tore away the tissue paper and lifted the lid of the box. There was key inside. Was it a metaphor? Had he given me the key to his heart? It would be like Carlos to offer a symbol of his love. But as I picked up the key I felt unsure. The key was ordinary. In fact it looked a bit like the key to Torte's front door. Carlos's romantic gestures were usually over the top. This looked like a functional key rather than an antique token of his enduring love.

I wasn't sure what to make of the key, but I could figure it out another day. It was time for a good night's sleep knowing that I was back on Ashland's firm and fertile ground.

Asian Noodle Salad

Ingredients:
8 ounces of spaghetti—boiled and cooled
½ head of purple cabbage—chopped
½ head of Napa cabbage—chopped
2 cups of bean sprouts
1 8 oz. bag of fine-cut carrots
1 bunch of cilantro—chopped
2 cups peanuts
2 cups of diced chicken breast

Ingredients for sauce:
¼ cup sesame oil
½ cup peanut oil
¼ cup soy sauce
¼ cup teriyaki sauce
½ cup of rice wine vinegar
¼ cup brown sugar
2 cloves of garlic—chopped

Directions:
Mix together cooked spaghetti, veggies, peanuts, and chicken in a large bowl. Whisk the sauce together in a separate bowl. Pour over the salad and stir with tongs. Top with chopped cilantro and peanuts. Serve cold.

Serves 6–8

Peach Coffee Cake

Ingredients:
    ½ cup butter
    ¾ cup sugar
    1 egg
    ½ cup milk
    2 cups flour
    2 teaspoons baking powder
    1 teaspoon salt
    2 cups of fresh sliced and peeled peaches

Crumble ingredients:
    ¼ cup butter
    ½ cup brown sugar
    ½ cup flour
    1 teaspoon cinnamon
    ½ teaspoon nutmeg
    Dried mangoes—chopped

Directions:
Preheat oven to 350 degrees. In a mixing bowl cream butter and sugar together, add milk and egg. Sift in flour, baking powder, and salt. Gently fold in sliced peaches. Pour batter into a greased 8 x 8 pan. In a separate mixing bowl

add butter, brown sugar, flour, cinnamon, nutmeg, and mangoes and combine with a fork until you have a crumbly mixture. Sprinkle over the top of the coffee cake and bake for 30 minutes.

Tropical Cookies

Ingredients:
 ¾ cup butter
 ¾ cup white sugar
 ¾ cup brown sugar
 2 eggs
 1 ¾ cups flour
 ⅔ cup of oats
 1 teaspoon baking soda
 1 teaspoon salt
 1 teaspoon cinnamon
 1 teaspoon vanilla
 1 cup white chocolate chips
 ½ cup dried papaya
 ½ cup golden raisins
 ½ cup macadamia nuts

Directions:
Preheat oven to 350 degrees. In a large mixing bowl or electric mixer cream together butter, sugars, eggs, and vanilla. Then gradually incorporate dry ingredients, saving the oats for last. Stir in white chocolate chips, papaya, raisins, and macadamia nuts by hand. Drop in teaspoons on a cookie sheet. For flat and crunchy cookies use an insulated baking sheet, for soft and chewy cookies use a shiny noninsulated baking sheet. Bake at 350 for 8 to 10 minutes.

Lemon Jelly Roll

Ingredients:
  2 eggs
  ¾ cup sugar
  1 cup flour
  ½ teaspoon salt
  ½ teaspoon vanilla
  2 tablespoons milk
  1 ½ teaspoons baking soda
  Fresh squeezed lemon juice
  Powdered sugar

For filling:
  1 jar lemon curd
  Whipping cream

Directions:
Preheat oven to 375 degrees. Beat eggs and sugar in an electric mixture until they become thick and pale (about 5 minutes). Stir in milk, vanilla, and fresh squeezed juice of one lemon. Slowly sift in dry ingredients. Batter will be thin. Grease a jelly roll pan and line with wax paper. Grease and flour the paper then pour batter over. Bake at 375 degrees for 8 to 10 minutes. While cake is baking dust a kitchen towel with powered sugar. When the cake is done and springy immediately loosen from paper and turn upside down on the towel. Roll cake and towel together, starting from the narrow end. Allow cake to cool completely. Once cool, unroll and slather evenly with lemon curd. Roll again and dust the entire cake with powdered sugar and serve with a dollop of whipping cream.

Monte Cristo Sandwich

Ingredients:
    Thick brioche bread
    2 eggs
    1 ¼ cups of heavy cream
    Ham
    Gruyère cheese
    Mustard
    Raspberry jam
    Powdered sugar
    Butter or olive oil
    Dash of salt, pepper, nutmeg

Directions:
Slice the brioche into thick pieces. Mix heavy cream, eggs, and dash of pepper, salt, and nutmeg. Heat a generous pat of butter in a skillet on medium-high. As the butter is melting assemble the sandwich by spreading a thin layer of mustard on both slices of bread. Pile with ham and cheese. Then dip the entire sandwich into the egg and cream mixture. Brown the sandwich on both sides until it's golden brown and the cheese melts. Dust with powdered sugar. Serve with a side of raspberry jam.

Mai Chai

Andy's tropical tea creation made with spicy Oregon Chai will have you dreaming of sunny beaches and warm, blue seas.

Ingredients:
  ½ cup Chai tea mix (Andy uses Oregon Chai, but any
       black tea blend will work)
  ½ cup coconut milk
  2 tablespoons pineapple juice
  2 tablespoons orange juice
  ½ of a fresh lime
  A splash of almond extract
  1 teaspoon of grenadine syrup

Directions:
Mix the juices, almond extract, and grenadine syrup in the
bottom of a clear glass. Squeeze in fresh lime. Add milk
and chai. Stir. Add ice and finish with a slice of pineapple,
an orange-rind swirl, a maraschino cherry, and a tropical
drink umbrella.

Read on for an excerpt from

Another One Bites the Crust

the next Bakeshop Mystery
from Ellie Alexander and St. Martin's Paperbacks!

They say that absence makes the heart grow fonder. After a week away from my beloved town of Ashland, Oregon I knew this to be true. The sidewalks along the plaza seemed merrier, the budding spring trees looked brighter and cheerier, and the southern Oregon sky glowed in warm pink tones as I made my way to Torte. It was as if Ashland had rolled out the welcome mat to greet me. I smiled as I passed sleepy storefronts and drank in the cool, early morning air. Our family bakeshop sat at the corner of the Elizabethan-inspired downtown. Huge Shakespearean banners announcing the new season at the Oregon Shakespeare Festival danced in the slight breeze. Torte's front windows had been decorated with matching maroon and gold banners, ribbons, and twinkle lights. Platters of cupcakes adorned with edible, hand-painted theater masks, busks, and scrolls made for a colorful and tempting display.

I'm home, I said to no one as I took a deep breath and unlocked the front door. Inside, the bakeshop was plunged into darkness. I flipped on the lights and surveyed the dining room. Torte was divided into three unique spaces. The front served as a dining room with red and teal walls, corrugated metal siding, an assortment of small tables, and cozy booths lining the windows. An espresso bar and pastry counter divided the dining room and kitchen. And a large chalkboard menu took up most of one wall. One of Torte's youngest customers had colored a stick figure family with a dog, cat, and what I could only guess might be some kind of a bird in the bottom corner of the chalkboard. We keep a basket of chalk, toys, and books on hand that's easily accessible for families. It's been a tradition since my parents opened the bakeshop to reserve a special section of the chalkboard for budding masterpieces.

The same was true for the rotating Shakespearean quote. My father had always been a fan of the Bard's work and enjoyed sharing his love of words with customers. When he died Mom continued the weekly quotes as an homage to him. This week's quote was from *Antony and Cleopatra*. It read: "Give me some music; music, moody food. Of us that trade in love." Not only was it a lovely quote, but it was also a teaser for the new season at OSF which kicked off in a week with the premiere of *Antony and Cleopatra*. Everyone in Ashland was buzzing with excitement. The commencement of another season meant that soon our calm streets would be packed with tourists in town to take in a show and shop and dine in our little hamlet. I liked Ashland's rhythm. Having a winter reprieve where things quieted down and assumed a more leisurely pace for a few months was always nice, but by February the entire town was ready and eager for an onslaught of guests.

I'd been away on a temporary assignment as head pastry chef for the luxury cruise ship, *The Amour of the Seas*, where I used to work. My estranged husband, Carlos, had begged me to fill in when the ship's pastry chef stormed off in a huff. At first I had resisted the idea, but the timing had been perfect. Plus Carlos had offered an all-expenses paid vacation for Mom and the Professor. A week at sea under the tropical sun had been just what the doctor ordered for all of us. Mom and the Professor got engaged and

I got some much needed clarity on my relationship and future.

Being back on the ship was a reminder of the life that I'd left behind. I didn't harbor any ill will toward my memories or my years spent sailing from port to port. In fact they had helped form me and make me into the chef I had become. Traveling the world had opened me up to new flavors and experiences. But I knew deep within that my heart belonged in Ashland. It was time to let go of the past, even if that meant saying goodbye to Carlos. The ache of leaving him this time felt different. I knew that things were shifting and I was ready to dive headfirst into my life here.

For starters that meant focusing on the task at hand—preparing vats of homemade soups, breads, and sweets for the incoming crowds. I tugged off my coat, grabbed an apron from the rack next to the espresso bar, and headed for the kitchen. In addition to gearing up for the busy season we were in the middle of a major expansion. The basement property beneath the bakeshop had recently come on the market and Mom and I had decided there was no time like the present to take the plunge. While we were on the cruise the first phase of construction had begun. The space had been waterproofed by adding special drainage and shoring up the foundation. With that project complete we could now turn our attention to the fun part—designing a state-of-the-art kitchen.

The current plan was to roll the remodel out in stages. Once the basement was complete baking operations would move downstairs. Then we would knock through the current kitchen, add stairs, and expand the coffee bar and dining room. Guests would be welcome in the new space to watch our team of bakers at work and nosh on a pastry in a small but cozy seating area next to the massive wood-burning oven. It all penciled out on paper, but I was nervous about how everything would come together and keeping the contractors on track. But with one glance at our current kitchen I knew whatever stress this project brought would be worth it. We had reached maximum capacity in the current space and if we wanted to expand our offerings, especially with weddings and catering, we had to have more square footage.

I fired up our shiny new ovens, which would eventually be repositioned downstairs, and studied my to-do list on the white board. There were wholesale bread orders, four custom cakes, two corporate pastry orders, and the daily Torte menu to complete. I quickly sketched out a plan of attack. Stephanie, our pastry protégé and Bethany, our newest recruit, could tackle the bread and corporate orders. I would work on the custom cakes. Sterling, our chef-in-training, would be responsible for soup and sandwiches, and Andy would man the espresso counter. As I began washing my hands the front door jingled and Stephanie and Andy arrived together.

"Morning, boss!" Andy grinned and waved.

Stephanie made some sort of grunting sound, hung her head, and shuffled inside after him.

"Someone needs a java—stat." Andy mimicked Stephanie's posture.

She shot him a harsh look. "Do you pound espresso before you get here?"

"Nope. But my mom always says that the early bird catches the worm." He winked and tipped his baseball hat at her.

Stephanie scowled. "Will you just please make me a coffee?"

I hid a smile. I was used to their unique personalities. They were both students at Southern Oregon University, but that was where their similarities ended. Nothing ever appeared to fluster Andy. He was perfect in his role as Torte's lead barista with his jovial attitude and easy ability to chat with anyone. Our customers loved him. They also loved his coffee. He had a natural talent for combining unique flavors and was a master at latte art. Stephanie might not have Andy's laidback attitude, but I had learned that sometimes there's a soft and sweet center under a steely exterior. Her goth style, shockingly purple hair, and tendency to dress in all black, paired with her sometimes surly smile, made her appear uninterested and aloof. But nothing could be further from the truth. She was loyal, dependable and a quick study. Mom and I had been teaching her the tricks of the pastry trade, and I was impressed by how much her skills had grown in the last few months. She often surprised me. Like the fact that she binged hours and hours of Pastry Channel baking shows for entertainment and her own education.

Andy removed his baseball cap and gave Stephanie a half bow. "My pleasure. I'm here to keep you caffeinated."

"You better make that a double," I hollered from the kitchen.

Stephanie tied on an apron and joined me while Andy began to steam milk and grind beans.

"Late night?" I asked, handing her the wholesale order sheet.

"Don't even get me started. A new girl moved into my hall. She's a music major and likes to belt out showtunes all night long."

I couldn't help but chuckle. "Showtunes, really? Somehow I don't think of your generation being big into showtunes."

Stephanie scowled. "We're not."

Andy turned to face us. "I second that! Man, I feel for you, Steph."

"Thanks." She rubbed her temples. "If hear *Oklahoma* one more time I'm going to lose my mind."

"Only in Ashland." I shook my head and laughed. "You know who would love this? Lance."

"No. Don't give him any ideas," Stephanie pleaded. "Can you imagine if she landed a role? That would only make her practice more."

"Good point." I gathered mixing bowls and nine-inch round pans. "I promise this will be a showtune-free zone today. Are you okay with working on the bread orders? Once Bethany gets in I thought the two of you could focus on the corporate deliveries too. They want an assortment of pastries, so we can double up our daily offerings."

"Sure." Stephanie's eyelids, which were coated in purple shadow, drooped as she read through the bread orders.

I felt sorry for her. Having a noisy neighbor was the worst. I'd been fortunate to have complete privacy in my apartment in Ashland. It was located above Elevation, an outdoor store, that closed at seven every evening. However I remembered my early days working for the cruise line when I had to bunk with three other women. The crew quarters were often an all-night party, which did not lend itself to bakers' hours. I had invested in an expensive pair of earplugs to get to sleep. I wondered if I still had them. I would have to check later and bring them in for Stephanie.

We worked in silence for the first thirty minutes. I creamed butter, sugar, eggs, and vanilla in the mixer and then sifted in dry ingredients for the first cake. The customer wanted a vanilla sponge with vanilla buttercream. A simple but classic request. They hadn't specified any design preferences so I planned to use an old method called spooning. After frosting the layered cake with generous amounts of buttercream I would pipe vertical dots all over the cake. Once the cake was covered with dots of buttercream I would use the back of a spoon and start at the base, making small swirls up to the top edge. Then I would repeat the process around the entire cake. The final product would look like fluffy clouds or flower petals. It's a gorgeous vintage look that was making a comeback.

Andy arrived with two brimming mugs of black coffee as I poured the creamy vanilla batter into the cake pans and slid them into the oven. "I went with a straight-up light roast. It's delicate and floral and I think it's best without any cream or sugar."

Stephanie, who was up to her elbows in bread dough, frowned and stared at Andy's offering. "Light roast. I need caffeine, man. I can't stop singing *Oklahoma* in my head."

Andy bit his lip to keep from laughing and rested the cup next to the mound of springy bread dough Stephanie was kneading. "Trust me. This will do the trick. There's no difference in caffeine when it comes to roasts. People assume that dark roasts have more caffeine because it's a bolder coffee, but it's a total myth that there's more caffeine in a dark roast. In fact there are some camps that think light roasts actually have more caffeine, since roasting beans for longer brings out oils, you could make an argument that more caffeine burns off in the process." He handed me a cup. "Right, boss?"

I shrugged. "Don't look at me. I had no idea. How do you know all of this?"

"YouTube." Andy's wide smile made his face look even more boyish.

"Really?" I cradled the coffee mug. The scent of floral notes hit my nose.

"Sure. I have to know what I'm talking about. When it comes to caffeine people get kind of crazy."

"Light roast, dark roast, I'll drink whatever you brew." I held up the mug in a toast and took a sip. As promised the coffee was smooth with a sweet complexity and a fruity tanginess. I inhaled its fragrant scent and took another sip. "This is fantastic."

"Glad you like it. I'm going to experiment with this blend today. It should be a nice spring drink. I'm thinking of trying to pair it with some infused rose water or maybe orange blossoms. I'll bring some stuff for you guys to try in a while." With that he returned to the espresso bar.

While I sipped my coffee I pulled out the next order sheet. The cake was a two-layer chocolate marble sheet for a kid's fourth birthday party. The customer wanted a unicorn and rainbow theme. That should be fun, I thought as the door jingled again and Sterling and Bethany arrived.

"Everyone's coming in pairs this morning," I said to Stephanie and waved hello to Sterling and Bethany.

Andy offered them a cup of his spring blend on their way back to the kitchen. They both gladly accepted drinks and joined the activity.

"Morning," Sterling said to both of us, but I noticed his gaze linger on Stephanie for a moment. Sterling had become like a brother to me. We shared a common love for food, we had both experienced losses, and had tender, romantic souls. He had been holding a torch for Stephanie for a while now, and I just hoped that she wouldn't break his heart. Not that he would have any difficulty finding someone new. Ever since we'd hired Sterling a rotation of young girls came into the bakeshop every day to catch a glimpse of the handsome, dark-haired chef. His brilliant blue eyes and poetic nature often sent groups of teenage girls into giggling fits in the dining room. Sterling was oblivious to the attention. He only had eyes for Stephanie.

"Are you up for a busy morning?" I asked Sterling and Bethany.

"At your service, Jules," Sterling said, heading straight for the sink. "Put me to work."

"Same here," Bethany echoed. She savored her coffee. "Have you seen social media lately?"

"No." I shook my head. Bethany had come on board initially to cover while Mom and I were on the cruise, but she'd been so helpful and blended in with our staff so well that we asked her to make her position permanent. She had started a brownie delivery service, The Unbeatable Brownie, so part of our contract had been a partnership where she retained a portion of the profits from those sales. She had also agreed to work with Stephanie to bring us into the twenty-first century and create a stronger online social media presence. They had been snapping pictures of cakes, pastries, customers, and life in the kitchen and posting them online. So far the response had been great. It was fun to have fresh ideas and energy in the kitchen.

"Well, Stephanie and I came up with this idea while you were gone, and it's been working really well. We've been posting a secret brownie flavor of the day. Anyone who comes in and mentions the flavor gets a free one. They have to take a picture and use the hashtag #secretsweets. We've doubled our followers in less than a week."

"That's amazing. I love the idea. It's so mysterious. How have you been deciding on flavors?"

Stephanie patted the last round ball of bread dough into a bread pan and brushed flour from her hands. "We started with a crazy flavor just to see if anyone would bite."

"Ha, bite!" Andy clapped from the espresso bar. "Well played."

"Anyway," Stephanie continued with an eye roll at Andy, "Bethany thought of adding Siracha to the brownie batter and we sold out in like an hour."

"Siracha brownies? Hmm."

"I know." Bethany gave me a sheepish grin. "It sounds weird, but they were good. We went easy on the Siracha. And don't they say that chocolate and spice go well together?"

"Absolutely." I nodded.

"Well," Bethany hesitated for a moment and fiddled with her hands. "You know my friend Carter? He's working in Portland now and they are doing all kinds of unique things with macarons. Like Doritos and Fruity Pebbles.

I've been wanting to learn how to make them, so I thought if you were up for it you could teach me and Steph, then we could mix it up and do macarons and brownies. I mean, only if you think it's cool. No pressure or anything."

"I think it's great. Yes. Let's do it, and I would love to teach how to make macarons. They're one of my all-time favorite desserts. We should definitely be offering them here."

"Awesome." Bethany reached over to Stephanie and gave her a fist pump.

We reviewed the task list and everyone started on their individual projects. I couldn't keep the smile from my face. Our team at Torte was more than I could hope for. They were hard workers, self-starters, and innovators. How had I been so lucky? The morning was confirmation of my decision. Ashland and Torte were home, and nothing— not even the stress of a major renovation—could get me down. That was until we opened a while later and Lance burst through, calling in a sing-song voice, "Oh Juliet, we need to talk—now!"